♠ ♥ ♦ ♣ **Tickets to the Devil**

♥ *To my favorite partner*

THE TITLE: According to *The Official Encyclopedia of Bridge,* the Puritans of New England used the term "Devil's Tickets" or "Devil's Picture Book" when talking about decks of playing cards. They may have been right.

♠ ♥ ♦ ♣ **TICKETS TO THE DEVIL**

Richard Powell

Charles Scribner's Sons
New York

♠ ♥ ♦ ♣ **Tickets to the Devil**

♠ ♥ ♦ ♣ 1

IT WAS USUAL for guests of the Xanadu, newest and most lavish of the hotels in Miami Beach, to arrive by airport limousine, taxi, or one of the better new cars. Mrs. Robert Lee Rutledge, of Richmond, Virginia, arrived by Collins Avenue bus. She was a thin birdlike woman wearing a hat like an abandoned nest. She carried a black handbag, an old suitcase and a large brown paper bag, and after getting out of the bus she patted it, as if it were her own special private bus, and cooed, "What a lovely trip!" In doing this she dropped her handbag, which spilled a small tin of aspirin, a piece of toast wrapped in a paper napkin, seventeen cents, an orange, a three-week-old letter from her married daughter, and a pale yellow card from the American Contract Bridge League that certified Mrs. Rutledge as a Master with twenty or more master points. The card was her most prized possession.

She collected the spilled items and looked up at the Xanadu, which was about to become the scene of the Spring Nationals of the American Contract Bridge League. The Xanadu perched on its twelve acres of beachfront land like an enormous wedding cake, frosted with spires and minarets and balconies. Across its front a slim river of gold flowed through neon tubes, tracing the letters X-A-N-A-D-U. The name came from the opening line of Coleridge's poem: "In Xanadu did Kubla Khan a stately pleasure dome decree." Hotel names that implied sinful luxury—Deauville, Fontainebleau, Versailles, and so on—were much in demand on Miami Beach. The complete word stayed alight for a few seconds; then it blinked out and the golden rivulet began flowing again from the beginning. Mrs. Rutledge studied twenty million dollars' worth of hotel and decided that it looked like a lovely place to play bridge.

As she started toward the entrance carrying her handbag, suitcase and large paper bag, a bell captain said, "Believe it or not, she's coming here. All right, one of you guys help her." Nobody moved, and the bell captain said sharply, "Okay, Juan, it's yours."

Juan Gomez, twenty years old and a recent arrival from Castro's Cuba, sighed and walked down the steps. In spite of limited experience he already knew that no worthwhile tip was likely to come from a guest who arrived by bus with an old suitcase and large paper bag. He said to Mrs. Rutledge, "Good morning Madam I take the theengs yes?"

"Oh, that's so nice of you," she chirped. "And you will be careful of that paper bag, won't you? It has clothes that need washing in it and I wouldn't want them spilled in front of everybody. There's a little rip in the bag and it might come apart. I'm here for the bridge tournament."

"Bridge?" Juan said blankly.

"Duplicate bridge. The tournament."

Bridge, Juan thought. He was starting to hear that word often today, and had better find out what it meant. "This way, plees," he said.

The ·hotel lobby that Mrs. Rutledge entered covered half an acre, and was bordered on three sides by a tropical jungle that soared sixty feet into the air. It was not a hostile but a livable jungle, held back by huge glass walls. Behind the glass, palms and orchids and hunter's robe and fiddle-leaf fig and other plants clawed upward on carefully placed rocks. Hidden lights revealed vistas of miniature pools and waterfalls. Within the lobby the decorator had grouped black vinyl chairs and couches around low black tables, accenting them with throw cushions in fire-red and tangerine and lemon. There was a quarter-acre rug the green of palm leaves; the rug was an inch thick and on it, floating like exotic lily pads, were large raised patterns in pink, purple and orange. To the east the jungle wall parted to reveal outdoor swimming pools and cabanas on the patio, and the Atlantic Ocean beyond.

The lobby made Mrs. Rutledge feel uneasy, a reaction that she seldom had. She wasn't sure that the Xanadu was going to be as nice as most hotels in dealing with the fact that she couldn't pay its rates. However, she was not a coward, except now and then when bidding slams, and so she marched to the registration counter and announced her name and that she had a reservation for the ten days of the bridge tournament. At the very least, she knew, her timing was right; it was only eleven in the morning and the crowds hadn't begun to arrive and so the hotel would have time to consider her problem thoughtfully and, she hoped, with sympathy. She registered, and waited until the clerk made out the white slip listing her room number and the rate, $16 a day.

"Oh my," she said in a soft plaintive tone. "I didn't realize it would be so much."

The clerk's head jerked up and he said in disbelief, "Too much? Sixteen a day?"

"I'm sure it's all my fault," she said, her soft Virginia accent flowing like Southern Comfort from a bottle. "I don't see real good these days and I looked at the confirmation you-all sent me and thought it said six dollars. But of course I didn't have the teensiest idea what a lovely place this would be or I would have known how silly I was. It's like Bobby used to say—that was my late husband, Robert Lee Rutledge—he used to say, Mary Rose, you as pretty as a hummingbird but you got no more brains than one of them. Of course, that was years and years ago when I maybe looked pretty, leastways to Bobby. Could I talk to one of your men about this, not the manager, goodness, I wouldn't want to bother a big important man with my little old problem, but somebody else?"

The frown on the clerk's face gradually faded as the soft voice caressed his ears. He was hardened to complaints, growls, sneers and accusations, but this was different. The old dame even started off by admitting she was wrong. And that bit about being pretty once, at least to her husband, it kinda got to him. "Just a moment," he said, and went away.

Presently another man came to the counter and said briskly, "Good morning. My name is Rothman, and I'm an assistant manager. Does there seem to be some misunderstanding?"

"Good morning to *you*," Mary Rose Rutledge cooed. "It's so nice of you to take time for little old me. The only misunderstanding is just me and my bird brain, and I wouldn't think of bothering you 'cept I saved so long and looked forward so much to this. It's my first Nationals. Now don't you go thinking I'm a country gal who can't play bridge, just because it's my first Nationals, account of really and truly I have a Master's rating, and right here's the card that says so." She brought out the pale yellow card from her purse and showed him. "It says I have twenty master points or more but I have to be honest and admit it's just exactly twenty, sixteen black and four red points. But a person who has any red points at all can play bridge pretty fair because you can't win red points except at a Nationals or Regional."

As he listened, cobwebs started to trap the thoughts of J. B. Rothman. He shook his head to try to sweep them out. Red points. What the hell were red points? As a kid in World War II he'd heard his mother talk about needing red points to buy meat. He tried to get back to the matter at hand. "The problem seems to be the room rate, doesn't it?" he asked. "Sitxeen dollars? Mrs. Rutledge, March tenth comes within our peak season. The room reserved for you has a regular rate in March of forty-eight dollars a day. We made very special rates for this bridge tournament."

"Oh, I'm sure of that, and I know the room would be lovely and worth just almost anything you charged, but like I told that nice young man I spoke to first I misread the confirmation you-all sent me as saying six dollars a day and not sixteen, and it's all my fault but I saved and saved to come here for the tournament and I just don't have more than six dollars a day for a room. What I have every month is seventy-eight dollars and forty cents from those nice Social Security folks, and two hundred from a trust Bobby set up 'fore he passed away—that was my late hus-band, Robert Lee Rutledge—and now and then my married daugh-ter up in Baltimore slips ten dollars in a letter to me, and that's every penny I have, and I did so look forward to staying in your lovely place."

"Mrs. Rutledge," he said, not quite as briskly as at first, "we set aside four hundred of our rooms at the special rate for this tournament, and every last one is gone and people are calling up from all over the country. If you walked in here cold I couldn't even give you a room for forty-eight a day."

"It's just awful of me to worry you like this," the soft voice said. "Like Bobby used to say when we were first married, Mary Rose, that's my name, Mary Rose, you are the most *worrisome* girl. Of course, it's a long time since I was a girl but I do fear I'm still worrisome. Wouldn't you maybe have some little old broom closet I could have? I don't need much."

The clerk had told J. B. Rothman that the old girl had a line that got to you, but it wasn't going to get to him, was it? He said weakly, "Madam, the Xanadu does not have broom closets. We have a built-in vacuum cleaning system."

She said gently, "I wouldn't be much trouble. Mercy me, I could even make my own bed."

It was unbelievable, Rothman told himself. She couldn't *do* this to him. He grabbed the sign-in card and crossed out the $16 and wrote $6 and initialed it and made the correction on her room slip. At the end of the month the auditor would question this and the manager would want to know what the hell, and J. B. Roth-man wouldn't be able to explain convincingly what the smile and molasses accent and pleading eyes did to you. "I hope you enjoy your stay," he said in a choked voice. "And please don't make your own bed, the maid will get upset. Boy, take the lady to her room." He turned away before she could drip thanks all over him.

Mrs. Rutledge followed Juan Gomez toward the grotto leading to the elevators, and Rothman growled to the clerk, "I think we've been had."

"Don't you feel good about it?" the clerk asked.

"No," Rothman said. "I just feel confused."

He watched Mrs. Rutledge vanish, and wondered what brought her so far to a bridge tournament. He could understand ordinary conventions, where people gathered for business that they couldn't transact in small groups. But you only needed four people to play bridge, didn't you? So why were they swarming here to sit on little gilt chairs four to eight hours a day and blow stale smoke in each other's faces? It was mysterious, like the lemmings scurrying across Norway to throw themselves into the sea. Well, he hoped it was worth it to Mrs. Rutledge. If she played bridge the way she played hotel she must be a champion.

Mrs. Rutledge, who did not play bridge the way she played hotel, and in fact did not even realize that she played a game with hotels and always won, trotted happily after Juan Gomez. Folks were so nice, she thought, when you explained your problem to them. She didn't know what she would do with herself if there weren't tournaments to go to, and on two hundred and seventy-eight dollars and forty cents a month, a body couldn't afford to pay those high rates for hotel rooms. Mercy me, there was food to buy, and bus fare to the next tournament *and* the fee for each session of bridge. In the Nationals, three whole dollars every time she played! She didn't think she could pay for more than five sessions. Six, if she was lucky with food.

Juan Gomez ushered her into the second-floor room and went around checking the setting of the air conditioning and opening the curtains, while Mrs. Rutledge made small cooing noises over the size of the room and the lovely furnishings and the *two* beds, both for her although naturally she would only use one. Juan finished his chores and turned hesitantly to her, not really expecting a tip. Mrs. Rutledge took a dime from her pocketbook and held it out to him with a doubtful smile, because sometimes bellboys were not pleasant about dimes. Juan looked at the coin; from some guests, a dollar was worth only a nod of thanks, but from the señora a dime was a large amount indeed. He didn't want to take the coin but that might seem insulting, so he accepted it and bowed and said "Mil gracias, señora," and left.

Mrs. Rutledge unpacked her things and did her laundry in the bathroom—it was almost a sin to do laundry in such a lovely place—and plugged in her small electric iron and got the wrinkles out of the dress she would wear that evening in the Charity Pairs, the first event of the tournament. Then she went to the door leading onto her balcony and stepped outside. The scene below took her breath away. The main building and wings of the Xanadu enclosed a large patio where palms foamed up in green fountains and three swimming pools caught diamond glitters from the sun. Two of the pools were filled with filtered salt water; almost nobody swam in the Atlantic Ocean beyond the seawall, because there was messy seaweed in the ocean and sometimes even the blue sails of the Portuguese man-of-war, a stinging jellyfish. One pool was enclosed and filled with heated fresh water, in case a guest did not care to rough it in one of the seawater pools.

She looked at the scene and felt the excitement of an approaching tournament bubble through her. Perhaps this would be another wonderful unbelievable thrilling time like the time two months ago in Boston. For years she had been going from one tournament to another, painfully gathering a black point here and a fraction of a black point there, and she had despaired of ever becoming a Master with twenty black points. She had hardly dared to think of ever winning a red point. She had not expected to win anything at the Regional Individual in Boston but she had at least hoped to have the thrill of playing with one or two Life Masters. In an Individual, you played each hand with a different partner—twenty-six hands in all—and if you had a lucky guide card you might find yourself playing with the sort of expert you could never hope to get as a partner in a regular pairs game. This time her guide card had been touched by magic. Every single partner was a Life Master! Of course they didn't display their gold Life Master cards, but she knew by the way they bid and played their cards, and she looked up their names afterward on the Recap sheet and saw that each one had an ACBL number that began with the awesome "L" or one of the other letters that meant they were bridge royalty with at least three hundred points, of which fifty had to be red points. During that magic session there were very few hands that Mrs. Rutledge had to play, and most of the time she held very few high cards, so all through the session the Life Masters sat across from her doing things like end plays and bath coups that an ordinary person wouldn't dream of, and at the end of the session the big red numeral 1 went up on the Recap sheet opposite her name, and she was the overall winner in that session out of one hundred and seventy-two tables and had won *four red points* and was a *Master!* In the other three sessions of the tournament she had no luck and ended with a poor total score, but nobody could take that first magic session and the four red points away from her.

It was time for lunch now but she did not touch the piece of toast and the orange she had saved from breakfast; they might be nice to have later on. She unpinned the small purse from inside her dress and counted the bills carefully—seventy-four dollars— and transferred nine dollars to her black handbag. She often dropped and sometimes lost things, and it would not do to lose all her money. Of course seventy-four dollars would not carry her through the tournament but sometime during the next week she could count on Beau—that was Beauregard Hollins, who had been Bobby's best friend in Richmond—sending her a certified check for one hundred dollars out of her monthly income. Beau was the nicest little old boy you ever met. He handled all her affairs for her and, since he owned the James Landing Hotel in Richmond, always gave her a room free whenever there were no tournaments she could afford to attend.

She went downstairs and asked the desk if there were any letters for her. No, there were none. For a moment her shoulders drooped. It had been three weeks since the last letter from her daughter in Baltimore. Now don't you go acting silly, Mary Rose, she told herself. Barby has that big house to run and a busy husband and three children, and just can't take time to write letters every whipstitch. She straightened her shoulders and hunted for the coffee shop on the lower level of the Xanadu and went in and took a place at a long table where many people were sitting, and ordered a thick nourishing soup and a pot of tea. When the tea came she opened five of the little paper containers of sugar —sugar gave you energy, and five papers of sugar cost nothing extra—and put the contents in her tea. While eating the soup and sipping tea she brought out Barby's last letter from her handbag. She read it again, hoping to find some overlooked hint that Barby wanted her to come up to Baltimore for a visit. But there were only references to how hard Barby's husband was working, and how young Jimmy might be getting the measles, and how much time it took Barby to run the house and be second vice president of the Women's Club.

One of the other people eating at the long table departed, leaving two of the four small triangles of a bacon and lettuce and tomato sandwich. Mrs. Rutledge reached over the table with no guilty side glances and no hastiness that might draw attention and pulled the sandwich plate to her own place at the table. It had become a lovely lunch, and tonight she could count on free food after the bridge game—coffee and pastry and maybe even sandwiches—and she had the orange and toast in her room for dinner and, yes, somebody was getting up and leaving several doughnuts within reach. She swept them into her paper napkin and shut them in her handbag.

Things were working out very nicely, except for no letter from Barby. She didn't know what she would do if there were no bridge tournaments. When you were sixty-seven years old, most of your friends had died or moved away, or only wanted to sit and talk about their ailments. Going to bridge tournaments saved her from, well, from just about dying. There were ever so many interesting people at tournaments. Away from a bridge table they might not even look at you, but while you were playing with or against them you were one of the most important people in the world. There was happiness and tragedy: the happiness of making a hand that should be set one or more tricks, the tragedy of losing one that should make. There was the hope that this time, as at Boston, a fairy godmother would hover behind your chair and touch you

♠ ♥ ♦ ♣ 2

THE MAN SIGNING IN at the registration counter had shoulders as rugged as a chuck wagon and eyes the color of the sky over Laredo and hands that looked capable of bulldogging a steer. His pearl-gray Stetson tilted back on his curly silver hair. He had big white teeth and a laugh like the rumble of a stampede. He wore tooled-leather boots and a beautifully tailored gray suit and a sport shirt and a cord necktie held by a large silver clasp. He signed his name with the vigor of a man branding yearlings. He gave the impression—and worked hard to do so—that he hailed from the open range in Texas. It was true that he came originally from Texas, but he had never been nearer a cow than to a glass of milk, and not often near a glass of milk either.

The clerk looked at the sharp black writing on the card and glanced at a special list of names: Oswald Jacoby, James Jacoby, Howard Schenken, Alfred Sheinwold, Gregory "Ace" McKinley . . . yes, this was McKinley. The names were those of bridge experts who wrote syndicated newspaper columns. Goren's name was not on the list; he lived in Miami Beach and did not need hotel accommodations at the Spring Nationals. The clerk beckoned to J. B. Rothman and handed him the card.

Rothman came to the counter and said, "Welcome to the Xanadu, Mr. McKinley. My name's Rothman. We're honored to have you with us. Good trip coming down?"

"Howdy, son," Ace said. "We flew through some junk over the Carolinas that got the plane bucking like a bronco. Bothered some of the folks, but I've rode plenty broncs."

"We certainly hope you'll enjoy your visit with us, Mr. McKinley. Anything we can do, let us know. We took the liberty of putting a few welcome offerings in your room, fruit, flowers, a little bar. Let us know if we failed to stock it with your favorite liquor."

"That's right nice of you folks, son," Ace said, knowing just as well as Rothman that a syndicated columnist who could plug the name of the Xanadu was worth courting.

"Planning to walk off with some of the big trophies?"

"Well I dunno. Might play, might not, depends how I feel. I won so many of them things in the past, kinda hate not to give other fellers a chance."

"Yes, of course," Rothman said in the proper respectful tone.

"Might just use the time collecting stuff to write about. That column of mine gobbles words like a coyote eating rabbit."

"Oh yes, speaking of your column, we had a phone call from your syndicate in New York." He got a phone slip from a box. "A Mr. Jackson would like you to call him back at your earliest convenience."

"Thank you, son. I'll do that. See you later."

He rode upstairs in the elevator with Mrs. Rutledge, who was so paralyzed by this brush with royalty that she could not open her mouth. She knew Ace McKinley because once she had watched him give his famous four-tables act; he sat in a swivel chair and played different hands at four tables at the same time, bidding and playing as rapidly and as well as if he were in a normal bridge game. To Mrs. Rutledge, who had trouble playing one hand correctly at a time, this was rather terrifying to watch. So Ace McKinley, who was always happy to be recognized and greeted, was denied that pleasure as he rode in the elevator with Mrs. Rutledge. He got off and followed the bellboy to his suite and slipped the boy two bucks. Juan Gomez gave him the same bow and thanks he had bestowed on Mrs. Rutledge earlier that day.

The hotel had stocked the bar nicely for him: a good Scotch, bourbon, and a couple of blends. Four in the afternoon was early to start drinking and he didn't approve of drinking alone, there were dangers in that, but one shot wouldn't matter. He put through his call to New York and slugged down a jolt of bourbon. The girl at the syndicate switchboard came on the line and he told her he was Ace McKinley calling Pete Jackson. On all suitable occasions he identified himself as Ace rather than as Gregory McKinley. Ace was a nickname that people remembered, and if you hoped to earn a good living at bridge you had to make people remember you. Old Ely Culbertson—rest his wild soul—understood that. It took showmanship to make a bridge expert seem exciting and colorful to millions of people; without it, a bridge expert was just a dull guy sitting for hours on his can scowling at a bunch of playing cards. It had been a fine stroke of luck when Ace won his first national event years ago and a reporter wrote: "When McKinley plays bridge, there are five aces in the game." He grabbed that as a nickname before you could say grand slam.

The nickname fit nicely into the Texas cowboy pose, which he had adopted soon after he began playing tournament bridge. Back in 1934 he was fresh out of college, teaching math at a high school in Dallas. The school board started running short of money —in 1934 they ran out of dough even in Texas—and as the newest teacher he was dropped. Fortunately he was good at cards, and an oilman who owned a hunk of the Spindletop field liked him as a bridge partner and bankrolled him for some tournaments, and he came out of Texas into big-time bridge like a charge of longhorns. Culbertson was at the top then, and Culbertson was The Man because among other things he had color, and McKinley saw that it paid off to be colorful and had patterned his career accordingly.

"Hello, Ace," the voice said in his ear. "Pete Jackson. You got my message, huh?"

"Sure did, Pete," he said, laying on the rawhide accent. "How's every little thing?"

"Oh, not so bad. How's it with you? Gonna knock 'em dead in the tournament?"

"Might not even play, Pete, depends how I feel. Takes a lot of time doing that column for you folks."

"Um, yeah, that's what I wanted to talk about, Ace. Three papers dropped your column this week."

His stomach started giving him a misdeal. "Oh well," he said uneasily, "they come and go, don't they?"

"Lately they just been going."

"Well, shoot, I must have nearabout a hundred still, don't I?" He couldn't have lost too many; the checks from the syndicate were still running fifteen hundred bucks a month.

"Ninety-six, Ace. But a year ago it was a hundred twelve. Three years ago, a hundred fifty."

"Reckon I better get busy and rustle some newspapers away from them other fellers."

"I think you better."

There was a pause after Pete made that remark, and Ace didn't like the length of it. "Might corral me a series on hands I played with famous fellers," he said. "Ike, Omar Bradley, Nimitz —I ever tell you about the night I played with Lauritz Melchior, who used to sing tenor at the Met? He holds the record for the lowest score anybody ever come in with at a big tournament. Average score fifty percent, he got thirteen percent. Well, him and me played—"

"Ace, you did a series like that two years ago. Now if you could work LBJ into it—"

"Aw, he don't play a thing in the world but politics, Pete. You think it's too soon to do another series on them others?"

"It's not too soon, but it won't solve the problem. That'll take something new. Trouble is, there are too many towns with just one or two newspapers. That means, out of the top three bridge columnists—you and Goren and Jacoby—one gets dumped. Lately you're it."

Ace had always run third in the competition with Goren and Jacoby but used to think time would bring him to the top. After all, he was only fifty-five, more than ten years younger than the others. Unfortunately Goren didn't act like a man getting ready to retire, and Oswald Jacoby had worked his son Jim into his byline, so *that* column was going to continue. "They just had a lucky streak," he grumbled.

"It's unlucky for us," Pete said. "Lots of papers buy your column in a package deal with some of our other features. They start dropping you, it hurts the sale of the package."

The slug of bourbon wasn't sitting quietly inside him; it was sending spurts of acid back up his throat. "I'll figger out something," he muttered.

"There's an easy answer. Knock off a big win in this tournament."

"Aw now rein in your cayuse! I play bridge all the time when do I write my columns?"

"Jacoby plays a lot and does a column. Wins plenty, too."

"Goren don't."

"Come on, Ace, you know how much he's got going for him. The Goren System. Thousands of accredited Goren teachers. That million-dollar title, the King of Bridge. Anyway he won a National event more recently than you did. How long since you racked up a big one, Ace?"

"Could be better than a year."

"Or better than three years, maybe?"

It was of course worse than that. Five years. He hadn't won any National event since 1963. "Could be," he said.

"Grab one for us this time," Pete said coaxingly. "You know what it does for a column. You slip in references to it: when Joe Blow and I were winning the Men's Pairs at the Spring Nationals, some mighty interesting hands came up, and here's one of them. Readers love it. And you know how to milk a big win, you used to milk the hell out of them in your column."

With an effort, Ace let out his rumbling stampede of a laugh. "All right, Pete, I might do that, if it'll take the burr out from under your saddle."

"Thanks, Ace. That's all I had on my mind. Good luck."

He hung up the phone and sat still for a minute. You wouldn't think a man could sit merely talking on the phone and end up sweating like he'd just outrode a posse and a hanging rope. You—goddammit, he told himself sharply, take off the cowboy suit, nobody's watching the act. It was time to quit doing rope tricks and start thinking.

He began analyzing his position. You made the top in big-time bridge in just one way, by winning national events. Of course that in itself didn't pay off; you had to exploit your wins. Invent a good bidding system, easy enough for the women in the afternoon bridge clubs. Write books. Do columns and magazine articles. Give lectures and high-priced lessons. Train bridge teachers. Peddle bridge accessories. You could make a fortune if you were a brilliant player, fine theorist, good writer, glib lecturer, an expert at business and a crack showman. In its forty-three years, contract bridge had produced one man who combined all those qualities: Ely Culbertson. Goren missed out on showmanship. He himself was no theorist or businessman. You could make a good living out of bridge without some of those qualities, but you always needed to be known as a brilliant player.

That was his problem now, the problem all top players always faced. How could you keep winning all the time? Culbertson didn't even try, after making his name and developing his system and writing his books and setting up his business organization. He simply stepped out of big-time competition and pretended not to hear challenges from upstarts like young Charlie Goren. Nowadays Goren could duck competition when he felt like it, because he had the name and system and books and organization. But there was room for only one person like that at a time; Goren was The Man now, and everybody else had to scratch for big wins.

He'd known for a couple of years that he better start winning again soon. The danger signs were clear: fewer papers running his column, fewer lecture dates. It was all very well to do his four-tables act and prove he could play with four partners at once, but he still had to prove that in tournaments he knew how to play with one partner.

He shaved and showered and went down to the lobby. It was too early for most of the top people to be arriving but he spotted a few and chatted with them, dropping hints about maybe looking for a game. Nobody seemed to be hunting for a partner. Finally he saw a lean young man, wearing a black suit and white shirt and dark unpatterned necktie. The man was lounging against a jungle background, as motionless as if he were a wooden tiki placed there by the management. For a moment Ace started turning away—why speak to Tony Manuto if you didn't have to? —but then he thought about the way Tony played bridge. Tony didn't have a lot of points, maybe only nine hundred or so, but that was because the guy played for pay, with dogmeat. He played very well with dogmeat, too; people said Tony had made more Life Masters than anybody in the country. If the guy ever played regularly with good partners he'd clean up. It wouldn't hurt at least to talk to Tony.

He started walking past Tony, so the guy could see him and speak first and it would all seem very casual, but Tony didn't say anything. Tony always wore black sunglasses, indoors and out, and you never knew whether he saw you or not because you couldn't tell where he was looking, if indeed he was looking anywhere. So Ace stopped with a display of surprise and said, "Why, howdy there, Tony."

Tony had seen him. Tony always saw everything. He had seen McKinley walk into the lobby twenty minutes ago, and chat with Jeff and Barry and Phil, and go through a moment of indecision before speaking to him. Tony hadn't been giving any special attention to Ace McKinley. He had merely been watching everything that happened in the lobby: people checking in, people greeting each other, Hank Duke and Harvey Ashcraft (of the Duke-Ashcraft bidding system, known to its fans as The Method) acting cool to each other, and Chief Tournament Director Waldo Starnes collecting a heavy package at the desk. None of this was of any real interest to Tony at the moment, but you never knew what might be useful. For example, if he played against Hank Duke and Harvey Ashcraft in some event, maybe he could get a couple of tops off them by knowing about that coolness. Maybe they would start to grab bids away from each other and he could sit back with a good hand and let them cut their own throats.

Tony said in a flat voice, "Hello, Ace." He was in no rush to learn what Ace had on his mind.

"I'm rounding up stuff for my column," Ace said genially. "Run into any good hands lately, son? Glad to give you credit if I use them."

If it was important to remember one hand, or a dozen or a hundred, Tony could recall them exactly. But after a hand was played and the Recap sheet went up and the protest period ended, he wiped them out of his mind. What was the percentage in remembering? He didn't give lectures or teach or write columns. "Don't remember any," he said.

"Well, if you get any good ones, let me know. How's business?"

"What business?"

"What the hell, aren't you still making dogmeat into Life Masters?"

Tony said, "They got a rule, ACBL Handbook, Chapter Eleven, Section Seven. It says don't hang around tournaments telling everybody, Hey, kids, I'm for hire. So all right, I'm not telling anybody anything. I'm just standing here."

"Sure, sure, son. Anyway I got nothing against playing for pay. We all got to round up a living somehow, don't we?"

"Uh huh."

"Thing is, though, you could make yourself a big name if you played now and then with a real good partner and grabbed off some championships."

"The idea of making a big name don't turn me on. Why should it?"

"Well, you could charge more when you play with dogmeat."

"I already charge every buck they'll pay."

"Don't blame you a bit. Got anything lined up for here?"

There was no harm, Tony decided, in telling the truth. Play-for-pay was legal as long as you didn't go after business too openly; lots of the top players did it, and prettied it up by saying they

were giving a paying lesson to a pupil. Besides, maybe McKinley
might steer some dogmeat his way. "I'm playing the Charity Pairs
tonight with a guy needs some red points to make Life Master.
And I'm lined up for the Vanderbilt next week."

Ace said casually, "I didn't figure on playing here, just bulldogging stuff for columns, but I kinda caught the fever. If you
got nothing better to do, maybe you and me could take a crack
at the Men's Pairs."

Behind the blank mask of the sunglasses Tony studied the
expression on McKinley's face, purposely delaying his reply, and
saw the casual smile get a big tense. Uh huh. Believe it or not,
McKinley was anxious. Tony said coolly, "Fifty bucks a session, you pay the entry fees."

"What!" Ace cried.

"Two qualifying sessions and two in the finals. That's two
hundred bucks. Cost you sixteen bucks more for my entry fees."

"You must be kidding! Who the hell you think you're talking
to? You know how many points I got?"

"Last time I looked, over seven thousand. You're in the top
ten of Life Masters. So what? I don't play bridge for laughs. We
go in the Men's Pairs, I get two hundred bucks. We win it, I get a
bonus. You want me to tell you how much?" He didn't really
want to set a bonus now, because he didn't know how much the
guy would go for.

"Take your bonus and stick it," Ace said, angry enough to forget
the rawhide accent. "You must think you're dealing with dogmeat."
He turned and stamped away.

Tony watched him go. Uh huh, he did think he was dealing
with dogmeat. When they came to him, they were dogmeat. He
eased away from the glass wall of the jungle and moved quietly
across the lobby, looking as if he had just come out of a much
more authentic jungle. It was time to find out when McKinley
last won a big one and how badly he needed another.

Ace went into the cocktail lounge off the lobby and sat at an
empty table and ordered a double bourbon on the rocks. His
hand was trembling when he lifted the glass. Who did that clown

think he was, asking *Ace McKinley* to pay him to play? Why, most anybody would feel honored to play with him. So all right, Jeff and Barry and Phil were already booked up when he talked to them earlier, that didn't mean he had to buy himself a partner. Hadn't he, twice in the past, taken the McKenney Trophy for winning the most master points in a year? He sure had. Not too many years ago, either. He started counting up how long and didn't like the answer. Everything seemed to have gone sour five years ago.

He happened to glance at the entrance of the cocktail lounge and saw the most important thing that had gone sour. Carola Clark was poised there rather uncertainly, much the way he had first seen her in 1948, in the doorway of Jacky Evans' office. Jacky produced shows on Broadway, and liked a good game of bridge. Jacky wanted him to come home for dinner with the wife and to play a couple of rubbers, and they'd made a few phone calls trying to round up a fourth, with no luck. So at last Jacky said, "Maybe somebody waiting outside can play bridge, God knows none of them can act." The chairs in the outer office were always filled with people hoping to get a tryout for one of his plays. Jacky sent out word, and pretty soon there she was in the doorway, a slim blonde named Carola Clark, looking as if she had forgotten her lines.

"You play bridge?" Jacky barked at her.

She gulped and nodded. It turned out later that her father, a fair enough actor when he wasn't drunk, had told her never to admit she couldn't do whatever was needed in a stage or screen role. Could she play the harpsichord? Yes. Turn cartwheels? Yes. Charm a cobra? Yes. Hell, maybe she could learn before she had to prove it. Unfortunately on this occasion she didn't have time to learn a passable game of bridge, and it was a weird evening at the Evanses. Carola played schoolgirl bridge and thought a strip play was something a girl only did in a burlesque show.

Near the end of the evening Carola said plaintively, "How should I have played that hand, Mr. Evans?"

"To quote my friend George S. Kaufman," Jacky growled, "you should have played it under an assumed name."

The kid was ready to bawl, and Ace said, "Lay off, Jacky. She's not so bad. She may not know much about the game but she has card sense."

"For playing what?" Jacky said. "Solitaire?"

"Well now shoot," Ace said, feeling annoyed. "I bet I could make her a Life Master in a year."

"Let's see if there's anything back of that Texas brag," Jacky said. "A thousand bucks says you can't."

"Make it two thousand," Ace said. "And a year from now the little gal and I will take you on in rubber bridge at five cents a point. That is, if—" he had a sudden thought, and looked at the kid "—if you're interested in giving it a try."

The tearful look had left her face and she looked at him as if he had just offered to star her as Shakespeare's Ophelia and Shaw's Saint Joan and Ibsen's Hedda Gabler. "I'll do anything you want, Mr. McKinley," she said breathlessly.

Everybody had hysterics over that statement, and Carola almost cried again, not understanding the joke. At the time she was twenty but in experience she was still wearing bobby sox and swooning over Frank Sinatra. What was back of her remark, he realized later, was just an overwhelming feeling of relief. She didn't want to be an actress. She didn't want to claw her way up in the world. She just wanted to have somebody take care of her and arrange her life. What she wanted, in fact, was a father, old man Clark never having tried out for that role.

So he took her in tow. He hadn't been wrong about the possibilities. She had a mind like a computer; you fed facts about bidding and play and percentages into it and the circuits clamped onto them and never forgot. But beyond that she had card sense. The computer mind would check the percentages on a bid or play and give her the answer, and then maybe she would reject it because something told her this time the percentages wouldn't work. In two months they were scoring above average in tournaments. In four months they were winning section tops. At eight months they won the Mixed Pairs in a Regional, and then there was no stopping them. Mixed Pairs was the easiest event anyway—usually a man and a woman didn't play as well together as did partners of the same sex—but he and Carola meshed like the gears of a Rolls-Royce.

Of course during the year there was a lot of gossip about Ace McKinley taking a young girl to tournaments and paying her expenses. He heard the gossip—"Ace is making a Life Master out of Carola, but when is he going to make an honest woman out of her?"—but he didn't mind. The whole thing was the most brilliant piece of showmanship in his career. Everybody was talking about the bet with Jacky Evans, and asking does or doesn't Carola sleep with Ace. Believe it or not, she didn't, although by the end of the year he was having to take cold showers rather often.

Jacky was a good sport about losing the bet. Jacky gave Carola her Life Master's party at the Plaza one night, and the next night gave her away at the wedding, old man Clark being in a sanatorium drying out at the time. Ace and Carola honeymooned in Bermuda and looked over the site where a new World's Team Championship, the Bermuda Bowl, was to be played in 1950. They decided that it would be nice to make the U.S. team and come back the next year, and by God they did, and on top of everything the team won the Bermuda Bowl, so the marriage was off to a very fine start.

It came to a very poor finish thirteen years later.

So there she was now, poised in the entrance to the cocktail lounge. The same slim figure. The same soft fluffy hair, like sunlight filtering through mist. The same faintly interested expression on her face. At least nobody could accuse him of having robbed the stage of another Lynn Fontanne or Katharine Cornell. Carola could cry when she was very sad, and smile when she was very happy, and that was it. She expressed all other emotions by looking faintly interested. She saw him now, and looked faintly interested. All right, why would she make a big deal of it, they saw each other at all the tournaments, didn't they?

He got up and beckoned to her. For a moment she hesitated, and then came to his table with careful steps as if walking a tightrope. "Hello, Carola," he said. "Sit down and have a drink and help me start a scandal."

"Hello, Ace," she said, peering around the lounge. "A scandal?"

"Ex-wife seen with ex-husband, what's the world coming to. Gin and it, like always?"

"Well, I had promised to meet Babs here."

Babs. That would be Mrs. George M. Hartley, chief lady-in-waiting of the little court of women who followed Carola around nowadays. Babs was the sort of woman who gave wife-beaters a good name. Not that she was a wife any longer; George M. Hartley had died some years ago, probably, Ace thought, of frostbite. Unfortunately he had left Babs four or five million bucks, and with that much money she could afford to do a lot of things she'd always wanted to do, such as be nasty to almost everybody. He wished he saw signs of her being nasty to Carola instead of possessive.

"You can meet her here and also have a drink with me. Gin and it, like always?"

"Well, all right. A little dry sherry, I think."

"Dry sherry? Not like always, huh?"

"Things do change, don't they, Ace?"

"Some things don't. You're still the best-looking woman I ever saw."

She sat down and suddenly gave him one of those smiles. "And you still tell lies as big as Texas. How are you, Ace?"

"Oh, fine, fine. Gonna do a lot of playing here?"

"I suppose. Babs wants to go into most of the events."

"She's not in your class. Why waste your time?"

Carola shrugged. "She asked me to give her some playing lessons."

"I hope you charge her a million."

"Oh, I make out all right, Ace. How have you been doing lately? Didn't I hear rumors that, well . . ."

"That what?" he said sharply.

"That . . . well . . . you know, Ace, I keep worrying about those alimony payments. It doesn't seem right."

"Two hundred a week? You need more?"

"Heavens no. I really earn quite a lot giving lessons and little talks. What I've been worrying about is, well, shouldn't that alimony be cut or even stopped one of these days? It doesn't seem fair for it to go on and on."

"What the hell, I keep worrying that maybe it should be more."

She reached across the table and touched his hand with her slender fingers, fingers that handled cards the way Da Vinci must have handled a paintbrush. "Really, Ace? You could afford it?"

"Why, shoot," he said, trying to make his tone strong and confident. "Say the word and we'll make it three hundred."

The fingers stroked his hand for a moment, and withdrew. "Thank you, Ace. I don't want more. I just want to be sure you can afford this."

"Afford it? Last year I must have made sixty-seventy thousand." That was absolutely true except for one word. Last year he *should* have made sixty-seventy thousand. What he actually earned was closer to thirty. "Know what, Carola? It's real nice having a little time with you again. Might be fun if we played in some event here. Just for kicks. I bet we could cut them to bits in the Mixed Pairs."

"Or cut each other to bits, like the last time we played?"

"That was five years ago."

"Ace, I don't know. I have a sort of date for the Mixed Pairs. And the Open Pairs, too. Let me think it over. I—"

"Oh, *there* you are," a voice said. It was a cool and cultured voice, as impersonal in sound as ice cubes tinkling in a glass. "And sitting with guess who!"

Ace looked up at Babs Hartley. She was probably a handsome woman, he thought, if you liked them thin and frosty and with lips that looked as if they were relaxing between sneers. She wore a simple black cocktail dress and a simple strand of pearls and, being Babs Hartley, the simplicity was probably from Balenciaga and Tiffany. He got up reluctantly and said, putting on the public accent, "Howdy, Babs. Set down and join us, I reckon you'll do it anyways."

"Oh, Ace!" Carola said.

"Think nothing of it, dear," Babs said, patting her hand and sitting down. "Ace always has been a little blunt, nobody ever told him that finesse is not exclusively a bridge term. Well, isn't this ever so cozy! What are we discussing over our tea and crumpets, is divorce the first step toward true love?"

"Oh, Babs!" Carola said.

"We were talking about maybe playing together here," Ace said. "Carola might enjoy a good partner for a change."

Babs turned to Carola and said, "Now don't say, Oh Ace, my dear. I can defend myself, weak woman though I am . . . yes, Ace, you certainly ought to play with her. Maybe you can come up with another hand that will go down in bridge history, like the last one you played with Carola. You remember it?"

"No," Ace said. He wasn't going to be needled into talking about *that*.

"You and Carola were defending against a four spade bid, I believe," Babs said.

"Oh let's forget it," Carola said. "Anyway it was four hearts."

"Four hearts, *doubled*," Ace said.

"I wasn't the one who doubled," Carola said.

"I had a perfectly good double," Ace said. "You overcalled and I had a right to count on you for at least one trick."

"I had two tricks," Carola said. "If you had played it right."

"Played it right!" Ace cried. "My God, woman, your opening lead was a singleton diamond king!"

"One of the best leads I ever made! All you had to do was overtake with your ace and return diamonds and I trump. Then I put you back in for your two club tricks and you give me another diamond ruff."

"All you had to do was make the safe opening lead of a club. I take my two club tricks and, since you hadn't led diamonds, I would automatically have played my diamond ace. Your king drops and I realize it's a singleton and give you a ruff for the setting trick."

"On the second trick I did put you in with your clubs. But would you lead your diamond ace? No, you decided I had king, queen, jack, small, and that declarer would get the ruff."

"Naturally I decided that," Ace said. "Who ever heard of leading a bare king when I hadn't even bid the suit! Sheer lunacy!"

"Yes," Carola said. "That's what you told me, right in public, after they made four hearts doubled."

"And you threw your cards in my face."

"Yes," Carola said, her voice starting to drown in tears, "and you couldn't resist turning to our opponents, a couple of horrid people, and saying, *Please excuse my wife, she's been throwing away her cards like this all night.* How colorful of you! What showmanship! It got you in all the gossipy books about bridge, didn't it? Oh damn, I didn't want to remember it. I—" She jumped up and hurried out of the lounge.

For a moment Ace sat stunned. How the hell had things gone so wrong just now? He knew why they'd gone wrong that last time they played. A lot of nasty remarks had been going the rounds, to the effect that Ace McKinley kept on winning only because Carola was such a good player and carried him. Of course you ought to laugh off remarks like that—there were always nasty remarks going the rounds—but it was hard to do. It was also hard to admit that Carola had become, well, *almost* as good a player as he was. Back in 1963 he was still trying to cling to their original relationship, to the picture of the wide-eyed girl looking at him and saying breathlessly, "I'll do anything you want, Mr. McKinley." All right, he thought, rather insanely, what I want is *Don't lead singleton kings.*

Across the table from him, Babs Hartley said sweetly, "So they were divorced on her charge of extreme cruelty, to wit, that he made the poor girl play bridge with him."

He glared at her, and said, "I sure went for that sucker bait of yours. I was stupid, wasn't I?"

"You merely acted like a normal red-blooded male idiot."

"And you acted like a cold-blooded bitch."

She got up lazily. "Perhaps I did," she said, with a small yawn. "Well, have fun in the Mixed Pairs with whoever you get to play with you. I doubt that it will be Carola."

He watched her depart, and thought about the way she had taken him. If she could play bridge that way she'd be hard to beat, but of course bridge had rules against that kind of coffee-housing. Well, as Babs said, he could give up any idea of playing with Carola. He was sorry about that. Even if they hadn't won he would have enjoyed it, provided, of course, that she didn't lead any more singleton kings.

Upstairs in her room, Carola gulped a couple of aspirin tablets, and took off everything but a slip and lay face down on the bed to wait for the thumping in her head to fade. Oh damn, she thought, it was so long since they'd had a talk and it started out so nicely—she really had kept her looks and figure, hadn't she?—and then it ended so badly. It would have been good to play with Ace again. It didn't really matter which of them was the better player, although of course she was, because the important thing was that their games fit so beautifully. At his best, Ace played bridge like a circus acrobat doing leaps and twists on the high trapeze, and she was the catcher who never let him fall, except when he simply closed his eyes and refused to watch what she was doing, as in the case of the singleton king. Didn't he realize that, with her lead, they could have set that contract *two* tricks instead of the one down that the safe club lead would have produced?

She thought back over their talk and found she was still worried about those alimony payments. There really were rumors that Ace wasn't doing so well lately. What was it he said? *Why, shoot, say the word and we'll make it three hundred.* He sounded very firm and confident. But that might not mean anything. When Ace made an opening bid you couldn't tell from his tone whether he had half the high cards in the deck or was psyching with a bust. You always had to make a careful exploratory response to find out whether he meant it or not, and downstairs she hadn't had enough time to do that.

A tapping sounded on the connecting door to Babs' room, and she called, her voice muffled by the pillow, "Come in."

"You poor dear," Babs said, coming into the room. "You're all upset, aren't you?"

"I just have a little headache."

"I can't forgive myself for bringing up that subject, Carola. I didn't realize what it would lead to."

"That's all right. It was my fault for getting angry."

Babs sat on the bed and began rubbing the back of Carola's neck. "It's probably just a tension headache, and this will relax you," she said. "Feel good?"

The fingers kneading the neck muscles worked softly and skillfully. "It feels wonderful," Carola said.

"We can have dinner sent up. There's plenty of time, the Charity Pairs don't begin until eight-thirty. Of course we can skip the game if you don't feel up to it."

She was starting to become drowsy under the touch of the long clever fingers. They moved down from her neck and began loosening the muscles of her back. It was pleasant to lie quietly and let somebody take care of her, the way Ace used to do. "This will fix me up," she murmured.

Babs said with a soft laugh, "My fingers keep skidding on this slip of yours and I can't get into the tight muscles. If I pull your slip down I can do a better job." Her fingers began to slide the straps of the slip off Carola's shoulders.

Carola stirred uneasily. Perhaps she didn't want Babs to take care of her as completely as this. "I feel fine now," she said, sitting up and adjusting the straps of the slip. "Just give me a half hour to wash and dress, and I'll be ready for dinner. And thank you, Babs, that was very nice of you."

Babs smiled and said, "Any time, my dear," and returned to her room.

For a minute Carola remained sitting on the bed, trying to sort her thoughts neatly, like a bridge hand. Unfortunately the suits kept changing color, and kings turned into queens, or an Ace McKinley became a Babs Hartley. She knew she wasn't clever about managing her relationships with other people. She tended to let herself drift. Once she let herself drift into a divorce that she didn't really want, and now a rather odd undertow in her relationship with Babs was carrying her to . . . well, she didn't exactly know where, or even want to know.

And about Ace. Were the rumors about him true or not, and what if anything ought she do about it? She didn't want to run around asking other bridge people about him; they would begin whispering that Ace couldn't keep up the alimony payments, or invent some other unpleasant reason for her questions. She wondered if she dare call the syndicate; somebody named Johnson, no, *Jackson,* used to handle Ace's column. But perhaps Mr. Jackson wasn't there any more, or maybe he wouldn't answer her questions and would tell Ace that she had been prying into his affairs. It could all get very complicated. Perhaps she had better do nothing.

At exactly this moment, downstairs at the bar of the cocktail lounge, her questions about Ace were being asked and answered.

Waldo Starnes, Chief Tournament Director, was having a drink at the bar. During the next ten days he would not have time for many drinks, because he would be in charge of organizing, supervising and scoring nine championship events of two or more sessions each, four consolation events of two sessions each, and thirty-five one-session side games, counting the Charity Pairs tonight. During these games nine thousand two hundred and forty-five tables would be in play. At least a thousand times, people would complain of the room to which they were assigned for a bridge session, or protest that they should have been seeded or demand to be north-south instead of east-west or explain that they couldn't play as Pair Six because six had a bad aura for them. Perhaps five hundred times, the firm or plaintive or angry cry "DIRECTOR!" would go up from a table and some decision would have to be made about an alleged breach of the rules. He had forty-four directors to help him, but in some ways this merely meant that he had forty-four more people to bring him problems.

He loved it all. He was a small elflike man who led a happy scurrying life in the world of big-time bridge. The giants of bridge kept him fascinated. He was filled with a quivering curiosity about their loves and hates and what they did at the bridge table and away from the bridge table. He enjoyed peeking into their bridge hands and into their private lives. He was very important to them because he ran tournaments better than anyone else could do, and in another way utterly insignificant because he did not play expert bridge. In fact he played very bad bridge, and this gave the giants a chance to get back at him for the authority he held over them in tournaments. They did this by coaxing him to play rubber bridge late at night after the duplicate events ended. He always wanted to refuse these invitations and was unable to make himself do so. It was like having a horrible urge to go for a swim among man-eating sharks. They never let him play for high stakes—a quarter of a cent a point, at the most—and so he would only lose nine or ten dollars, but the sensation was that of being mouthed by terrible jaws and then of being flung contemptuously aside. Oh yes, the giants of bridge were strange and wonderful creatures. He never tired of spying on them and picking up every bit of gossip about them that went the rounds.

This, of course, was the reason why Tony Manuto now joined Waldo at the bar, in the course of seeking information about Ace McKinley. "Hi, Waldo," Tony said. "Can I buy you a drink?"

Waldo's nose began twitching with eager interest. Tony Manuto wanted to buy him a drink. Oh how wonderful! How fascinating! Tony never did anything without a purpose. If Tony asked you for the time, maybe he wanted to see if your watch was worth stealing. That was only in a manner of speaking: just a way of indicating that Tony must want something from you besides the time. Tony didn't steal watches or anything else of normal intrinsic value. That is, as far as Waldo knew. He hugged his arms to his sides ecstatically. What a shame there were never any big jewel thefts at these tournaments! Tony would be the perfect suspect: dangerous, unprincipled, quiet and sneaky as a cat. But of course Tony wasn't an ordinary thief. The only things Tony stole were tops on duplicate hands. Waldo knew he did it. After an event was scored, Waldo always studied the Recap sheet to see how some of his most fascinating giants had done. When Tony's name was listed, you could usually find two or maybe even three hands on which Tony had obtained an extraordinary result. Perhaps Tony made an overtrick at four spades when everybody else was down one. A cold top: twelve match points out of a possible twelve, or twenty-five out of twenty-five, if they were pairing the sections. Expert players sometimes got remarkable scores when their opponents made errors, but to do it several times a session with dogmeat partners, that had to be cheating, didn't it? Perhaps a quick peek into an opponent's hand? Of course Tony was clever. With those dark sunglasses nobody could tell if he peeked. Also Tony made his amazing scores against poor opponents who might be expected to give away tops, and so the experts didn't get suspicious and start wondering how Tony managed it.

"A drink?" Waldo said. "Oh yes indeed, Tony. I'm having Scotch and soda."

Tony gave the order, and said, "Looking for a big mob? Will it beat last year?"

Oh, this was delightful! Tony had no interest in attendance as long as there were enough paying partners to keep him fairly busy. "I'm sure we'll go over eight thousand tables," Waldo said. "Maybe even nine thousand. I look for eight hundred pairs just in the Charity game tonight. You playing in it, Tony?"

"I might make the scene, I might not."

Waldo hid a giggle. Tony didn't like being asked questions, even one as innocent as that. There were dozens of lovely and not-at-all-innocent questions he would like to ask Tony. How much do you really make, Tony? Besides peeking, how else do you cheat? Were you really in one of those New York street gangs as a kid? Do you have a sex life, Tony, and is it with men or women? "Well, good luck if you play," he said.

"Are we gonna be using those juke-box hands?" Tony asked.

"You mean the ones dealt by computer? Yes, we are. In all the big events and even a lot of the side games."

"What happens if the printed copies of the hands don't come in time?"

"I could call the ACBL office up north and have duplicates sent airmail special. But I already have all the hands. They were waiting when I got here, a bit box that came by certified mail."

Tony nodded. That was the package he saw Waldo collect earlier that day. He said, "I see a lot of the big shots already showed up. Saw Hank Duke and Harvey Ashcraft in the lobby. What's with those guys? They acted like they didn't quite catch each other's name. After all they did invent The Method, a lousy system if you ask me. They gonna be playing together?"

"Oh, they haven't been getting along at all well, Tony. I'll be surprised if they do any playing as a pair. Of course they'll be on the same team in the Vanderbilt, I expect, but playing with their wives."

"Glad I got no wife. Must be hell carrying all those fights home from the bridge table, like I guess Ace McKinley and Carola used to do. That guy hasn't been with it lately, has he? How long since Ace won a big one?"

"He took the Men's Pairs at a regional five years ago," Waldo said. "That was just before his divorce went through. He hasn't won a thing since except, you know, consolations and little stuff."

"Does he still make much dough from his column and other things, now that he don't win big?"

"Well, I suppose his income must have gone down, because he's lost a lot of newspapers and he doesn't get the lecture dates he used to. But he still seems to spend money rather freely, and of course he pays quite a good alimony to Carola."

Tony finished his drink, and slid off the stool and said, "Like I said, glad I got no wife. Carting fights home, paying alimony, not for me. Save me a north-south for tonight, Waldo, in case I decide to play."

"I will certainly do that," Waldo said.

He watched Tony leave, and hugged his arms to his sides. How lovely, lovely, lovely! Now, what did Tony really want to know? Which were the real questions and which the smoke screen? Was Tony involved with the Dukes and Ashcrafts, say, with Miggsy Ashcraft or Olga Duke? Both were attractive women, in very different ways, of course, and both showed a slightly tense look around the eyes, as if something had gone out of their marriages, such as maybe sex. Or did Tony have a special interest in Ace McKinley? Or—oh heavens, how shocking and delightful!—did Tony have some dark and devious ideas about the computer-dealt hands? If anybody ever managed to steal copies of those hands in advance, think what a score he could make! Of course it wouldn't be easy to steal them. Each set of hands was sealed in a big Manila envelope that had to be examined and opened in the presence of a special committee. And, at the moment, the envelopes were in a locked box in a locked closet in Waldo's locked room. But perhaps sealed envelopes and locks were no harder for Tony to finesse than a guarded queen.

So what had Tony really been curious about: Ace McKinley's finances, or the problems of the Dukes and Ashcrafts, or the computer-dealt hands? Which of Tony's questions had been a type of false-carding, designed to hide the facts? Waldo had often been fooled by false-carding, during those fascinating and frightening sessions of rubber bridge into which the experts liked to lure him. But this time he was sure he had seen through the ruse. He hurried upstairs to get the box of computer-dealt hands and to put it into the hotel safe.

Meanwhile Tony Manuto, having collected the information he needed about Ace McKinley, went off about his business.

MANY AMERICANS WHO play bridge have subconscious feelings of guilt about it. This is a heritage from Puritan times, when cards were looked on as things of the devil. The Puritans called them Devil's Tickets or the Devil's Picture Book, and pointed out that the commandment against making unto thyself any graven image obviously included the face cards of a deck. The ban against cards ended but the feeling of guilt about card playing became embedded in the national memory, where it was strengthened by inherited worries about doing anything that did not have a serious, moral and improving purpose. The playing of duplicate bridge is a serious activity—a point in its favor—but nobody can claim that it helps the morals of its devotees, and it certainly does not improve such things as their dispositions.

It has been customary in the United States to atone for guilt feelings by engaging in good works: in early days, perhaps by sending long cotton garments to nude Polynesians; in later days, perhaps by sending a hundred million dollars to an emerging African nation. Thus in 1934 the officers of the American Contract Bridge League started a charity program. By the time of the Spring Nationals at the Xanadu, the ACBL was raising more than a quarter of a million dollars yearly for various good works. An important part of this program was the first event at the tournament, the Charity Pairs. Simultaneously, hundreds of other charity games were held throughout the country, using the same computer-dealt hands played at the Nationals. So it was possible for people to play bridge without a twinge of conscience on this particular evening.

One player who never felt guilty about bridge, or about anything else, was Tony Manuto. He came up to the table where Waldo Starnes was selling entry slips, and gave him six dollars for himself and his partner, and said, "You were gonna save me a north-south."

"Playing with anybody good?" Waldo said.

"Guy named Ensley Worthington, standing over there looking at the schedule," Tony said, jerking a thumb at his partner.

Waldo saw a slender young man whose crew-cut hair looked tough and whose full red lips looked soft. He was beautifully dressed in a sport jacket checked in black and white, a pale blue shirt with a darker blue tie, dark trousers and mirror-finish black shoes. As the young man studied the schedule, his slim fingers constantly adjusted his gold collar pin and the three points of the white handkerchief in his breast pocket.

"I've seen him around," Waldo said. "Ensley Worthington, hm? What's his background?"

Tony could have said that his partner lived in Palm Beach, didn't work because his parents were loaded, yearned to be a Life Master, acted like a nance who hadn't met the right guy yet, and in general was a real creep. But Tony did not give out information needlessly, so he merely said, "His background is that everybody calls him Bubba."

"What a revolting nickname!" Waldo said. "Is he a Life Master?"

"No. He's got the black points but he needs twelve reds."

In tournaments it is the practice to seed strong pairs through the sections, so that they will not be grouped closely and kill each other off. For this purpose the entry slips for tables 1, 6 and 11 were reserved, table 1 north-south being the prize position. When Waldo was in a mischievous mood he sometimes gave a strong pair not only an unseeded number but also an east-west position that made them keep moving all evening. But he was pleased with Tony for having been so fascinating at the bar before dinner, so he reached into the pile of reserved slips and gave him Section D, table 1, north-south.

Tony looked at the entry slip with mild surprise. Playing with dogmeat, he did not often get 1 north-south. Top seeding gave you a psychological edge over some opponents, and sometimes made dogmeat like Bubba play better. "Okay, thanks," he said, and went away.

While this was happening, another player who did not feel guilty about playing bridge, but who had a much deeper and more painful reaction to it, approached the Partnership Table. He was a tall gaunt man, aged fifty-nine, with large bulging eyes like those of a St. Bernard dog on a rescue mission.

"For the Charity game I am needing a partner," he said to one of the committeewomen. "I am hoping you have somebody good, and if they also play the Hoffmeister No Trump I am asking nothing better. I am P. J. Hoffmeister, of the Hoffmeister No Trump, approved as a Class Two convention."

The woman looked at him with awe. To develop a bidding convention and have it approved and carry your name was, in a way, to achieve immortality. But she could not understand why an immortal should be reduced to coming to the Partnership Table. Also she could not exactly place the Hoffmeister No Trump, although she was fairly well up on her conventions. Obviously the convention existed, however, because the man wore a large plastic badge that announced I PLAY THE HOFFMEISTER NO TRUMP.

"We'll do our best for you," she said, and then added rather apologetically, because it was hardly the question you asked an immortal, "Um, how many points do you have?"

Hoffmeister believed in honesty, although this had not always helped him in his business as an accountant, and so he replied sadly and accurately, "Fifty-three."

Well, the woman thought, how lucky I asked! Suppose I had assumed that I must get him a Life Master? People were often unhappy with the partners she obtained for them, but at least if she matched up the point holdings she could always defend herself by saying, well, he has as many points as you do. "I think we have just the person for you," she said. "Do you see that nice lady standing by the doorway, the one who just dropped her handbag and—mercy, are those a couple of doughnuts that fell out of it?—anyway she is Mrs. Robert Lee Rutledge and needs a partner. Come back and tell me if it isn't all right."

Hoffmeister walked up to the lady and looked politely elsewhere while she recovered a doughnut that had rolled under a chair. When she straightened up, flustered and pink in the face, he said, "To you a very good evening. I am P. J. Hoffmeister, of the Hoffmeister No Trump, and the lady at Partnerships says a game you are looking for."

"Oh," Mrs. Rutledge said, and then, "Oh! The Hoffmeister No Trump!"

"Ah! You are hearing of it? Maybe even you play it?"

"Well of course I've heard of it," Mrs. Rutledge said, because it could be fatal to admit ignorance when trying to arrange a partnership. "But maybe I'm the least little bit rusty on it."

"You should excuse me for asking, how many points have you got?"

"Forty-seven," Mrs. Rutledge said stoutly. She was not going to admit she only had twenty, and perhaps lose a splendid partner. Even forty-seven might be far too few. "Maybe you have just bundles of points and wouldn't want to play with little old me."

"Such a thing don't cross my mind. You should worry, I have only fifty-three points. But it is busy with the theory of the game I have been, it gives not enough time to play. Of the fifty-three points, two red points I got already."

"Only two?" she said happily. "Why, I have four red points!"

"Maybe a good game we are having, and we are sitting down somewhere and going over the Hoffmeister No Trump so it will get us a couple tops. But first I am getting our entry slip."

"Oh good," she said, making no move to open her handbag.

Several times she had played with real southern gentlemen who did not ask for her entry fee. "I'll wait right here."

He said firmly, "From you it is three dollars for the entry fee."

Of course he wasn't southern, sort of foreign by his way of speaking, so she hadn't really hoped that he would pay for her. She dug out three dollars for him.

Hoffmeister walked to the long directors' table and waited in the line in front of Waldo Starnes. He knew Waldo, and in fact almost everybody important in the ACBL, because he had been obliged to plead and argue with them for years to get Class Two approval for the Hoffmeister No Trump. They had been very blind about it. Year after year he had painfully made out the application for approval, and sent it in with the required seventy-five copies of a document describing the convention and showing how it was used in sample hands, and year after year they had rejected it. Last year, grumpily and with the air of men wanting to get rid of him, they approved the Hoffmeister No Trump for a two-year test. After that they would decide whether enough people were using it to justify extending the approval. So he couldn't relax. He only had one year left to prove its value. There was also the problem that Class Two was not automatically allowed at the convention in any given tournament. Class Two was optional, and before each tournament he had to beg the tournament committee to allow it, as he had done here. He did hope that Mrs. Rutledge played fine bridge and would help prove the value of the Hoffmeister No Trump tonight.

"Hello, P. J.," Waldo said, as Hoffmeister reached the head of the line. "Good luck to you tonight." He sold him the entry slip for Section D, table 2, east-west. This would move P. J. Hoffmeister and Mary Rose Rutledge around the fourteen tables of Section D throughout the evening and, for the last two hands, pit them against Pair 1 north-south, Tony Manuto and Ensley Worthington, with consequences that would affect the lives of a dozen people. Of course Waldo did not know this, which was too bad, because it would have been one of the most delightful experiences in his career.

Hoffmeister went back to Mrs. Rutledge and led her to Section D, table 2, east-west, and said, "Half an hour we got, you and me should know each other better. The—"

"Oh yes, it's much nicer when you know something about each other," Mrs. Rutledge said. "Well, I'm from Richmond, Virginia, and if you want you can call me Mary Rose." She pronounced it Mayrose.

"It's all the same to you, I am not getting so familiar. What we should get to know better, it is how the both of us play bridge."

"Oh. Well, what I usually play is just plain old Goren with non-forcing Stayman and Blackwood for aces."

"The Hoffmeister No Trump you are forgetting," he said. "And now I am telling you about it. I am looking at you and asking, how many times are you holding a sixteen-to-eighteen-point no trump count when the right-hand opponents has opened the bidding?"

"Oh dear," she said, with a vague feeling that she was being accused of something. "Would . . . would that be bad?"

"Bad has nothing to do with it. Percentages we deal with, and percentages don't know from good or bad."

"You know all about *percentages?*" To her, they were among the mysteries of bridge.

"An accountant I am, a little business of my own, in Newark, New Jersey, just an accountant, I don't claim a C.P.A., but an accountant you got to know percentages. Like Oswald Jacoby he wouldn't play such good bridge except he was an accountant, maybe you don't know he was an accountant?"

"I really never thought of it one way or another."

"A fact it is, you should be thinking of facts, Mrs. Rutledge. So a fact we got here, how often do you hold a sixteen-to-eighteen-point no trump count when the righthand opponent has opened the bidding, I could give you the percentage, it would just confuse you, but I'm telling you such a hand don't come up often out of the 8,122,425,444 different hands you can hold in second position at the table. So a regular no trump overcall you don't get to make often, so the regular no trump overcall we are not making, so we are looking for a chance to overcall with . . . with what, Mrs. Rutledge?"

His questions sounded so ominous that they drove thoughts clean out of her mind. "I—I don't know," she said.

He tapped the large plastic badge on his coat. "So we are looking for a chance to overcall with the Hoffmeister No Trump, Mrs. Rutledge! An artificial bid we are making. What do we need for this bid? A hand we are getting lots more than we are getting a regular no trump count after the righthand opponent makes an opening bid. We are looking for a hand of nine to thirteen points, and out of the three unbid suits we are looking for two suits of four-card length or longer. Right away we are saying, One No Trump, and the opponents they are looking at us like a mother they just lost, account of we have bid the Hoffmeister No Trump and the percentages say we are going to give them a bad board. You are remembering what we need for this bid, Mrs. Rutledge?"

Nine to thirteen points, and a pair of four-card suits. Why, it was going to be easy! Yes, she could remember that, and it sounded like such fun. "Oh yes!" she cried. "I've got it, I really have!"

"Comes now," he said, "the important part. Comes now what the partner does after the Hoffmeister No Trump."

"The . . . the partner?" she said weakly. One moment it had been so lovely and easy, and now it was going to get ugly and complicated.

"The partner," he said sternly. "Bridge a partnership game is, Mrs. Rutledge. So you shouldn't got to remember it from talk, I am giving you the facts the way a bridge writer, he makes his living at it, for me in print did it up." He took a printed card from his pocket and handed it to her.

Mary Rose understood that she was expected to look at the printed card intently and intelligently, and at least she could look at it intently. The card said:

THE HOFFMEISTER NO TRUMP

Over an opening bid, second hand bids The Hoffmeister No Trump with 9-13 points, balanced hand, and four cards or more each in two of the unbid suits.

Partner passes with a balanced hand and less than 12 points.

Partner raises to Two No Trump with balanced hand and 12 or more points; this allows first No Trumper to bid game with 13 points.

Partner passes with less than 6 points and no long suit.

With unbalanced hand and six cards or more in an unbid suit, partner bids and rebids that suit regardless of points.

With two unbid suits of four cards or more each, regardless of points, partner bids lower-ranking suit. If this doesn't match one of No Trumper's four-card suits, the No Trumper bids other suit; the chance of finding a four-four fit is very good.

THE HOFFMEISTER NO TRUMP HAS GREAT VALUE IN EITHER SHUTTING OPPONENTS OUT OF BIDDING OR CRAMPING THEIR BIDDING ROOM!

Mary Rose studied the card and nodded thoughtfully, just as she would have done if asked to read an explanation of how the Doppler Effect accounts for the red-light shift in distant nebulae. "Does it always work?" she asked.

"Always we are not talking about, there is no always in bridge, percentages we got. Seventy-two percent of the time a good score the Hoffmeister No Trump gets you."

Mary Rose nodded again. She too could work percentages, if they were simple enough. They would be playing twenty-six boards tonight. Only fifty percent of the time would he or she be in the second-hand position needed for the Hoffmeister No Trump. *She* certainly wasn't going to bid it. That left the twenty-five percent of the hands when Mr. Hoffmeister was the second bidder, and maybe he would never have the right hand to bid it.

The percentages were very much in her favor. "It's just lovely," she chirped. "I don't think we'll have the teensiest bit of trouble."

"Good," he said. "Then we are fixing up our convention cards and getting ready lots of tops to make."

When Hoffmeister talked about making tops he was referring to the scoring system that helps to make duplicate a different game from rubber bridge. In rubber bridge, the full score that partners earn on any deal is carried on their tally throughout the play. In duplicate, the initial score made on a board is translated into match points by comparing all north-south scores with each other and all east-west scores with each other. A pair of partners gets a match point for every pair beaten, and half a match point for every pair tied. It makes no difference if Pair 1 north-south sets a spade grand slam thirteen tricks vulnerable, doubled and redoubled for a profit of 7,600 points, while all the other north-souths allow the grand slam to make, vulnerable, doubled and redoubled, for a loss of 2,890 points, or a combined difference of 10,490 points; the winning north-south pair only gets one match point for each other north-south pair beaten. The north-south pair could get exactly the same number of match points by making one no trump and 90 points while all the other north-souths are making one spade and eighty points.

If the scores of thirteen north-souths are being compared on a board, the top match point score is twelve and bottom is zero. And if a north-south gets a top on a board, obviously its east-west opponents are going to get a bottom.

So it was in the hope of tops and the fear of bottoms that P. J. Hoffmeister and Mary Rose Rutledge set out to play in the Charity Pairs, along with eight hundred and thirty-nine other pairs divided into thirty sections of fourteen tables each. Waldo and twenty-nine assisting directors handed out printed copies of the computer-dealt hands, and hovered over the duplicating of these hands with cards, and snatched back the printed copies, and made sure that each pair of duplicated boards was passed to another table where the printed hands for these boards had not been seen. During the course of the evening the Mitchell Movement would send the boards in one direction around the section and the east-west pairs in the other. The mathematics of the progression would prevent any pair from playing the hands they had seen when duplicating them. Mary Rose did not understand the Mitchell or the scrambled Mitchell or the Howell or Rainbow or any of the other movements used in duplicate, but one of the reasons why directors were paid from $20 to $25 a session was to keep people like Mary Rose from playing the wrong boards at the wrong table, which otherwise she would have done.

Hoffmeister and Mary Rose began having a magical evening. Everything went well. There was no way to be absolutely sure—caddies grabbed the pick-up scorecards after every round, so you had to guess what others were doing on the same boards—but there were ways of making an estimate. Hoffmeister did it the hard way, by calculating the best normal result on a hand and comparing it with the result he and Mrs. Rutledge obtained. Mary Rose did it the easy way; she knew that if opponents were snapping at each other when she left their table, they must have done badly and she must have done well.

In his happiness over the game they were having, Hoffmeister began noticing what a nice smile Mrs. Rutledge had, and the way her soft brown eyes glowed. These were things he had not noticed in a woman since his wife left him fifteen years ago.

"A fine woman," he told himself. "Looks she has got, and a brain. I should have been so lucky with my Reba, that idiot, she should run off with one of my clients why don't she pick a smart client, not that Herman, I bet he still don't make two hundred a week."

It was after Reba left him that he had begun trying to develop a new convention for bridge. A man had to do something to put his mark on the world. Were you going to die and leave nothing to mark your passage through life but the dent in a mattress, and the hollows in the wooden stairs outside your walk-up office? A man had to aim higher than that. If he couldn't leave behind such monuments as children or a novel or an opera or a fine business, he had to try to scratch his name elsewhere for coming generations to read. Perhaps in the records of bridge: the Hoffmeister No Trump.

Maybe tonight, he thought, the scratch would go deep enough to stay. He and this fine woman were having a big game. Seventy percent of the match points they were winning, enough to take first in section east-west, maybe even first overall out of all the thirty sections. Seventy percent was a monster; most sections you could win with sixty percent of the match points. If only the Hoffmeister No Trump would come up, so that later he could show how it helped them win first overall out of eight hundred and forty pairs!

At that moment, more than halfway through the session, the strong current of his thoughts dragged his attention away from the cards, and he failed to follow suit and was charged with a revoke, costing two tricks. It was a sure bottom, and killed the chance of first overall. But first in section was still possible and maybe even seventh or eighth overall. He made no mistakes at the next table, number 11. Unfortunately he and Mary Rose arrived there at the wrong time. Playing north-south at table 11 were Carola Clark and Babs Hartley, and Carola was furious with herself. All evening Ace McKinley had been on her mind and she had played stupid bridge. Now she yanked her thoughts back to the game and began using all her icy skill. She bid a shaky little slam and made it with a trump coup. She gambled on a bid of three no trump with one suit unguarded, and got away with it. Hoffmeister and Mary Rose left table 11 with two more bottoms, and now first in section was nearly out of reach.

The hands at tables 12, 13 and 14 went smoothly. Their opponents made several errors, and first in section fluttered closer again, a bluebird of happiness. Then they came to the final table, 1, to which Waldo Starnes had assigned Tony Manuto and Ensley "Bubba" Worthington, with consequences that were about to be realized. Hoffmeister did not know either of the north-south players at table 1. North was a young man with sleek black hair, thin lips and black sunglasses. His face was clean, hollowed at the temples and under the cheekbones, the effect being that of a carved and polished primitive mask with large blank eyeholes. South was a young man with brown hair worn in a crew cut, brown eyes and full red lips.

"To you a very good evening," Hoffmeister said politely.

Neither of the young men answered or even looked at him, which was not unusual in tournament bridge. They were talking earnestly to each other. "Cool it, man," North said, North being Tony Manuto. "You almost blew that last one."

"But Tony, Tony, Tony!" South cried, South being Bubba Worthington. "It came out all right, didn't it?" His voice teetered up almost to a soprano level.

"They could have kicked our teeth in. We were just shot with luck."

"But Tony, we've got it nailed down, haven't we? Haven't we really?"

Hoffmeister recognized the boiling excitement in the tone and in the way the young man quivered. When one or both of a pair acted like that, they were having a monster game, tops all over the place.

"Got what?" Tony said in a voice like glass crunching underfoot. "A lousy first in section? Two point eighty red points. I thought you wanted twelve. Only one score gets us that. Not fourth overall. Not third overall. Not second overall, that's just eleven point twenty. You want twelve red ones, we need first overall. That pays sixteen red points. Now put away your dolls and play bridge."

Bubba Worthington trembled and yanked his cards from the pocket of the board, his full red lips pouting. He was angry and hurt, which was what Tony intended; some creeps had to be slapped to make them concentrate. Tony drew his cards smoothly from the board, like a man easing out a knife. Mary Rose looked at Hoffmeister, and shrugged as if to say, "The folks who play bridge!" Hoffmeister gave a grimace that said, "Such manners they got, I don't think." Hoffmeister disliked the two young men; he was not vindictive, but it would be a pleasure to keep the young men out of first overall.

On the first hand, Tony opened with a big pre-empt—three spades—and stole the bid from Hoffmeister and Mary Rose, who could have made four hearts. The spade bit should have been set but somehow Tony made it. A top for north-south. A bottom for east-west. And now, Hoffmeister knew sadly, first in section east-west really had flown away on its bluebird wings. Maybe even second and third in section also. But there were still fractional master points for fourth and fifth places, if they did well on the final hand.

Bubba, in the dealer's position, sorted his cards and said, "One spade."

Hoffmeister looked at his cards, and squeezed his eyes shut, and looked again, and tensed his muscles to keep the deep tingling thrill penned inside his body. There it was at last. He controlled his voice carefully, because the Laws of Duplicate Bridge, Part 7, Proprieties, section 2b, state that it is a breach of ethics to make a call with special emphasis, inflection, haste or undue hesitation. "One no trump," he said, without special emphasis or inflection or haste or undue hesitation. Nonetheless, in spite of the tonelessness of his call, banners were flying from battlements and armor gleamed in the sun and drawn swords glittered. He had just bid the Hoffmeister No Trump.

Behind the black sunglasses Tony's eyes flickered toward the bidder. What the hell was this? Bubba had opened a spade, and Bubba had promised not to open with less than thirteen points and two and a half quick tricks. With dogmeat, you had to make sure that their opening bids were sound. So Bubba had thirteen points at least. He himself had eight points and a little spade support, not enough for game unless Bubba had a big hand, and how could Bubba have a big hand with a no trump overcall from this jerk? Tony looked at the badge the jerk wore. He hadn't bothered to read it before, but now he saw it announced I PLAY THE HOFFMEISTER NO TRUMP. A jerk with a lousy new convention he'd put over on the ACBL. There was a printed card in front of the jerk that probably explained the convention, and Tony had a right to read it now if he wished.

Tony also had the right to ask the jerk's partner what the bid meant. But doing either of those two things meant calling attention to the fact that the bid was artificial, and often dogmeat players forgot what conventions they were playing.

So Tony asked no questions and merely bet that dogmeat would probably act like dogmeat. "Double," he said.

Mary Rose huddled over her cards as if she were cold and hoped they would warm her. She did not like to hear an opponent double a low-level bid. Was the double for take-out? For business? Were she and her partner in trouble? She did not have a good hand, which was to be expected since the bidding indicated strength in all the other hands. She could not redouble, because that promised at least ten points in high cards, and she only had six points. She held the king-queen of diamonds and seven clubs to the jack-ten-nine, and nothing else of value. She did not dare bid two clubs, because that was the Stayman convention asking partner to bid a four-card major. If she bid three clubs her partner might go to game. She sighed. Well, at least the double gave her partner a chance to bid again, so she would leave it up to him.

"Pass," she said. She had not recognized the Hoffmeister No Trump.

Hoffmeister played one no trump doubled and went down two tricks. He played slowly and sadly, because on this hand the Hoffmeister No Trump should have taken them to three clubs, which could be made for a fine score, maybe a top. At best the opponents could only have made two spades. But down two doubled at no trump was a top for north-south, a bottom for east-west.

As soon as the last card was played, Bubba jumped up, quivering like a palm frond in a breeze, and cried, "Tony, we made it! We made it we made it we made it!" He tried to shake hands across the table.

Tony looked at Bubba's extended hand as if it needed washing, and did not take it. "We got nothing until the Recap sheets go up," he said. He wrote the score carefully on the pick-up slip and made sure that Hoffmeister initialed it.

"Let's go get a drink!" Bubba said. "Tony, I must do something to celebrate or I'll explode!"

"Go ahead and order me a Scotch and soda," Tony said. "I'll join you there soon as they collect the pick-up slips." It was silly to walk away leaving two pick-up slips with tops on them, you never knew what might happen.

Bubba hurried off, and Hoffmeister and Mary Rose got up and smiled at each other. There was pain in Hoffmeister's smile and pleasure in Mary Rose's.

"It's been such a nice evening," Mary Rose said. "I surely did enjoy playing with you, and maybe we can play again some time. Do you think we came in somewhere, maybe fourth or fifth in section?"

"I should be guessing at it, no facts I got, we are maybe a couple points above average, that don't bring us in."

"Well, above average, that's something. I just think I'll hurry over to the table where they're putting out the food, sometimes people grab things so fast there isn't much choice when you get there a bit late. Are you staying around to see the scores posted?"

"From the scores I got no interest."

"Well, thank you again," Mary Rose said. "And I do think your convention is just wonderful. I wish it had come up."

For a moment he wanted to say, so it did come up, such a pass you made, you should take up pinocle. But he didn't, because a nice woman she really was. He merely nodded, and shuffled away through the crowded ballroom. For a moment, a brief moment in the middle of the session, the letters of the words HOFF-MEISTER NO TRUMP had gleamed and glowed and quivered as if incised on tablets brought down from a mount. They were having a monster game and the Hoffmeister No Trump was going to come along and help them win first overall out of eight hundred and forty pairs. The big red 1 was going to go up beside their names on the Recap sheet, and people would stand around saying, such a big score they got, we should find out how to use that Hoffmeister No Trump. Later there would be a photograph in the ACBL Bulletin and maybe a little box showing the hand on

which the Hoffmeister No Trump made a top for the winners. But
the glow faded from the lettering on the tablets and the stone was
blank and empty, not a scratch even.

It would not be so hard to find himself always paired up with
defeat, he thought dully, if victory had not come so close, so
achingly close.

♠ ♥ ♦ ♣ 4

WITHIN ANY FLOCK of chickens there exists a social system that biologists call a peck order. Chicken A has the right to peck all other chickens in the flock. Chicken B has the right to peck all but Chicken A, and so on down the line. In tournament bridge the peck order is called master points.

The awarding of master points to players was started in 1936, and the program is given much credit for the growth of the ACBL, which by the time of the Spring Nationals at the Xanadu had reached a membership total of more than two hundred thousand. People who do not waste time on tournament bridge tend to be sarcastic about master points whenever the practice comes to their attention. A Russian commissar, for example, may regard it as an illustration of the decadence to be found in capitalist states, because he is only interested in winning the Order of the Red Star. A golfer may snicker at bridge players and then try to work a mention of his low handicap into the conversation. A professor may shake his head sadly over such infantilism, and write a learned paper on it in the hope of being awarded an honorary degree.

The ACBL master-point plan is complicated; seventy-seven pages of packed columns of figures are needed merely to list the tables of point awards for sectional and regional tournaments. But the more complex the plan becomes, the more it fascinates bridge players. Points are awarded according to the importance of the tournament (club, local, sectional, regional and national), the presumed caliber of play (lowest awards for novice games,

highest for games limited to experts), and the number of contestants. Thus the winner of a small club game may only receive
thirteen-hundredths of a master point. The winner of a major
championship may get 125 full points. The ACBL maintains complete records and notifies members by computerized postcard of
each addition to their hoard of points.

In itself this would appeal hugely to the human collecting in-
stinct, which always responds to such offers whether they be travel
stickers, trading stamps, or pictures of athletes in packs of bubble
gum. But the ACBL devised an improvement. This involves the
ranking of players into Junior Master (less than 20 points), Master (20-49), National Master (50-99), Senior Master (100 or
more), Advanced Senior Master (200 or more, of which at least
20 must be red points), and Life Master (300 or more, of which
at least 50 must be red points). Red points can only be won in
certain events at regional and national tournaments; all other
points are black. The name of the originator of this ranking system is not known, just as there is no record of the genius who
suggested to Napoleon the establishment of the Légion d'honneur
and its classification into Chevaliers, Officiers, Commandeurs,
Grands Officiers and Grands Croix. The results in both cases
were and are excellent. In Napoleon's era the French cuirassier
charged with more élan against the bayonets of the British square,
and today the bridge player marches more grimly into more tournaments.

Among the bridge players on whom the master-point plan had
the desired effect was Bubba Worthington. After finishing play
in the Charity Pairs he went to the bar and had three drinks, two
of them in the company of Tony Manuto. In this way he managed to use up forty minutes, while waiting for the directors to
score the event. The wait made him feel like a giant alarm clock
that wouldn't stop jangling. Tony was no help to him; the fellow was impossible, a mess, really, except across a bridge table.
Bubba returned to the ballroom and found that the scores had
not yet been posted. The big room was half empty. Nothing but
crumbs and spilled coffee and sandwiches rejected after one bite

remained of the food. A few post-mortems were still going on; many players could recall every card in hands that they had played brilliantly or their partners had played badly. Everybody was waiting for the scores. These were being compiled in a private room, where a director could work without being obliged to sit inside a tent of spectators.

For the thirty-second time, Bubba said to Tony, "We made it, Tony! Didn't we?"

"How the hell do I know?" Tony said.

They had to make it, Bubba told himself, they *had* to. He adjusted his necktie nervously, making sure it was centered above the gold collar pin. He did not care for buttoned-down shirts; a collar pin was neater. He had been on the verge of making Life Master for a year. He had a hundred more black points than necessary but only thirty-eight of the fifty required red points. He wanted to be a Life Master for many reasons, one of which was connected with his father, a leading surgeon in the Palm Beach area. Father was always asking in a grumbling way, "When are you going to do something besides loaf, Ensley?" Father did not call him Bubba, which was Mother's pet name for him, a nice old girl, Mother. How fortunate that Mother had so much money of her own! Otherwise Father certainly would push them around. When Father asked again when he was going to do something besides loaf, Bubba wanted to be able to reply, with quiet dignity, "It happens that I *have* been doing something. I have become a Life Master."

A platoon of directors entered the room and began taping the Recap sheets to the wall. Each sheet carried the pair number, names and ACBL numbers of each pair in a section, the plus or minus game score made by each pair on each of the twenty-six boards, the match points (zero to twelve) resulting from the game scores, and the total match points for each pair. In addition, the top five pairs north-south and the top five east-west had their standings listed in small red figures to the left of their names. They would get from two point eighty red points down to fifty-six hundredths. Here and there on the sheets, in the column farthest to the left, were big red numbers beside the pairs who had placed first to ninth overall out of the eight hundred and forty pairs. There were 312 possible match points, and in most sections it took a score of 190 to 200 to win first in section north-south or east-west, or about sixty to sixty-four percent of the possible match points. Tonight a score of 224 had won first overall.

Mary Rose Rutledge, who was very nimble, got to the sheet for Section D before anyone else, and saw that she and Mr. Hoffmeister scored 159 match points, or fifty-one percent. She went away contentedly; it was always nice to come in above average, and she also had a lovely feeling in her stomach from the four sandwiches, five cakes and two cups of coffee she had managed to get at the buffet. Carola Clark did not bother to go to the Recap sheets, and learned her score when Waldo Starnes came by and said, "You were third in section, Carola, 178 points." Carola thanked him and said to Babs, "Well, at least that's something, after that hideous start."

Bubba Worthington, rather hating himself for joining the mob, pushed his way to the sheet for Section D. He was so excited that the tiny figures kept blurring even when he got up close. He squinted, and pressed a hand against one temple, which sometimes sharpened his eyesight. Some day, he admitted, he would have to get glasses. But glasses for men were such ugly things, not like the attractive ones women could buy, and they would make him look like a goldfish or lemur monkey or something equally dull. At last the figures came into focus. Anthony Manuto and Ensley Worthington, Pair 1, north-south, 224 match points. To the left of that, in a small red figure, first in section north-south. To the left of that, in the column for overall standing, the big red numeral 1.

Bubba let out a hoarse scream, although he was not aware of doing it. He fought his way out of the crowd and looked for Tony and saw him lounging in a chair, cleaning a fingernail on his left hand with the nail of his right index finger. "We made it, Tony!" he cried for the thirty-third time that evening. "First overall! Good

Lord, what a game we had, 224! Tony, you said that would be sixteen red points?" For a moment he had a twinge of fear; suppose the payoff was only ten or eleven, when he needed twelve? He knew from sad experience that he might go months and months before winning another red point or two.

"Yeah," Tony said. "Sixteen red ones. So you're a Life Master." He said it exactly as he would have said, "You're a lousy creep."

"I've got to do something to celebrate!" Bubba gasped. It was suffocating to have all these emotions boiling inside. He wanted to fling his arms around Tony or . . . or somebody, it was unthinkable of course with Tony.

"One thing you can do is pay me off," Tony said.

"I did pay you the fifty dollars and the entry fees earlier, didn't I? So . . . oh yes, *yes,* the bonus! Please forgive me, Tony, I wouldn't try to get out of it, I'm just so excited I forgot. It was to be a hundred if we came in second or third and two hundred if we made first overall, wasn't it?" He got out his wallet and began counting twenties. "Because it was such a wonderful game," he said, "let's make it three hundred. Is that all right, Tony?" What he wanted, although he did not realize it, was to buy something warm and friendly from Tony with the extra money: a big happy smile, an arm thrown over the shoulders, perhaps Tony saying, "You were great, kid."

Tony said in his flat voice, "Sure, why not?"

"Maybe I'll give a party," Bubba said. "A new Life Master should always give a party, shouldn't he? I think I'll have a cocktail party in a day or so, up in my suite before dinner. You'll come, won't you?"

"Could be."

"And I know what I'll do now! I'll call Mother, she'll be so happy!"

"At one-thirty in the morning she'll be happy?"

"Why, of course. Mother always wants to know just everything I've been doing, and if it's really important, like this, she'll love me calling her. Well, I'll see you, Tony. And thanks just awfully."

"Don't give it a thought," Tony said, yawning.

Bubba hurried upstairs and put in his call to Palm Beach. Presently a man's voice, thick with the dregs of sleep, said, "This is Doctor Worthington."

"Hello, Father," Bubba said. He should have remembered that his parents would be in bed in their separate rooms and that the bell did not ring in Mother's bedroom, the shock would upset her. "How are you?"

"How am I, at one-thirty? I'm sleepy. I thought it was an emergency at the hospital. What's wrong, did you have an accident? Cops grab you for something?"

Bubba said indignantly, "You know I don't have accidents or get arrested."

"Did you get a girl in trouble?"

"Father!"

"It was only a hope, Ensley. All right, why the call?"

"Well, I wanted to talk to Mother, but perhaps you'd like to hear the news too. I have just become a Life Master."

"Let me get this straight," the voice said heavily. "You have just become a life master. Excuse me if I sound envious. I myself have never managed to master life, rather the contrary."

You never knew whether Father was being ignorant or sarcastic. "Life Master in *bridge*," Bubba said. "It's like getting a ten-goal rating in polo."

"Polo," Father said. "Did you ever think of taking that up, Ensley? Of course people sometimes break their necks at it. I will let you guess whether that is a fond parental warning, or encouragement. If you will hold the line I'll rouse your mother, and for once she will pardon me for doing so. I would like to continue this stimulating talk but I have a bit of surgery to do at eight a.m."

Bubba waited, and at last Mother's soft warm voice came over the wires, enfolding him cozily and creating a world in which nobody mattered but Mrs. William Worthington (née Sandra Ensley, of Southampton and Palm Beach, and of the Ensley Battery fortune) and Bubba Worthington, her son, Life Master of the American Contract Bridge League.

Downstairs in the ballroom Tony Manuto still lounged in his chair, cleaning his fingernails. Nobody could claim he was advertising for dogmeat; he was just sitting there. If people wanted to know who won the Charity Pairs and somebody wanted to point him out, there he was, and try to make something of it. In itself the attention he was getting meant nothing. What was big about winning a lousy Charity game and sixteen red points? Except for the chance to sign up more dogmeat he wouldn't care if he never won an event. What he got out of bridge was the feeling that came when he played a tough hand like he was inside everybody's head. It was an odd feeling, you could almost call it sexy, like going to bed with a broad. Only it was better than having a broad. He'd got the feeling out of three hands tonight, and how many guys could make the scene with three broads in three hours?

Earlier in the evening Waldo Starnes had unwittingly forged the first link in a chain of events by selling Tony Manuto the entry slip for Section D, table 1, north-south, and soon afterward selling P. J. Hoffmeister the entry slip for Section D, table 2, east-west. This had brought Hoffmeister and Mary Rose Rutledge to table 1 for the last two hands, during which they gave two tops or twenty-four match points to Tony and Bubba. Except for those two tops, Tony and Bubba would not have won the Charity Pairs. And if Tony had not won, Ace McKinley would not have forged the next link in the chain. Ace was looking over the Recap sheets casually, to see who did what. If he had not seen the big red 1 beside Tony's name he would have moved on and never done more than nod to Tony in the future.

But there was the symbol beside Tony's name. Ace paused, and muttered to himself, "Shoot! That coyote can play bridge. And with dogmeat, too."

He thought for a moment about the hints he had dropped during the evening, while chatting with top players, about how he might be coaxed into playing in one of the championships. Nobody seemed ready to act on his hints. So finally, with that big red 1 blinking like a stoplight in his mind, he walked to the table where Tony was lounging.

"Well, I see you made it," he said. "Nice going."

From behind the dark glasses Tony studied the guy's face. Yes, he thought, maybe that win was going to get him another hunk of dogmeat, and maybe right now. "Wasn't much," he said. "Bunch of clucks in the game."

"Won't do you any harm in rounding up customers, son. Wouldn't surprise me if a couple people had talked to you already."

"Could be."

Ace took a deep and slightly painful breath. "You and me talked about maybe taking a crack at the Men's Pairs."

"Uh-huh. But you didn't go for the idea of paying."

"Well, shoot," Ace said, feeling angry and miserable at the same time. "How do you think that made me feel?"

"I wouldn't know."

"I never played with you," Ace said, halfway hoping to find some reason for not hiring the guy. "What system do you follow?"

"Name it and I play it. Standard American, Kaplan-Sheinwold, Duke-Ashcraft, Roth-Stone, Momma-Poppa bridge, anything I have to. I can play the Neapolitan or Roman systems as good as that frigging Italian Blue Team, if that's what my partner likes, but they don't allow those systems here."

Ace said weakly, "Well, uh, I have a sort of style all my own."

"That's news? I watched you a dozen times. You play Standard American with ruffles and bows. You open light, in-quick out-quick, if partner don't show much. You throw in a psych, usually in first position, about once a session. You like to gamble, what I call a look-Mom-no-hands act. Some guys say you invented the Gambling Three No-Trump and some guys say the hell you did."

"The hell I didn't!"

"It's not my fight. Anyway, that's how you play."

"Wouldn't have thought you knew my game that well."

"My business is knowing how guys play."

Ace opened his left hand and slugged it several times with his right fist. "All right, shoot," he said finally. "Let's play in the Men's Pairs. You said fifty bucks a session and I pay the entry fees."

"Plus a bonus if we win."

"Yeah, you mentioned something about that. How much?"

Here goes, Tony thought. Smack between the eyes. He said coldly, "Five thousand bucks." It knocked the guy right off his saddle onto a bunch of cactus.

Ace made squawking noises, like a public address system that had gone sour, and finally gasped, "You must be nuts!"

"Nuts, am I?" Tony said. Suddenly the sleek patent-leather surface that he usually presented to the world began buckling and cracking. Here he was, the best bridge player alive, scrabbling for nickels and dimes while this Wild West ape and Goren and Jacoby walked off with the jackpots. "I'd be nuts not to try to make it when I get a chance," he said bitterly. "What have I got to sell? The way I can play the game, that's all. I can't write a book on it. I can't write a lousy column in the papers. I can't give talks or run bridge cruises or sell clucks the Manuto System even if I had one or do a goddam thing but get more out of the cards than any other guy can. You want to buy that, it's five grand and you don't pay the bonus if I don't come through."

Listening to him, Ace forgot some of his own shock and fury. You never knew what went on inside a guy. This character was an iceberg on top and a volcano underneath. You could understand why he wanted to make it when he got a chance. But five thousand dollars! Fifty bucks a session didn't mean much, just a matter of sweeping his pride under the rug, but five thousand wasn't play money. He began figuring how long it might take to get back five grand. Well, actually, a few extra lecture dates, ten more papers added to his list, and he'd be home free. Winning a championship would pay off. And of course a big win would also rate as insurance against losing some of the income he already had.

"No win, no bonus, huh?" Ace said slowly.

"No win, no bonus."

"And you'd keep your mouth shut about it?"

"Nobody ever pays me to talk."

"All right," Ace said. "It's a deal. I'll see you at the first session of the Men's Pairs tomorrow afternoon." He walked away quickly, because he didn't want to see any grin sliding over Tony's face.

He need not have considered that possibility, because in Tony's mind five grand was a serious matter. Tony merely permitted himself to feel good; for once he was going to be playing for the big green stuff. Now he had to figure how to get it. Best bridge player in the world or not, and even playing with a fairly good partner like Ace, you had no guarantee of winning the Men's Pairs in the Nationals or even of coming in high in the overall standings. Ace would have to be on his game, and they'd need luck. You always needed luck to beat good competition. Maybe they wouldn't have the luck. That was all right, Ace would be back at him to play in other events. And then, if the luck didn't start coming their way, he'd have to figure how to give it some help. For five thousand bucks, they were going to win one of those championships.

♠ ♥ ♦ ♣ 5

THE GIRL IN THE LOBBY of the Xanadu was waiting for one
person and hoping to see another. It was Saturday morning, on
the second day of the tournament. The girl's name was Victoria
Summers. She had lived for twenty-nine years and had not enjoyed any of them very much. She was five feet eight inches tall
and weighed one hundred and eight pounds. Her body did not have
the elegant lean lines of a fashion model, flaunting bones and
angles at the world of overweight women, but was thin as a home-
less cat. There were other ways in which she did not resemble
a fashion model. Her clothes always looked out of shape, as if
they preferred to keep the outline of the clothes hanger rather than
adjust to her body. Also she was not clever in selecting colors,
being somewhat color-blind. The tailored suit she wore, bought at
Lit Brothers in Philadelphia, marked down from $29.98 to $7.98
(it had been in two other clearance sales without moving) was
the color of a slightly decayed orange. Unfortunately Vicky Summers thought the color was pale yellow. While she waited she
stood on one of the large raised patterns that floated like exotic
lily pads on the inch-thick green rug, and unfortunately her lily
pad was pink. Vicky thought it was gray. Several people in the
lobby who were not color blind noticed the combination of the
pink lily pad and the decayed-orange suit, and winced. They did
not actually notice the girl, but then few people ever did.
    She could of course have waited sitting down, perhaps on a
black vinyl couch, where she could have surrounded her orange
suit with lemon-colored cushions, but she rarely sat when expect-

ing to meet someone. She waited standing, moving her weight awkwardly from one foot to the other, a girl consumed by an inner heat. She hoped that Ben would walk through the lobby before Mrs. W. B. Edmunds rolled into sight and carried her off to lunch. She knew Ben had arrived; the desk clerk said he checked in an hour ago, and at any moment he might come down from his room.

She remembered every detail of their only meeting. It was at the Regional in Boston early in January, a unique tournament consisting of a two-day four-session Individual in which you played every hand with a different partner. The Rainbow movement had brought her a strange young man for the last hand of the last session. After the game ended, the other two players left the table but the young man remained seated across from her, his long body slouched in the chair. He took off his thick-lensed glasses and chewed gloomily at one of the ear pieces.

Vicky asked hesitantly, "Did . . . did I do something wrong on that hand?"

"Lord no," he muttered. "We must have made a top on it. Just about the only one I've had this session, too. I shouldn't have wasted money coming here. An Individual is all luck, if you don't get good partners you're dead. But I wanted some points badly and I had two days off and this was the only Regional."

Vicky said earnestly, "I know what it's like to want points badly. I have a hundred and ninety-six, still a long way from Life Master. Is that what you're trying to make?"

"No," he said.

Something in his tone set off a warning bell in her head. "Oh dear," she said. "You *are* a Life Master."

He shrugged and gave a nod. He rubbed a hand over his forehead, as if he had a headache, and she saw that the cuff of his jacket was frayed and a button missing from the cuff.

"But why do you want points so badly, then?" she asked, giving way to an unfortunate habit. She had told herself time and again to stop trying to get a man's life history the moment he showed any readiness to talk to her.

"Just a hobby," he said. "You wouldn't be interested."

"Oh but I am," she said helplessly. "I really am."

He put on his glasses and peered at her, and shrugged and said, "All right. I don't get many chances to bore people with my problems. To start with, I teach and direct the bridge games at a big hotel in the Catskills, you know, the Borscht Circuit."

"You do? Why, I run a bridge club just outside Philadelphia!"

"Hey, that's a coincidence."

"Yes," she said breathlessly, "isn't it?" She told herself not to start babbling at him but to let him do the talking. A small bond had been spun between them, thin as a cobweb, and anything might break it.

"Well then, you know the setup," he said. "It's fun if you love bridge, and sometimes it's a living, but you can't get very far in the world doing it. Of course maybe I'm the kind of guy who won't get very far anyway."

"Oh, I'm sure you will!"

"Well, I'm trying. I love the game, see? Always have. I understand it. And I have a knack, or I think I have, of being able to show people how to play it. And I kid myself that I write in a sort of interesting way. You follow me?"

Follow him? Who couldn't follow anybody so intense and solemn and wonderful? She could follow him to . . . oh stop it, Vicky, she told herself. In a moment of intuition she said, "You're writing a book!"

"Hey, you're a real sharp cookie," he said. "All right, I am. Matter of fact, Prentice-Hall saw the first four chapters and gave me an advance. I have a title they think is great. *How to Beat Your Friends—and Enemies—at Bridge.* Like it?"

"It's just wonderful!"

"Thanks. Well, I'll get it written and published, but then what? Lot of bridge books on the stands. No matter how good your book is, you need a reputation if you hope to sell many copies. So I'm trying to get myself a rep this year."

"You will," she said. "I just know you will. You play such a wonderful game."

A grin skidded across his face and vanished, like a small boy careening through a roomful of solemn adults. "We play one hand together and you're the declarer and my game is wonderful, huh? You're crazy. Of course I am too. Maybe we could play together at some tournament, huh? My name's Ben Aarons, what's yours?"

There wasn't much more to remember about those few minutes together, late on a Sunday night in Boston. They were both leaving early the next morning and Ben was the kind of person who needed his sleep. They traded addresses, and she said she hoped to get to the Spring Nationals at Miami in March. Ben said, she was sure she remembered this correctly, to look him up there. Later she wrote him several letters, and he replied first with a friendly note and next with a friendly postcard and then not at all.

Of course he could have been very busy. He could also have put her out of his mind, a casual slough of an unimportant card. There had been so little to fix her in his thoughts, so few cobweb strands. Perhaps he would have remembered more clearly if she had dared suggest getting her needle and thread and sewing the button back on his coat sleeve, that is, if he still had the button, which he probably didn't. At the moment, as she waited on the pink lily pad in the Xanadu, her handbag held a needle and thread and a little collection of men's buttons in black, gray and brown, in four sizes.

Then she saw him. He was shambling across the lobby, tall and stooped, peering through his glasses and bumping into someone and apologizing and coming on. He was wearing the same suit, which had been too light for January in Boston and was too heavy for March in Miami. Vicky ordered her legs to stop trembling, and stepped forward and said softly, "Hello, Ben. Remember me? Vicky Summers, in Boston?"

He looked down at her from his considerable height like a heron peering into clouded water. "Huh?" he said. "Oh. Vicky, sure, hey, how are you?"

"Just fine," she said, and peeked at the cuff of his jacket. The button was still missing. "How has everything been going?"

"Oh, fine, fine."

"You're making progress on the book?"

"Oh yes. Yes indeed."

"Well," she said, hinting as strongly as she dared, "I did get down here, didn't I?"

"Fine, fine," he said vaguely. "Sure wish you lots of luck. Uh, I got to meet a guy. I'll see you around, huh?"

"Yes," she said, and smiled and stepped backward to let him pass, feeling as if she were deliberately backing off a steep cliff.

He jerked a hand at her in a sort of wave and shambled off.

Vicky's eyes started getting hot and tight, preparing to drench her face in tears, and she fought against it. She hated the way her eyes gushed whenever she let herself cry, so unlike the neat effective method some girls had of merely allowing their eyes to fill and a couple of drops to overflow and ornament their cheeks. It was just as well she did control herself, she realized, because Mrs. W. B. Edmunds was approaching. It was important to present a happy face to Mrs. Edmunds, who was paying her way here. Mrs. Edmunds came through the crowded lobby with regal power, like a tugboat. She was a woman who might have passed for stylish stout in a foundation garment, but she refused to wear one. She had silvery-purple hair, a complexion like cottage cheese, and keen blue eyes.

"There you are, my dear," she said. "What a hideous thing you're wearing. It looks as if the dye had run. And I must say, I wouldn't blame the dye for running from such a garment. Sheer fright, no doubt." She laughed, a sound like a fire gong clanging.

Coming from Mrs. Edmunds, any comment about the style and suitability of clothing was unfair, because Mrs. Edmunds herself was the sort of person who could make mutation mink look like dyed rabbit. But Vicky was unable to look at the comment from that point of view, and began crying.

"Oh my God, children and their tears," Mrs. Edmunds said.

"I'm sure I could never have stood any children of my own, not that it was my fault we didn't have any, frankly, I always thought the late W. B. was undersexed, or perhaps nothing excited him but a big business deal, which I wasn't. Now stop it, Vicky, one little remark about that suit of yours doesn't warrant all this."

"It's not that," Vicky wailed. "It . . . it was Ben!"

"Ben?" Mrs. Edmunds said with sharp curiosity. "Young Ben Aarons? I saw you talking to him. What on earth would he say to you to bring on this flood?"

"We met in Boston, at the Regional Individual," Vicky said, sniffling. "We had such a nice talk and I thought he said something about wanting to play with me the next time we met at a tournament, maybe here, and I don't want you to think I meant to cheat on you, Mrs. Edmunds, when you invited me to come you did say we needn't play together all the time, but now he . . . he hardly remembers me!"

"Heavens, girl, aren't you aiming a little high?"

Vicky blinked at her rapidly. This was not a way of drying her eyes but a nervous habit, the speed of the blinking geared to her emotional state. "Well, I know he's a Life Master," she said. "But you are too, Mrs. Edmunds, and you don't mind playing with me."

"My dear girl, have you ever heard of the McKenney Cup?"

"It's a sort of trophy that goes to whoever wins the most master points in the country each year. But what has—"

"The McKenney race," said Mrs. Edmunds, who knew everybody and everything about tournament bridge, "runs from the end of one Fall Nationals to the end of the next one. So this one is almost four months along. The young man you expected to play with merely happens to be tied for the lead right now."

"Oh, how wonderful for him!" Vicky cried, forgetting that it was the opposite for her. "But he didn't say a word about it in Boston."

"That was two months ago, and he hadn't hit his streak then. Don't you keep up with tournament news?"

"Not really. He actually has been on a streak?"

"Oh, it's the talk of the bridge world. Absolute unknowns, Ben and his partner, another Jew boy named Sammy Rothberg, please understand I have nothing against Jews, the Jewish mind is perfectly fitted for bridge. Of course everybody knows them now, except I suppose you. Starting seven weeks ago they began mopping up every Regional in sight—four altogether, I think. They've picked up more than four hundred points each, and all three Nationals still ahead of them. An amazing start on the McKenney."

"No wonder he hardly remembers me."

"No wonder, indeed," Mrs. Edmunds said. "Now let's go to lunch, I'm quite famished. By the way, I haven't mentioned the most interesting angle about those boys, everybody is speculating about it. You see, they're tied in points and have done it all together, but there's only one McKenney Cup, so which boy is going to break up the partnership? When are Damon and Pythias going to go for each other's throats? Isn't it fascinating . . . ?"

It was not correct that Ben Aarons hardly remembered Vicky Summers from their meeting in Boston. He remembered her very clearly, and as he walked away from her he disliked himself for what he had just done. It was odd how you could get interested in a girl for no special reason. There didn't seem to be anything brilliant about her mind, and Lord knows she wasn't pretty. Maybe it was because she was so real. Most girls put on masks to hide their real selves, if indeed there was any. One girl might insist, with each giggle and every twitch of her body, that she was the cutest thing you ever saw. Another might pretend to be deep and mysterious. A third would play Sexy Susie. Then there were the girl-pal types, the wife-mother types, the let's-hold-hands-on-a-picket-line types, and so on. Vicky wasn't any of those types and didn't use a mask. She wore her emotions in public for anybody to see, not proudly, not aggressively, just sort of helplessly, in about the same way he wore a frayed suit, because there was nothing else to put on. In one way, he couldn't claim to know much about girls, but after all he worked at a Catskills hotel where often there were more girls than men. Now and then a girl took him on merely to keep in practice, like dealing herself bridge hands and playing the cards double-dummy.

He knew perfectly well that Vicky had hoped to be his partner at some event here. And, for the first couple of weeks after Boston, he had looked forward to it. But then he and Sammy started on that incredible streak. The girl was for real but something else became much more real: if he won the McKenney race, he was made. The book would sell and he'd be on his way. He had to be on his way; thirty years old and what was he, a bridge director in resort hotels, eighty a week and a room and meals, and fifty of those bucks going to Mom in the Bronx. Pop never made much money. You didn't find a fortune running a dry cleaning shop, just small change that customers forgot to take out of pockets, and if you were Pop you put the coins in neatly marked envelopes and gave them back when the customer returned for his clothes. His parents had worked hard to put him through C.C.N.Y. He was going to be a professional man, a doctor or anyway a lawyer, yes? Sorry, folks, no. You weren't going to be much of a doctor if the sight of blood made you sick, and he didn't have the razor-edged mind you needed to climb from a dry cleaning shop to a big law firm. What he had, it turned out, was the right mind for bridge. So now Pop was dead and Mom sat in the one-room Bronx apartment, waiting for him to do something about which she could boast to her friends. This was the year he was going to do it, and don't kid yourself, Ben old boy, you're not winning the McKenney playing with that real little, plain little Vicky.

One thing about her wasn't plain. Her eyes. They were large and soft, set like jewels in enormous dark lashes, real ones, not the kind that girls stuck on. She did a lot of blinking, and when he gave her the knife just now her eyelashes went into a blur of fluttering. He headed downstairs to the lower level, holding the banister so he wouldn't stumble. Each step was six feet below the level of his eyes and he didn't see things clearly at that distance. Now he would go to the coffee shop and see if Sammy Rothberg would also blink when he gave Sammy the knife.

Half an hour ago somebody had told Sammy about seeing him arrive, and Sammy phoned him in his room and said, in a typical explosion of words, "Ben old boy! You're here! You didn't think you could make it. Hey, we got a lot of arrangements to make. I won't keep you now, you're unpacking and all, let's have lunch in the Kubla Khan room, half an hour, okay?"

"The coffee shop is my speed," Ben said.

"It's on me, Ben old boy. The food's better upstairs."

"We go Dutch and the coffee shop," Ben said.

He saw Sammy at a corner table as soon as he entered the place; it was always easy to spot a guy as good-looking as Sammy. Except for the name nobody would figure Sammy for Jewish, and in fact his ancestry was at least as much goy as it was ghetto. Sammy had blond hair and blue eyes and soft clear skin that infuriated Sammy by the ease and frequency with which it blushed. Back in 1937, the year before Sammy was born, Sammy's father had been smart enough to read the message on the outside wall of the family bank in Stuttgart, Germany—the message being a crudely daubed swastika—and got out while there was still time. The Rothbergs came to New York and now the senior Rothberg owned the controlling interest in the management firm that ran a very nice mutual fund. Sammy peddled shares in the fund whenever bridge didn't interfere, and to be honest sometimes his excellent game of bridge helped him as a salesman.

He and Sammy had become friendly in their first year at C.C.N.Y. They started playing bridge together—it was an In thing to do at C.C.N.Y., anything intellectual, from chess to Zen Buddhism—and got to be pretty good. When the Duke-Ashcraft bidding system came out they took it up before it became a feverish cult known as The Method. Just for kicks they took the new system to the Men's Pairs at the Asbury Park Regionals, a couple of brash college kids, and played some experts who didn't yet know how to defend against The Method, and shocked everybody by winning. That was nine years ago. They had done all right since then but nothing sensational until the streak began this year.

"Ben old boy!" Sammy cried, jumping up and grabbing his hand. "This is just wonderful! I had no idea you were coming. You remember I even offered to stake you to it, and pay me back when your book comes out if you insisted. But no, you proud bastard, you won't take help from anybody. You rob a bank to get here?"

Ben sat down. In the past it had always been fun to get together with Sammy and watch the sparkle in his eyes and listen to the bubbling talk. He had never resented the fact that things came easily to Sammy: money, high marks, girls. Well, there *had* been one moment of resentment, in Senior year, when a little soft quiet girl who majored in sociology showed an interest in him and Sammy came breezing along and swiped her. But he didn't hold the resentment very long, how could you, it was just Sammy's way. "If you had only *told* me you liked the girl!" Sammy mourned, when he learned how Ben felt. "She meant nothing to me." By then she meant nothing to Ben either, so it didn't really matter much.

Ben said, "I talked Prentice-Hall into another advance on the book."

"That's right, do it the hard way. Spend the dough before the book earns it, don't ask your friends for anything. Now look, Ben, you put me on a spot, showing up without notice."

"That so?" Ben asked. Of course he knew what was coming; Sammy was going to be very generous in his good-hearted thoughtless slightly maddening way.

"Well, now I got to bust some dates to take care of you, Ben. One date I can't bust is for the Vanderbilt, because that would let a pretty fine partner down. You know her, Runa Montez, from L.A."

"Oh yes," Ben murmured. "The Nylon Cobra. Whee!"

"She's a very nice person and all those stories about her are crap!"

"O.K. Who's the rest of your Vanderbilt team?"

"Jake Jacobs and Tony Manuto. I suppose Jake's paying Tony, good as Jake is. Quite a team, huh?"

Yessir, Ben thought, quite a team: Little Red Riding Hood Sammy and three Big Bad Wolves. "I certainly wouldn't want to break that up," he said. "It ought to be a real experience for you."

"Yeah, we might do nicely. Tell you what, Ben, I'll play with you in the Open Pairs the end of next week, that gives the partner I was going to play with plenty of time to get someone else. And I think I can work you into the Men's Team I lined up, although I may have to step on some toes. The big problem is the Men's Pairs, gosh, that starts in an hour and a half, doesn't it? I took on a guy for that just for business reasons, he's working on his mother to buy a hunk of shares in our mutual fund. Don't think you know him. Worthington, Bubba Worthington. Hell, if I bust that date . . . dammit, I will, just for you, and kick a nice commission away."

It was now time, Ben thought grimly, to start kicking a nice friend away. "Don't bother," he said. "I have a date for the Men's Pairs."

"Well good for you," Sammy said, sounding disappointed. "You must have done it at short notice and I hope you didn't get some clown."

"I'm playing with Harvey Ashcraft."

"You what!"

"Uh-huh. Now if I only don't forget how to play The Method with one of the two guys who invented it—"

"Oh hell, that's ridiculous!" Sammy said angrily. "Harvey always plays with Hank Duke. How could you possibly get Harvey?"

"Prentice-Hall said O.K. to the advance three days ago. I made up a list of people I'd like to play with and sat down at a phone and started calling long distance. Harvey was on the list and said yes and you could have knocked me over with a pick-up slip."

"You get him for the Men's Teams too?" Sammy asked, the color blinking red in his face.

"Yes. Hank Duke will be on the team but playing with somebody else. I must have hit Harvey right after some disagreement with Hank."

"You lucky bastard. The Vanderbilt too?"

"Nope. Harvey and Hank play with their wives in that. I'm an alternate, if anybody gets sick or tired."

Sammy was studying him as if wondering how many more aces he had up his sleeve. "The Mixed Pairs? Don't tell me, I bet you got Carola Clark. You've played the Mixed with her before."

Ben nodded. "And she's playing with me in the Open Pairs too."

Sammy's skin went through a white phase, with a small red stain over each cheekbone. "Let me ask you just one thing," he said tensely. "Where on that list of yours was the name Sammy Rothberg? Where, huh? Right at the bottom?"

Ben shook his head and gave the knife the final twist. "No," he said. "It wasn't on at all."

"Let me get this straight. We've been partners how long, twelve years, and without any warning you dump me. There has to be some good reason, doesn't there? What the hell is it?"

"It's called the McKenney Cup."

"But Ben! We were doing so well in it, tied for first and all and . . . oh, I get it! Ben! Ben old boy, why didn't you talk it over with me? I'd have figured out some way to make it a nice clean fight. You didn't have to go in for this back-alley stuff, pretending you weren't coming here and letting me get lined up with a lot of third-raters."

"I didn't pretend I wasn't coming. Up to three days ago I wasn't. And I had nothing to do with who you lined up. For all I knew, you could be playing with Barry Crane and Alvin Roth and Helen Sobel Smith."

"But you knew goddam well I wouldn't be playing with Ben Aarons. So we're through, huh?"

"That's right. Anyway until this thing's finished."

"Well, we'll be through after that, too!" Sammy cried. "And if you're playing dirty, I can play rough. I just might go in every goddam tournament from now till the end of the Fall Nationals, and pick my partners carefully. How will you like that, huh? Where can you get the dough to go in every tournament?"

"Oh, you'll have an edge there, all right. But if I do well here, maybe Prentice-Hall will at least back me in all the big ones."

Sammy's face was crimson now, the blood surging under the fair clear skin so that you could time his heartbeat. "Jeez, what confidence!" Sammy said. "You'll take me, playing part-time? What a laugh! Why, you never saw the day your game could touch mine. You know that, don't you? Don't you?"

"No," Ben said calmly.

"O.K., we'll see about that," Sammy said, jumping up from the table. "We'll see." He rushed out of the coffee shop.

Ben let out a sigh that left him feeling like an empty rubber balloon. The talk had gone very badly, and at the same time very well. Badly from the point of view of friendship, trust and loyalty. Very well from the point of view of winning the McKenney. Like most other excellent players, Sammy thought he was probably the best in the world. You had to feel that way to play top bridge. But now Sammy might start thinking: *Am I really the best in the world, or even among the best, if that bastard has the nerve to dump me?* Ben knew Sammy quite well indeed. That worry was going to haunt Sammy's thoughts, and Sammy would start playing emotional bridge, trying to get more out of the cards than was in them. A couple of bad sessions (and everybody had them) would make the worry grow. It was called psyching an opponent. It wasn't the nicest thing you could do to a friend.

Nonetheless, he told himself firmly, it wasn't as bad as it seemed. If things had gone on in a normal way, he and Sammy would have played together in some more big tournaments and maybe would have done very well and might have opened up an even bigger lead in the McKenney. But somewhere along the line Sammy, who had all the time and money he needed, would go into a few smaller tournaments without Ben and pick up a bunch of points and put a lock on the McKenney. Sammy would do it in his usual good-hearted thoughtless slightly maddening way. And afterward Sammy would say, as he did once about the little soft quiet girl who majored in sociology, "But Ben, if you had only *told* me you wanted the McKenney. It meant nothing to me."

All right, Ben told himself, he was merely trying to do to Sammy what Sammy would have done to him. What was the difference? He studied that question carefully and could not avoid finding the answer. There *was* a difference. Sammy would have knifed him without intending to, like a kid playing mumblety-peg and letting the knife slip. He, Ben Aarons, was doing it deliberately.

♠ ♥ ♦ ♣ 6

PEOPLE PLAY TOURNAMENT bridge for many reasons. For players like Ace McKinley it is a business. For those like Mary Rose Rutledge it satisfies a need to feel important to somebody, even if only to a bridge partner. Still others play the game in order to release primitive urges: at a bridge table you can get away with actions that bear a gratifying resemblance to assault and battery, mayhem and manslaughter. Mrs. W. B. Edmunds, who had paid the way of Vicky Summers to the tournament, liked to commit assault and battery with that blunt instrument, the spoken word. Runa Montez, who was going to play with Sammy Rothberg in the Vanderbilt, was more inclined to manslaughter.

Another group of people use bridge much as other people use liquor or narcotics, as a way to escape unpleasant realities. Bridge has an advantage over liquor and narcotics in that there is no hangover. Also, if the addict cannot obtain the necessary supply of bridge games, the withdrawal symptoms are not as severe.

Finally there are people who play tournament bridge in order to act out imaginary roles or fantasies for which ordinary life does not provide a stage. The fact that the fantasies are unreal makes no difference; the satisfaction is real enough when the fantasy is enacted successfully. In the case of failure, there is the hope of success in another bridge hand or session or event or tournament. It is always possible, of course, for continued failure to destroy both the fantasy and the person who holds it. None of this group at the Xanadu realized that they were acting out fantasies. P. J. Hoffmeister did not know that in his subconscious mind he was a minor Hebrew prophet, lonely and scorned, crying in the wilderness the message of the Hoffmeister No Trump. Sammy Rothberg did not realize that he was acting the part of a young and handsome crown prince, admired by men and loved by every attractive woman in the kingdom. He had played this role with almost unbroken success—bridge really had helped him with women, and coronation in the form of the McKenney Cup was within reach—until the moment when a trusted general, Ben Aarons, launched a revolt. Bubba Worthington did not know that he played bridge in order to prove his virility. When he won the Charity Pairs with Tony Manuto, the big red 1 indicating first overall was a phallic symbol, and becoming a Life Master marked the attainment of manhood.

Jake Jacobs, who would be playing with Tony Manuto in the Vanderbilt Team matches, along with Sammy and Runa, entered tournaments to act out the fantasy that he was a ruthless captain of industry. The unusual thing about this was that he already *was* a captain of industry, even though the I. I. Jacobs Company could hardly be compared to General Motors. Jake was the product of a New York slum and a broken family. At age sixteen he dropped out of high school. Then he proceeded to upset the neat charts of sociologists by refusing to become a statistic in the probation or welfare files. At seventeen he was a stock boy at S. Klein. At twenty-one he was an assistant buyer of cosmetics at Gimbel Brothers. At twenty-seven he was buyer of cosmetics at Macy's. At thirty-one, having learned the business thoroughly, he rented the fourth floor of an old warehouse and hired a chemist and a dozen girls and began putting four cents' worth of lipstick into cases that looked as if they cost a dollar (by the gross, they cost twenty-nine cents each) and wholesaling the result for fifty-eight cents.

The new company grew rapidly, and Jake had visions of climbing the heights to join firms like Revlon and Max Factor and Helena Rubinstein. But this called for a gamble: the borrowing of much money, the setting up of a big sales organization and the spending of millions on advertising. Jake couldn't force himself to take the gamble. He played it safe and kept his overhead low and became a private-brand supplier for chain stores. At his present age, forty-eight, he had a good but limited business. It was too late now to think of climbing higher, because the major companies had become too big to fight. He didn't dare compete with them; they'd kill him with their huge ad budgets and special deals and highly-trained demonstrators and the push money they paid to salesgirls in stores.

In tournament bridge, Jake took the gambles that he avoided in real life. And when he won a section top it was as satisfying as if he actually had taken on Charlie Revson of the Revlon Company and knocked him for a Naked Pink loop. In addition to bridge he had one other major interest: women. No fantasy or play-acting was involved in that interest. Where women were concerned, Jake was for real.

He prepared for the first qualifying round of the Men's Pairs in somewhat the fashion of a young squire of medieval times purifying himself before receiving knighthood. After his breakfast had been digested he worked out for an hour in the gym of the Xanadu, took a steam room treatment, and went to the barbershop for a haircut, shampoo, facial massage and manicure. He studied the manicure girl as she worked over his nails. She had the sort of knockers that made you wish you were still in diapers. Just for kicks he tried out one of his tested approaches to girls: "Look, honey, I own a cosmetics company. You got real fine hands (or eyes, or mouth). Maybe I ought to send a photo of your hands (or eyes, or mouth) to the boys at the ad agency, and see what they think of using you as a model." It didn't get him anywhere this time. He hadn't thought it would, because too many guys tried their approaches on manicure girls. This girl didn't believe in the cosmetics company. She thought that made her pretty smart. Of course if she really were smart she would believe in the cosmetics company and disbelieve the ad agency. The I. I. Jacobs Company did not advertise. Why waste money on ads when you only sold private brands to chains? He gave her a dollar tip and one of the flashily-cased lipsticks he always carried in his pocket, and enjoyed watching her begin to worry that maybe she had turned down a good thing.

Before leaving the barbershop he checked his appearance in a mirror, and admired his glossy black hair, smooth tanned face, easy smile and white even teeth. They ought to be good teeth, he thought; the recapping job had cost eighteen hundred bucks. He appraised the effect of his light yellow shirt, rust-colored necktie, dark yellow sports jacket of Italian silk, rust-colored slacks and alligator-skin shoes. Very nice, very nice, he told himself, and went upstairs for lunch in the Kubla Khan room.

As he stood in the entrance of the dining room, waiting for the hostess, a woman at a nearby table waved to catch his attention. The waving hand was ornamented with bright red fingernails and a huge silver and turquoise ring, and belonged to Mrs. W. B. Edmunds. A plain-looking girl built like a bed slat (Jake always thought of women in terms of bed) was with her.

Jake walked to the table and said, "Hello, Katy. Good to see you, except now I won't be able to keep my mind on bridge. Is it still *No,* honey?"

Katy Edmunds rattled out her fire-gong laugh. She and Jake had known each other long enough to recognize certain traits that they shared. Both of them were well-adjusted, confident, predatory animals. Neither of them wanted anything from the other, and so they were able to pass each other on the hunt with mutual respect and consideration. "Watch yourself, Jake," she said. "Some day I might take you up on that, and will you start doing backflips! I want you to meet my little friend, Vicky Summers. We're playing in some of the events. Vicky, this is Jake Jacobs. You can trust him at a bridge table but not near a bed."

Vicky's thin body jerked as if her chair were equipped with electrodes and somebody had tested the voltage. The word "bed," pronounced in the presence of a man, had a painful effect on her. She blinked rapidly and managed to stammer, "H-how do you do, Mr. Jacobs?"

Ordinarily Jake would have said something polite and put her out of his mind, but her eyes caught his attention. They were large glowing eyes that never seemed to stop blinking. There was something helpless and appealing about the constant flutter of her thick dark lashes, and he wondered how her eyes would look blinking up at him from a pillow. "Hello, Vicky," he said. "Don't believe all you hear. You can't trust me at a bridge table either. You're playing with Katy, huh? You got a good partner."

"Oh, I know!" Vicky said quickly, as if she might be suspected of having a different opinion. "I feel so lucky about it."

Jake allowed himself a tiny shrug. Lucky? Katy always brought a partner to tournaments, sometimes a thin nervous youth and sometimes a thin nervous girl, and usually they ended up wearing Katy's teeth marks—in a manner of speaking, that is. As far as he knew, Katy no longer had physical urges.

"Have lunch with us, Jake," Katy said. "A boy turned Vicky down and so she's acting like a guest at the Last Supper. I need somebody to cheer me up and you're not after my money, like most men, just after my fair white body, and that's something nobody can snatch because I don't have it any more, right?" Her laugh went off like a four-alarmer.

Jake chuckled and sat down. He enjoyed Katy's talk, even at the price of having his eardrums lanced with that laugh. "If I'd only met you when I was twenty years younger," he said.

"Wouldn't have done you any good," she said comfortably. "I was too busy trying to salt away money before the late W. B. could lose it."

"Lose it? I heard he was a real sharp operator."

"Oh, sharp enough in his way. He made plenty on those developments of his, horrible sleazy houses with all the value on the surface. But when the housing boom ended he wanted to keep right on building, a dreadfully stubborn man, and he'd have gone broke. But he died before he could lose much, the most considerate thing he ever did for me. Are you playing in all the events here, Jake?"

"Haven't quite decided. I don't have to ask about you. How long since you missed an event in one of the Nationals?"

"Not since W. B. died, ten years, I guess. But I don't know. I need a change. I'm planning to take a year off and travel around the world."

"Think of the lousy bridge partners you'll get."

"Not me," Katy said. "I'll take a bridge partner with me. Maybe—" She looked at Vicky as if the thought had just occurred to her, although she had been considering it for a month "—it might even be Vicky."

"Me?" Vicky cried. "Oh Mrs. Edmunds, it's wonderful of you to think of me, but I couldn't get away from my bridge club and—"

"Don't refuse before you get asked, my dear," Katy said. "As for your club, while I've never played in it, I know that Philadelphia Main Line crowd of yours and I bet you can't handle them. To do that you either have to come from a better family than theirs, or have a lot more master points, or just be all-out nastier than they are." She turned to Jake and said, "Vicky inherited her club from the woman who owned it. Vicky was her assistant and the woman died." She turned back to Vicky. "Be honest, now. How many members have you lost since you took over?"

"Well, a few," Vicky said, huddling lower in her chair.

"And furthermore," Katy told Jake, "Vicky needs a man, and who do you meet at a local bridge club who doesn't have arthritis and a heart condition, or at the very least a wife who's on the alert? On a world tour I could get Vicky a rich widower who has a few good years left. Want to bet I couldn't, Jake?"

Jake saw that the girl was very upset, and decided to change the subject. "Except at a bridge table," he said, "I never bet against a woman. And Katy, I wouldn't bet against you even there. I remember one hand you played against me at the Nationals in Chicago, I thought we had you for an eight hundred set, you held the king, jack, ten and nine of clubs, the ace third of diamonds—"

"Oh yes!" Katy said with a happy screech, taking the bait as expected, and going on to describe the hand and the play in detail.

After that there were other bridge hands to discuss, and they had a nice lunch with no further comments to make the girl squirm. It wasn't that Jake wanted to interfere with Katy's business, it was just that he didn't want to watch a slave trader poke at the merchandise. Also the girl did have the most astonishing eyes, with lashes that looked soft as a bed. They finished lunch and signed their checks and started to leave. Katy paused on the way out to chat with friends, and Jake had a minute alone with Vicky and decided to poke the merchandise himself, but of course in a nice way, not Katy's way.

He took one of the special lipsticks from his pocket and said, "Katy forgot to mention I own a cosmetics company. I'd like you to have this, just a reminder of a pleasant lunch. It's our best lipstick. And you know, honey, you got—" he meant to go on with the line about the fine eyes and the photo and the boys at the ad agency, but she didn't give him a chance.

"Oh, I couldn't!" she gasped. "Thank you so much, but I really couldn't!"

"Couldn't what?"

"I—I couldn't accept a gift from a man. Not when we only met an hour ago. I do thank you so much, but . . . but . . ."

"That's all right," he said, giving her his easy smile. "I understand, honey. Well, I'd better run along. Good luck today, and I'll be seeing you."

He intended to do that little thing, too. Bed-slat figure or not, this was an interesting kid, with those eyelashes that seemed to be wigwagging frantically for help. Maybe he could provide some help. He took a deep happy breath, and put one of his interests in life temporarily out of his mind and headed for the ballroom and the Men's Pairs and his other interest.

The Xanadu was filled with bridge players for the first major events of the Spring Nationals. Tables crowded the ballroom, every available meeting room and even part of the garage. Three hundred and seventy-four pairs entered the Men's event and four hundred and forty-two pairs entered the Women's. These were four-session events. The afternoon and evening sessions on the first day were qualifying rounds, and about half of the contestants would go into the final rounds the next day. In addition to the

Men's and Women's Pairs there was also a side game, entered by one hundred and eighty pairs. There was always a side game at every championship session; these were not very important and drew players like Mary Rose Rutledge and P. J. Hoffmeister. The competition in side games tended to be rather bloodless, like children squabbling in a playground, while the championship events were more reminiscent of fights with bicycle chains and knives and zip guns. The Men's event was especially notable in this respect. Without women in the game, the men reverted to a violent and reckless type of play. It was almost as good as having a war.

Ben Aarons was playing with Harvey Ashcraft, using the Duke-Ashcraft bidding system, The Method. Their styles meshed perfectly, and they went through opponents like expert swordsmen cutting their way through rabble. Also they had luck. During the two sessions they made the fourth best score of the one hundred and ninety-six pairs who qualified.

Sammy Rothberg played with Bubba Worthington. Sammy would not have done his best in any case, after being psyched by Ben Aarons, and he was unfortunate in playing on this day with Bubba, who thought that his new rating as Life Master would both improve his own game and daunt opponents. Bubba even told several opponents that he was a new Life Master. These set out grimly to prove that Bubba's rating was a big joke, and succeeded. Sammy and Bubba failed to qualify. Sammy went upstairs to bed, and had bitter thoughts about Ben, and finally took a sleeping pill in order to get some rest.

Tony Manuto and Ace McKinley had two erratic rounds. Tony could play well with anybody as long as he knew what his partner was likely to do, but Ace was inconsistent. Tony would figure Ace had joined him in a dark alley, ready to do a mugging job on the opponents, but instead he would find Ace walking down the middle of the street like a crummy cowboy hero on TV, ready for an honest shoot-out. There were other times when they had the drop on opponents and Ace wouldn't pull a gun, and times when Ace came whooping into the bidding with six-guns blazing like a drunken cowhand. Tony did the best he could but it wasn't enough. They qualified, of course, but so what? If your carryover score wasn't big enough, you needed a miracle to win in the final two rounds.

"I don't think we got a prayer tomorrow," Tony said.

"Reckon you're right," Ace muttered.

"You can play better than that. What the hell was wrong?"

Ace said miserably, "Looks like I'm kinda rusty. Well, it'll be good practice in the finals tomorrow, and then maybe we can try another event, what do you think?"

"I'm free for the Men's Teams and the Open Pairs."

"We'd need another pair if we go in the Men's Teams. Know anybody good?"

"Yeah," Tony said. "Jake Jacobs and that jerk Bundy who made the North American team a couple years ago, I still don't know how. Want me to set it up?"

"Go ahead. And save me the Open Pairs."

"Don't forget you're paying fifty a session, and that bonus if we win."

"Sure, I know," Ace said gloomily. "Only goddam it, we got to win one of these!"

"Get the rust off your game and we'll have a better chance," Tony said, and walked off to locate Jake.

Jake had enjoyed the two qualifying rounds. He did not expect to win a trophy the next day—he and Phil Bundy were going to qualify with too low a score—but several hands had given him real satisfaction. Once he overcalled an opposing spade bid with three no trump, holding nothing but a seven-card club suit to the ace-king, and the guarded king of spades. The opponent led spades, Jake got in with his king, the club suit broke and let him run seven tricks, and he picked up the ninth trick with the ace of hearts in his partner's hand. If the opponents had opened diamonds and then led through his spade king instead of up to it, he would have been down a million. It was a classic gambling bid, worthy of him.

Now he was ready to forget bridge for a while and take up his other interest in life. While everybody waited for the Recap sheets to be posted, Jake watched the table where Vicky Summers sat with Katy Edmunds. He wanted a chance to get the girl alone and try a couple of forcing passes, and he didn't mean that in the bridge-table sense, either. While he waited, Tony came by and suggested a Jacobs-Bundy-Manuto-McKinley combo for the Men's Teams. Jake agreed casually, and kept watching the girl. Finally he saw her hurry out of the room. He went after her, hoping that he wasn't going to end up at the women's john or something stupid like that. The girl walked outside onto the big patio next to the ocean. Very nice, he thought, and followed. He couldn't have asked for a better setting. The trade wind was coming off the Gulf Stream in little warm puffs, like the breath of a woman in bed, and the palm fronds were rustling like new cards being shuffled and the Miami Beach Chamber of Commerce had shined up the stars.

The girl sat on a bench in the shadow of a palm, and Jake walked past and faked a start of surprise and said, "Well, hello there, Vicky. Getting a little air?"

"Oh!" she gasped, looking up. Then she said hesitantly, "It's Mr. Jacobs, isn't it?"

"Call me Jake," he said. "How did you do today?"

"J-just awfully," she said.

He sat on the bench and offered her a cigarette. The glow of his lighter picked up the quick flutter of her eyelashes, and his skin tingled as if the eyelashes were stroking it. "We all have days like that," he said easily. He tried to figure the best way to get on with his business. The boys-at-the-ad-agency approach wouldn't make a nickel; if you couldn't even give her a lipstick she wouldn't go for that fame-and-fortune bit. Of course there were other approaches. When he ran into a really gorgeous number he sometimes did all right by pretending to be attracted by her brilliant mind, but Vicky missed being gorgeous like the Battery missed being in Central Park. When he got interested in a girl who was long on brains and short on looks, he made like she was Venus, but this kid wasn't smart either. Another type of approach was to

work the health angle. You pointed out that intercourse was a
normal part of human life and necessary for good health, and
ought to be as regular an activity as taking vitamins. Jake always
felt very honorable when he used the health approach because he
believed every word of it; the only thing that kept him from using
it exclusively (he liked to feel honorable) was the fact that it
rarely worked.

The most effective approach, of course, was to make like you
were falling in love. Jake absolutely refused to go in for this. He
tried it once in his life, back when he first became a buyer at
Macy's, and what did it get him? It got him Sadie, who held out
for marriage like it was a mink coat, and got it, and wrapped herself luxuriously in the name Mrs. I. I. Jacobs and from then on
asked nothing more from life, except not to be bothered too often
in bed. After the first few years she got that wish too, because it
was discouraging to marry a cute little cupcake and end up with
a sack of flour.

While Jake considered various approaches, and felt baffled by
the complexity of this problem, Vicky made things simple for
him. She turned on the tears.

"Well, now, what's all this?" Jake asked soothingly.

Vicky gasped, "She told me I come to a bridge table as if it
were a guillotine!"

Jake put an arm around the thin quivering shoulders and let it
rest there, warm and comforting. Was it really going to be this
easy, just a little friendship and sympathy? "You don't want to
take Katy seriously," he said. "That's just her way."

"But I want her to like me!"

He pulled her a bit closer, putting across the message: That's
all right, honey, somebody down here does like you. "I'm sure
she does," he said, although he didn't believe it at all. Katy looked
on people either as sparring partners or as punching bags, and
liking or disliking really didn't enter into it.

Vicky wailed, "Probably it was my fault, because I must have
hurt her feelings at lunch when I didn't act pleased about maybe
going on that world trip with her. And I've thought it over and it

would be a wonderful thing. Mrs. Edmunds is right, that bridge club of mine is doing very badly, and sooner or later I'm going to have to find something else. But I'm so stupid and I've never made a go out of anything and I just don't know what to do!" There was a large warm shoulder close to her face, and she nuzzled against it for solace.

Jake stroked her hair, feeling her sobs as a pleasant tingle inside his chest. She would be very emotional in bed. To make it really good there had to be an emotional response. The best was when the woman tried to rip you to shreds, but women of that sort were scarce and you couldn't hope to find one often. This kid would probably go off like a Roman candle, very nice indeed. His hand slid down from her hair and stroked her cheek and throat.

Vicky became slowly aware that something odd was happening in her body. A soft and pleasant lassitude was creeping over her, blotting out hurt and shame and worry. Her senses began reporting strange new things from the outside world: the scent of after-shave lotion, the nubbly texture of the Italian silk against which her face pressed, the feel of hard muscles prisoning her shoulders, the sound of a man's heartbeat against her ear, loud and fierce as kettle drums raging in an orchestra. It was becoming more and more difficult to get her breath, and she raised her head and looked wonderingly at the man who was responsible for all this.

"You're a very lovely and charming girl," Jake said softly, and bent and kissed her. It was a nice friendly kiss, none of this wet open-mouth stuff to startle her, and that was just as well, because it turned out that anything more would have sent the kid into orbit.

For a moment her lips felt soft and quiet and childish under his, but then a gasp forced her lips apart and she pressed close and clung to him with a lovely little moan. This only lasted a couple of seconds. Then she broke away and jumped up and stared at him and said, "Oh!" She turned and ran into the hotel.

Jake smiled, and stretched out his legs luxuriously, and lighted a cigarette. He told himself to relax, there was plenty of time. Probably tomorrow night would do it, if Katy Edmunds would just be her usual nasty self and upset the girl again. He stayed outside for another half-hour, enjoying the warm breeze and playing a mental game in which he had a harem and was allowed to choose seven women for it, one for each night in the week. Tomorrow night was Sunday and so Vicky would start off the week. He got up finally and went into the hotel, passing Carola Clark heading out into the patio, and said hello to her and kicked a movie star out of Monday night and gave it to Carola, lucky girl. He chuckled; it was a fun idea but ridiculous, because he doubted that any approach would work on Carola, who had everything a woman could want and so ought to be completely satisfied and happy.

Jake did not always bat 1.000 when he appraised women, and in the case of Carola Clark he did not even get a piece of the ball. She walked onto the patio and wondered what was the point in going outside. The breeze off the Gulf Stream smelled of dead fish and decaying seaweed, and the palm fronds went clickety-clack like women jabbering, and the stars were bits of sharp glass that hurt her eyes. There was certainly no point in going outside, just as there was no point in staying inside. She could also go upstairs to her room, where Babs would want to come in and dissect every hand played that evening, and that was even more pointless.

Probably this was unfair to Babs, because they had done quite well and it was only natural for Babs to want to talk about it. They placed third in section that afternoon and first in section this evening, and would have a nice carryover for the finals. But Carola hadn't enjoyed playing. Once it had been gratifying to sit north at table 1, calm and regal, with three or four women watching in awed silence, but lately it made her feel hemmed in and suffocated. It was amazing that they made such a good score tonight, because on many occasions her thoughts wandered away from the game. Once in the middle of a hand she caught herself trying to decide whether to wear the blue chiffon or the Chantilly lace tomorrow night. Another time she felt a sudden inexplicable dislike for the upswept hairdo balanced on Babs's head. She found herself wondering how Ace was making out in the Men's Pairs, and whether he was actually paying that creature Tony Manuto. So it had gone all day, her thoughts wobbling around like new kittens.

She sat on a bench in the shadow of a palm and squeezed her eyes shut and watched the stars arrange themselves in brittle new patterns against her eyelids. A few seconds or hours went by, and a voice said to her in an uncertain tone, "Hi." She thought: At least it's a man's voice. She opened her eyes and looked up at Ben Aarons. "Hello, Ben," she said. "How did you make out?"

He said glumly, "We got the fourth best carryover."

"You make it sound like mumps. Goodness, Ben, you don't have to be first all the time, to win the McKenney."

"That isn't the problem," he muttered. "The problem is, maybe I shouldn't try to win it. You got a moment to talk, Carola? Maybe you can solve this problem for me. You have a good clear mind."

"I do? It's been acting very fuzzy lately. But sit down and tell me anyway."

He distributed his long thin body on the bench in a series of sharp angles, like a tangle of stepladders. "Let me put a hypothetical case to you," he said. "Let's say two young guys are in business together. They're doing all right, but one of them thinks he'll make out better alone. So he walks out, sets up in business for himself, and uses his knowledge of the other guy's weaknesses to kick him in the teeth. Would you call that ethical?"

"I'd call it human nature."

"Well, maybe human nature is a mess. Now let me give you another hypothetical case. Suppose—"

She gave a small laugh and said, "Why don't we save time by calling your hypothetical people Ben and Sammy?"

"Huh? Well, all right, you guessed it, I said you had a good clear mind. So you know what I'm doing, huh? What do you think of it?"

"I don't think much of your hypothetical case, Ben. You two

boys in business could have stayed together and been a big success. You can't stay partners with Sammy and be a big success, because only one of you can win the McKenney. There isn't an unlimited amount of room at the top in bridge."

"Right," he said. "You're so right, Carola. Now we come to the ethical question: is it right to dump a friend in order to win success?"

Oh dear, she thought, was she supposed to act like an advice columnist in a newspaper? If he weren't so terribly young she'd be tempted to say, look, Ben, if you're frightened by knives don't try to carve the turkey. But she liked him very much, and even if she couldn't help at least she could listen. "How good a friend is he?" she asked.

"Well, it's like this," he said, and began giving her the full story of life with Sammy.

It was a pathetic little tale, she thought, although of course Ben didn't see that. You took a solemn boy who had no money or looks or social graces, merely ability, and threw him in with a golden boy. You let golden boy exploit solemn boy, doing it with the utmost charm and irresponsibility and lack of awareness. Golden boy used solemn boy as a mirror in which to admire himself, as a foil to make himself seem even more attractive, and as a crutch to help get over rough spots in the road. Now solemn boy was tired of being a mirror and a foil and a crutch, and hated himself for feeling that way.

"What I want to know is," Ben said finally, "why can't I either do the right thing and feel good about it, or the wrong thing and not give a damn?"

"I don't know," she said helplessly.

"Also," he mumbled, "just because I'm such a heel, I'm doing the wrong thing to a girl, too. A real nice girl."

"You . . . you've made her pregnant?"

"Oh my God!" he cried. "I haven't even kissed her!"

"Maybe I'm crazy. What *have* you done to her?"

"I busted a date to play bridge with her, just because it would hurt me in the McKenney."

"Oh Ben, Ben, Ben," Carola said in a choked voice. "You make me want to cry." She put a hand under his chin and lifted his head until she could look into the large dark painful eyes behind the thick glasses. "You idiot," she said, and leaned forward and kissed him.

After she drew back he stared at her, and gulped and said, "You didn't have to do that, just to make me feel better."

"I probably did it to make *me* feel better."

"You know, I could fall in love with you very easily, Carola. I guess that would be bad, huh?"

"I'd find it very flattering, but it might not be the best idea you ever had."

"You're right," he said, considering it thoughtfully. "For one thing, I'd want to go to bed with you, and I've never done that with anybody, and I bet I'd be kind of dull and clumsy, what do you think?"

She fought back a burst of rather hysterical laughter. Did a woman ever get such a sideways, reverse-English, unromantic proposition? And yet in an odd way it was quite appealing. She was tired of sleeping alone. More than that, she was tired of living in a women's world, a shrill and untidy and overly scented place, like a giant ladies' room. It might be nice to have Ben around, running to her with his stubbed toes and small-boy troubles. Every woman needed a small boy in her life, just as in her early years a woman needed a father and later on a husband. So why didn't she take Ben's hand and lead him up to her room and . . . and . . .

Oh no you don't, she told herself. You made that sort of mistake once before. When Ace came along you tried to get two for the price of one: a husband, and a father. Now you seem to be expecting another two-for-one bargain: a husband, and a small boy. Well, they don't come in one package, and what you really want is a husband.

She patted Ben's cheek and said, "I think you'll be a wonderful man for the right girl, and she won't think you're dull or clumsy at all."

"You don't think I'm sort of revolting to women?"

"You're a love," she said. "I have a feeling that things are going to work out very nicely for you."

She wished she had a feeling that things were going to work out very nicely for herself.

7

ON SUNDAY MORNING Harvey Ashcraft lay in bed in Room 408 in the Xanadu, yearning for coffee. He thought of how gaily it danced in the percolator and how sensuously the steam curled from the cup and how it kissed him back to life like the Prince waking the Sleeping Beauty. There was a percolator on the bureau, a can of coffee, a jar of cream substitute, sugar, cups and saucers and spoons. He always brought coffee-making equipment on trips. Room Service coffee was likely to be too strong, too weak, too hot or too cold. Or, worse yet, too late. Unfortunately one bit of coffee-making equipment was missing: somebody to get up and make it.

He peeked at the other twin bed. Miggsy lay on her side facing him, eyes closed, fluffy hair tousled, lips soft and slightly pouted, looking like a pink-and-white doll waiting for a child to pick her up. One plump little shoulder and a round little hip put curves in the sheet. He studied the way the sheet stirred to her breathing, trying to decide whether or not she was awake. She was completely capable of pretending to be asleep, in the hope that *he* would get up to make the coffee. He was willing to bet that Olga Duke, in the adjoining room, was the kind of wife who would get up to make coffee for a husband.

He tried a small experiment now, closing his eyes and moving uneasily and letting out a faint moan. A thoughtful wife would awake and hear this and get up softly and plug in the coffee and sit on his bed and stroke his forehead to coax the bad dream to go away. He opened his eyes to see if the experiment had produced any result.

Miggsy Ashcraft was also awake. She thought how nice it would be, just once out of the sixty-two hundred mornings of their married life, to awake and hear Harvey bouncing happily around the room, plugging in the coffee, beating his chest under a cold shower, and then coming to her bed to give her a hug and maybe to nibble her ear with fierce pretended growls. It was so hard to face a new day unless your man had it under control. But Harvey never seemed to have anything under control.

There was just one time when she had thought he did. That was when they first met, seventeen years ago in Chicago. She was a dental technician, a job she hated, all those gaping jaws looking ready to bite you. One morning when she was doing an errand her taxi had an accident and it hurt her neck just awfully, a sort of whiplash injury. The taxi company was mean and unsympathetic; at the hospital the company tried to get her to sign a paper releasing it from any liability and admitting she wasn't hurt. But she *was* hurt. She came back to her job, hardly able to *walk,* and noticed once again the lettering on a door down the hall from the office of her employer. The lettering said: Duke & Ashcraft, Attorneys-at-Law. Now and then she had seen a big gorgeous bear of a man going in and out, as well as a smallish chubby pink-and-white man. Nobody else ever seemed to go in or out, except a dark-haired girl, thin as lemon peel, who was probably the secretary. On an impulse, Miggsy opened the door of Duke & Ashcraft and went in, holding her neck a bit askew so the big lawyer could see what a nasty old whiplash injury she had.

Nobody was sitting at the desk in the tiny reception room. The door of the inner office was open and Miggsy peeked in, enjoying a delicious shudder at the idea of walking into a bear's den. But the big man wasn't at one of the two desks. Nobody was there but the smallish pink-and-white man, studying some playing cards that had been dealt into four hands.

She was about to creep away when the young man looked up

and said, "Oh, sorry, I didn't hear anyone come in. May I help you?"

"I—I was looking for your partner," Miggsy said, not knowing which was Duke and which Ashcraft. If she had known anything at all about them, she realized later, she could have guessed. Naturally the big man was Mr. Duke, whose name was of course the *first* on the office door.

"Sorry," the man said cheerfully. "My partner will be away for two weeks. He and Olga, that's our secretary, got married yesterday. The only way we could keep a secretary was for one of us to marry her. Can't afford to pay her. You wouldn't be a possible client, would you?"

"Well, I wanted to talk to your partner about something. You see, I work down the hall for Doctor Evans, and, well—"

"Say," he cried, peering at her. "What's wrong with your neck?"

She had intended to leave, but there was an eager note in his voice that held her. "It . . . it hurts," she wailed, her eyes filling with tears.

He came quickly around the desk. "Well I just bet it does," he said, touching her neck very gently with the tips of his fingers. He had long slender fingers, like a girl. "Could it," he said, "have been an accident? Is that why you came here?"

"Y-yes," she sniffled.

"Not your own fault? Maybe somebody else was *negligent?*"

She nodded, trying to look just as miserable as she could. "A car accident," she said.

"Who was the other party?" he asked. Then he added gloomily, "I suppose it was some ape in an old jalopy."

"I was in a taxi and it skidded and hit a telephone pole and . . . and it hurt my neck!"

He said almost reverently, "The taxi company. A telephone pole." He looked up at the ceiling and presumably to the sky beyond and said, "Lord, thank you very much." Then he took her hands and moved her slowly, as if she were made of lovely fragile crystal, to a chair. "Tell me all," he breathed.

"I don't want to bother you," she said, still not sure she wanted to be *his* client, maybe she could wait until the big man came back from the honeymoon, and wasn't it a shame the way those dark intense lemon-peel girls got all the men. "You seemed to be busy," she said, pointing somewhat reprovingly at the cards on his desk.

"Oh, that? My partner and I are bridge nuts. We've been trying to work out a new bidding system, and at least it helps pass the time. My name is Harvey Ashcraft, and you'd better give me your full legal name, because we're going to need it in suing that taxi company for one hundred thousand dollars."

She gasped. He was certainly not much to look at, but he had just spoken the most beautiful four words she had ever heard from any man. One hundred thousand dollars!

To the best of her knowledge, that was the last time he ever had anything under control. She tried a small experiment now, seventeen years later, to see if she could appeal to his better nature and get him up to make coffee. She wriggled in bed and uttered a plaintive noise, like a hungry kitten. By chance she did this at the moment when Harvey moaned as if having a bad dream, and so neither heard the other. She opened her eyes to see if the experiment had produced any result. This was when Harvey looked to see if *his* experiment had succeeded. The two pink-and-white people stared at each other reproachfully, and neither moved. The eighteen inches of space between the twin beds deepened into an abyss.

"*You are so awake,*" Miggsy said accusingly.

"I'm awake," he groaned, "but not alive. Is there any coffee?"

"How could there be coffee? You haven't made it."

"How could I make it?" he said. "I'm not up." He was proud of that reply; it was the sort of logic that would have made him a notable figure in the Cook County Bar Association, if bridge had not claimed him by a sort of writ of mandamus.

"Hank Duke would be up making coffee."

"He would indeed," Harvey said mournfully. "When Hank and I were bachelors, sharing an apartment, he had coffee ready for me every morning. In those days he was a wonderful wonderful guy."

"You could be wonderful to me, Harvey."

"Oh damn," Harvey said, because she could always outwait him. He pried himself out of bed and felt his way to the bureau and started the coffee and headed for the bathroom.

"Harvey, you haven't kissed me."

"If you had been up, you could have kissed *me*," he said grumpily, and stumbled into the bathroom.

In the next room, beyond the connecting door that could be opened to make Rooms 408 and 410 into a suite, Hank and Olga Duke were doing their morning exercises. Unfortunately the room was only of moderate size and each of them exercised violently and in a spirit of independence, so there was always a danger of collision. Hank touched his toes with sweeping movements of his arms, and did jumping jacks and a bit of shadow boxing. Olga had studied ballet; when she first rose that morning she was in a reflective mood, calling for choreography of a gentle graceful nature, suitable for *Swan Lake*. But Hank was taking up even more space than usual and so she did a few resentful leaps from Stravinsky's *Firebird*.

Finally she paused for breath, and said, "Aren't you overdoing things a bit this morning, Hank?"

"Certainly not," he said. "A man has to keep in shape."

She looked at his bare chest, on which sweat gleamed and hair coiled like rolls of barbed wire, and winced. "Hank, you're forty-five," she said. "I wouldn't want you to go plop with a heart attack one of these mornings. You ought to stay in bed a little longer."

"Never felt better in my life," he said, striking his chest with a booming noise. He looked at the dew of perspiration on her upper lip, and wished she weren't so athletic. A man didn't want a ballerina soaring through the room every morning, he wanted somebody to protect and cherish. When you got up in the morning it gave you extra strength to know that somebody was depending on you to get things organized and accomplished. He remembered how vigorous he used to feel long ago, in his bachelor days, preparing coffee and breakfast in the apartment while poor Harvey tried to summon up enough courage to face life again. Back then Harvey was a real sweet guy; too bad he had become querulous and peevish as the years went on. Harvey wasn't equipped to take care of the lovely helpless girl he married, and that made Harvey insecure and unhappy.

"If you slept a little later," Olga said, "you'd be in better shape to play bridge."

Her tone sounded much too casual, and he knew there was something back of it. "What's wrong with my bridge?" he growled.

"Didn't Harvey and Ben come in way ahead of you and your partner yesterday?"

"Sleep has nothing to do with it. Harvey plays a good enough game to beat me when he has lots of luck, as he did yesterday. Are you going to take your shower first, or am I?"

"Let me go first. You'll splash up the whole bathroom, as usual."

"All right, go ahead," he grumbled. "At least then I won't have to watch you parading around naked afterward, catching your death of cold. After all, you're forty, Olga. You ought to watch your health."

"Thirty-eight, thank you," Olga said, and peeled off her pajamas and walked into the bathroom, her lean body quivering with indignation. Forty, indeed! The man was almost as inconsiderate as her birth certificate, which insisted that she was forty-two.

Just before she turned on the shower, making sure it was set for cold, she heard water running in the next-door pipes. It was a nice warm feeling to know that Harvey was only a few feet away. It would of course be Harvey, because Miggsy always managed to make poor Harvey get up first and slave for her. Olga did not dislike Miggsy—how could you dislike a kitten that kept twining around your ankles and mewing to be picked up?—but the girl was completely unsuitable for Harvey. As on many occasions, Olga wished she had not been away on her honeymoon when Miggsy first came in the office. She could have headed the thing off before it got started. But by the time she came back,

Miggsy had twined herself so firmly around Harvey's ankles that the poor man had no chance.

The first morning after the honeymoon Olga had come to the office wondering how Harvey had managed in her absence. She hadn't liked abandoning Harvey for two weeks, but after all when you got married you were supposed to go on a honeymoon, and Hank insisted on it. He was a very insistent person. She hadn't been sure she wanted to marry him, but he insisted on it. Now and then, in the course of their lives together, she wondered if Hank would have wanted to marry her if there hadn't been another man in the office, competing for her attention and posing a challenge that Hank couldn't resist. But of course that thought was unfair. Hank loved her, and she loved Hank, and she was not and never had been in love with poor Harvey.

She walked into the office that first day after the honeymoon and saw a fluffy little creature in a chair very close to Harvey. Olga said, "Who on earth are you?"

"I'm a client," Miggsy said proudly.

Harvey said, "She has a whiplash injury, the fault of the soulless and negligent taxi company, and I'm suing for a hundred thousand dollars."

Hank brushed past her and took the fluffy creature's hand and said in a rumbling tone, "*We're* suing, little girl, because I'm Hank Duke and Harvey is my partner. Now let's hear the full story and consider if we shouldn't sue for a hundred fifty grand."

In a way that was rude of Hank but of course it was necessary, because by himself Harvey couldn't have won the case. Harvey was clever in looking up law and preparing the brief, but it took Hank to try the case, his voice roaring when he denounced the taxi company and dropping to a whisper when he called the attention of the jury to the girl shrinking in the witness chair, her pretty head a bit askew from the whiplash injury.

Olga was never able to decide whether or not it was a real injury. The Duke-Ashcraft medical experts said yes, and the taxi company doctors said no. The taxi people hired private detectives to trail Miggsy, trying to get photos of her with her head on straight, but they never succeeded. In fact if they had kept trying for seventeen years the result would still be the same; even today the pretty head tilted a bit to one side, so either it was a real injury or Miggsy knew that the tilt was rather attractive.

The jury brought in a verdict of $123,750.50, which an appeal finally cut to $87,500. Duke & Ashcraft, working on a contingency basis, earned a fee of one-third. Of course it was ridiculous to let the rest of that money get out of the family, in a manner of speaking, and so poor Harvey had to marry the girl. This produced a lasting joke—"We had to marry our only client in order to keep her"—to go with the other lasting joke about having to marry our secretary because we couldn't pay her.

Miggsy really had been their first and only client. Hank decided that the wait between clients was too long, and that bridge offered a better livelihood. The money from the whiplash injury financed them while Hank and Harvey hammered out The Method and wrote a book and went in tournaments and became famous.

Olga took her shower, arching her body disdainfully into the cold needle spray, and came out and began drying herself. From beyond the party wall came another gurgle of plumbing and then the sound of a thin tenor voice trying to sing "Londonderry Air." The voice was not sure of the words, and stopped. On an impulse, Olga sang the next line in her flat and slightly harsh contralto: *The pipes, the pipes are calling.* Suddenly she realized the implication of the words, and laughed. The pipes in the song were bagpipes, but it was amusingly and somewhat shockingly evident that the words could also apply to the sounds of back-to-back plumbing.

From beyond the party wall came a faint giggle, and the tenor voice sang another line.

How ridiculous can you get, Olga thought happily, and finished the song with the concluding line: *Oh Danny Boy, I love you so.*

The bathroom door snapped open and Hank poked in his head and asked, "Were you calling me?"

"Why, no," she said. "What gave you that idea?"

"I was doing pushups and couldn't hear well but I thought I heard you calling my name."

"I was singing the Londonderry Air. Maybe the words Danny Boy sounded like Hank to you."

"Oh. That explains it. You getting out of here soon? I'm ready for breakfast."

"Right away. Look, why don't we have breakfast sent up, and ask Harvey and Miggsy to join us."

"Good idea. Soon as I shower and shave I'll invite them. Why don't you phone in the order now, to save time?"

"All right," she said, and turned the bathroom over to him.

Beyond the party wall, Harvey came out of the bathroom smiling. That was an amusing thought about the plumbing pipes calling to each other. He looked at Miggsy, still snuggled under the covers, and said, "Why don't we have breakfast sent up here, and ask Hank and Olga to come in? I don't want Hank to get the idea I dislike him, just because we're not playing together any more."

"That's a wonderful idea," Miggsy said, getting up immediately. "You call in the order, and I'll wash and throw on a robe or something."

"It would be more proper if you dressed completely," Harvey said. "I must say, that shortie nightgown and your negligee are very revealing."

"Revealing? Me, Harvey? What about Olga and those thin tight sweaters she wears, with absolutely nothing on underneath. After all, I don't suppose anybody has a bra with two buttons sewn on it."

Harvey thought about those buttons and decided that, well, in this modern day one had to be broadminded. "All right," he said. "I suppose it doesn't matter."

He called in the breakfast order, changed into a clean and neatly pressed pair of blue nylon pajamas, tied a yellow scarf around his neck, and put on a blue satin robe and knotted the cord neatly. Meanwhile Miggsy washed and put on her negligee.

"I'm all ready, Harvey," Miggsy said, with a caroling note in her voice.

In the next room, Olga had put on a light tailored suit and a thin sweater that clung to her figure. Hank wore slacks and an open sports shirt that revealed a triangle of muscular chest and coils of black springy hair.

"I'm all set, Hank," Olga said, with a husky throb in her voice.

Hank went to the door connecting the two bedrooms and unlocked his side and rapped softly. He waited eagerly for it to open and let him smile down at the soft fluffy pink-and-white girl who needed somebody to take care of her and unfortunately had married Harvey. In the other room, Harvey heard the soft knock, and hurried to unlock his side of the door. He opened it, ready to exchange a knowing smile with the girl whose pipes had called to him that morning.

Both men found themselves staring at each other, and both smiles warped into grimaces. Each felt a twinge of anger and frustration, as if a partner had laid down a Yarborough when there was reason to expect an ace.

"Oh, hello," Hank said coldly.

"Hello yourself," Harvey snapped. "Did you want something?"

"Yes," Hank said. "I wanted to tell you not to figure on breakfast with us. We're going out right now."

"Good," Harvey said. "We're having breakfast in bed."

Two hands closed the door firmly and two locks clicked shut.

8

DIRECTLY BELOW HANK and Olga Duke in the Xanadu was Room 310, occupied by Sammy Rothberg, who also had partnership troubles. Sammy got up slowly and painfully, as if pulling himself out of quicksand, because he had taken one more sleeping pill than was prudent before going to bed. He always carried a supply of pills for use if an evening session of bridge left him overstimulated. He wandered around the room, taking off his pajamas and dropping them on the floor, where they joined the clothing discarded at bedtime. As he began dressing he faced decisions as to which necktie or slacks or socks to wear. It was hard to make these decisions, and sometimes an item of clothing slipped from his fingers onto the bed or a chair or the floor, where he let it lie. He thought resentfully that Ben Aarons was no doubt dressing with fireman speed, eager to get to the finals of the Men's Pairs. But of course Ben had few decisions to make about clothes; the guy wore the same things day after day.

Finally, when lunchtime was getting close and he had made little progress, Sammy unscrewed the top of another pill bottle and took a Benzedrine pill. Maybe there was something symbolic about that: bennies, and Ben Aarons. Ben used to stimulate him, too. Soon the amphetamine drug began working, and Sammy soared up from the quicksand and orbited into a high chill world where everything was very clear and precise, and energy boiled in him like rocket fuel. He hurried downstairs, knowing that at least he and Bubba were going to win the consolation event today.

Sammy was wrong. He and Bubba played poorly, and ended

below average. Sammy waited around to see how Ben came out with Harvey Ashcraft in the Men's Pairs finals, and after looking at the Recap sheet went back to his room and, for the second night in a row, took one more sleeping pill than was prudent.

Harvey Ashcraft had also played rather poorly, at least for him. Miggsy had acted upset that morning after he shut the door in Hank Duke's face. Among other things, she asked plaintively who was going to eat the two extra breakfasts they had ordered. Harvey ate them grimly, hoping he would die of acute indigestion before her eyes. However, it merely made him feel puffy, and hurt his play that afternoon and evening. But Ben played very well and they came in seventh overall, a gratifying distance above Hank and his partner.

Ben Aarons looked at the Recap sheet late that evening and checked the Awards placard and saw that he and Harvey would get 10.33 red points each. So now he led Sammy in the McKenney. He didn't feel especially good about it. He debated looking up Sammy and calling the whole damn thing off, but rejected the idea. He considered looking up Carola, but after a battle threw out that notion also. He couldn't go running to her all the time.

Carola did not find out immediately that she and Babs placed tenth in the Women's Pairs, because she was waiting to check the ranking in the Men's Pairs. Finally she saw that Ace and Tony made ninth in the Men's, a good showing considering their carry-over score. She sighed, and wished Ace would win something.

Miggsy and Olga had qualified for the final rounds of the Women's Pairs. Their husbands had started teaching them The Method early in their married lives. It had not been easy. The Method was complicated and featured a very slow approach to the final bid. Nearly all low-level bids were artificial, designed to uncover facts about the distribution as well as the point count.

"I'll never learn it!" Miggsy used to wail.

"I hate the thing!" Olga used to cry.

Teaching Miggsy was like trying to knit with wet spaghetti; at the least excuse, everything came apart. But Harvey and Hank persisted, and finally Miggsy memorized The Method without really understanding it. She was not a bad partner. She could always produce the exact book bid; it might not be right for the situation but she made it anyway, and it was always of some value to know just what she was going to do. She never made a mechanical error in the play and never made an inspired play. When the percentages were working in her favor she was not easy to beat. When the short end of the percentages showed up, she was a sure bet for bottoms.

Olga also had been a difficult pupil. Teaching her was like knitting with guncotton; the tiniest spark, and everything vanished in a hot puff. Harvey and Hank persisted with her too. She learned The Method but never submitted completely to its rules. She was like a falcon obeying a trainer while remaining basically wild, always likely to go soaring off in untamed flight. As a partner she could be either brilliant or maddening. She tossed away rules at the drop of a hunch, and her score card tended to be studded with tops and bottoms.

Miggsy and Olga always played together in Women's Pairs. After years of experience each had learned one thing about their partnership. Miggsy knew it was no use to play with extra caution to compensate for Olga's reckless game, because Olga would simply get more reckless. Olga knew it was no use to play more cautiously in order to shame Miggsy out of her cowardly ways, because Miggsy would just get more cowardly. So each played her own game. The faults of caution canceled the faults of recklessness and produced a well-balanced partnership. In spite of that, they had never come close to winning a major title. This was because they played together absentmindedly, as if the other did not really exist, a reaction that psychologists call wish-fulfillment.

Today, however, they were very much aware of each other. Before they began play in the afternoon, Miggsy said, "I don't understand what happened this morning. Harvey and I agreed to ask you in for breakfast, and Harvey suddenly changed his mind."

"That's odd," Olga said. "We were going to invite *you* in for breakfast, and Hank suddenly changed *his* mind."

"Harvey said he was hungry, and ate all the extra food we had ordered sent up."

"Did he really? Hank said he lost his appetite, and didn't want a thing."

"Poor Hank. You shouldn't let him go without his breakfast."

"What about you letting Harvey overeat?"

"Hank is a big strong man who needs his food."

"I sometimes wonder if Harvey overeats to make up for something missing in his life."

Miggsy said, with a hint of tears in her voice, "I wish you'd stop worrying about my husband."

"Then stop worrying about mine," Olga snapped. "Let's drop the subject and find our table, shall we?"

They began playing, and for once each was alert to everything the other did and said. Olga was familiar with all Miggsy's little mannerisms, and could usually ignore them, but today she was painfully conscious of the tilt of the head, the twitching walk that Miggsy must think was beguiling, and the way Miggsy gave people little pats as she talked to them. It was as if Miggsy wanted to keep reminding people by touch that she was really and truly there.

Across the table, Miggsy kept watching Olga. She rather hoped Olga's sweater was scratching the two small buttons that dented the fabric. She wished that Olga's dark hair, piled in two mounds on her head, one on top of the other, would collapse. Olga always carried a chiffon handkerchief tucked under a bracelet on her left arm, and when Olga had nothing else to do with her hands she often yanked out the handkerchief and whipped it around nervously, like an amateur matador flapping things at a bull. Was there a chance, Miggsy thought wistfully, that Olga might hit herself in the eye with the end of that handkerchief?

And so, throughout the afternoon and evening, Miggsy and Olga kept their full attention on what the other was doing. This produced a remarkable result.

After the evening session ended, each joined her husband and waited for the results of the Men's Pairs to be posted. Each stood by attentively while her husband copied the match points from the Recap sheets and began analyzing each hand to see why he had done well or poorly. While this was going on, Chief Tournament Director Waldo Starnes came bouncing up to Harvey and Miggsy, his small body aquiver with glee. He looked like an elf who had just learned a new trick, such as turning milk sour.

"Hello there," he cried. "Miggsy, I haven't seen you getting your own score."

"Oh, I'm not interested in my score," Miggsy said. "Our carry-over wasn't much. Did Olga and I come in somewhere?"

"Well, sort of," Waldo said, hugging himself with his elbows. He saw Olga and Hank studying another Recap sheet of the Men's Pairs, not far away, and called, "Olga! Hank! Can you come here a moment?"

Hank and Olga came over, Hank frowning slightly, because he did not care for Waldo and furthermore he had been interrupted in explaining a hand that his partner had butchered. "What is it?" Hank said irritably. "I hope it's important, Waldo. I was telling Olga something that might improve her game."

Oh, this was too too wonderful, Waldo thought. "Maybe," he said, "you ought to let Olga tell you things to improve *your* game, Hank. May I introduce you two gentlemen to the Women's Pairs Champions, Mrs. Olga Duke and Mrs. Margaret Ashcraft?" He looked at the expressions on the four faces, and went away seething with happiness.

"Oh no!" Miggsy said, peering almost in fright at Harvey and Hank.

"I can't believe it," Olga said, peering at the fluffy pink-and-white idiot with whom she had been playing.

"Could it be a mistake?" Harvey said hopefully.

"Let's look for ourselves," Hank growled, and led the way to the Recap sheets of the Women's Pairs.

There was the big red 1 circled beside Miggsy's and Olga's names, and there were the scores they had made that afternoon and evening: a good sixty percent game in the afternoon, and an enormous, unbelievable, preposterous seventy-four percent game in the evening. These, added to a modest carryover from the previous day, put them two full boards ahead of the field. Miggsy and Olga and Harvey and Hank looked at each other warily, and knew that things were never going to be quite the same from now on.

Miggsy's soft plump fingers fluttered with an urge to start patting the other three in order to reassure herself that she was there and they were there and everything was in order. But everything wasn't in order, and she didn't know who to start patting. She rummaged in a collection of ragbag thoughts, and found an expression that had been used by millions of people millions of times, so it must be safe to repeat, and said, "Oh well, lucky in cards, unlucky in love."

Then she peeked around and saw that had not been the right thing to say after all. . . .

Jake Jacobs was wearing black with white accents tonight. His suit was of dull black silk, made in Hong Kong, and his shirt was of glossy black silk, made on Seventh Avenue in New York. He had a white silk necktie, a white silk handkerchief in his breast pocket, and white buckskin shoes. He looked as smooth and polished as if he had just come out of a giant buffing machine. He had done only fairly well in the Men's finals and had no interest in his score. Tonight he was interested in scoring with a dame. He watched alertly while Katy Edmunds checked the Recap sheets of the Women's consolation. Katy turned to the thin girl and made some comments that seemed to hit the kid like a slap. The girl flinched, and hurried out of the room. Jake caught up to her in the main lobby.

He put a firm hand under her arm and said, "Vicky, you need a drink."

Her eyes felt like boiling teakettles and she had to blink hard to get the man into focus. It was Mr. Jacobs, who wanted to be called Jake. That reminded her of a slang term: everything's Jake. It meant that everything was all right, but in her case it meant everything was all wrong, because he always showed up when she felt ready to die. She took a deep shuddering breath and used it to push out a tumble of words: "Thank-you-very-much-but-I-have-to-go-up-to-my-room."

"Let's go up to my room," he said easily. "We can have a drink there."

She stared at him and tried to speak and failed to produce a sound. All evening Mrs. Edmunds had been complaining about her play, and just five minutes ago Mrs. Edmunds snapped, "There must be *some* card game you're good at, Vicky. Could it be Old Maid?" It would have been bad enough if Mrs. Edmunds said Authors or Michigan, but there was a special hurt in Old Maid because that reminded Vicky of a problem not connected with cards. Now Mr. Jacobs—or maybe she ought to think of him as Everything's Jake—was reminding her even more painfully of that problem. He seemed to be a nice man and perhaps didn't mean anything by his invitation, but considering the way it affected her he might just as well have said, "Do you want to go up to my room, or do you want to spend the rest of your life playing Old Maid?" The choice left her paralyzed.

Jake didn't give her time to choose. He suspected that the kid had probably not gone to bed with a guy more than two or three times in her life, and if you gave such a girl time to think you might end up dealing yourself a game of Canfield. His hand tightened on her elbow and he propelled her gently across the lobby and up the stairs, talking soothingly about how she needed to relax and he had a suite with a living room and they would merely have a friendly drink and friendly talk and if she had to wash she could go in the bedroom and lock the door and use the bathroom and everything would be proper and she was a nice kid and he was sorry Katy had been chewing on her.

Vicky was not used to having men act masterful with her, except back when she worked in an office and a man might say, "Miss Summers, I need an original and four carbons of this letter in fifteen minutes." She had never displeased a man by refusing to do the letter in fifteen minutes and she did not want to displease a man now. Also the soft flow of his meaningless words kept washing thoughts out of her head. She allowed herself to be guided to the second floor and down a corridor and into the living room of his suite, her legs as wobbly as an old card table. He sat her on a couch (she was not experienced enough to take a chair) and she pressed her knees tightly together to stop them from trembling. Her eyelashes fluttered like small frantic wings.

Jake made a stiff drink for himself and a light one for her; he was not one of those apes who couldn't score unless they got the girl drunk. Anyway this kid was upset, and would either get sick or pass out if she did much drinking. He gave her the glass and sat on the couch, leaving a reassuring amount of space between them. The kid took a sip and didn't say anything, just stared at him with a steady beat of eyelashes.

"Katy said you run a bridge club outside Philly," he said, trying to get her to relax. "What's it like doing that? Is there any dough in it?"

For a moment she continued to stare wordlessly at him. Her thoughts and emotions were locked together like jumbles of ice in a frozen river; enormous pressures were at work on the ice jam, and it would have taken very little more to send her into hysteria. But his questions were calm and friendly and made no further demands on her thoughts or emotions. She began answering in a flat toneless voice, like a child reciting in school.

"I have two afternoon and one evening session a week," she said. "It isn't bad except some of the women don't seem to like me. I average ten tables a session and get a dollar and a quarter from each player, so I average fifty dollars a session."

"That's gross, of course," Jake said. "What do you net?"

"I have to provide tables and chairs and cards and scoring material, and pay ten dollars a session rent. I have to pay franchise and sanction fees to the ACBL. Each session has one master-point game a month, and the ACBL charges five dollars for the first master-point game and three dollars for the other two. Then I have to buy a book of one hundred certificates for fractional points, that's three dollars. If I hold a club championship or a special winners' game I pay thirty cents a table to the ACBL as a sanction fee."

"You're not getting rich, that's for sure."

She realized in surprise that she was beginning to feel better. Nothing awful had happened to her, and the ice was starting to thaw. She couldn't remember when a man had ever coaxed her to talk about herself. Usually she tried to get them to talk. That was her biggest failing when she worked as a secretary; she would allow herself to get feverishly interested in the life of her boss, and sooner or later that made him uneasy and he looked for ways to get rid of her. But Jake wasn't like that.

"I net twenty-five or thirty dollars a session," she said. "I'd make more, but I have to pay a woman to take the money and keep the books, and when we have a charity game I only get expenses. I do make some money out of giving lessons. I guess Mrs. Edmunds would say that I . . . t-that I . . ." The ice jam suddenly broke and a flood of tears began. "She would say," Vicky sobbed, "that I'm t-taking money under false pretences!"

"There, there," Jake said soothingly, and slid close and put an arm around her.

Everything came out then in a rush. All the mean remarks Mrs. Edmunds had made. How Mrs. Edmunds had teased her about Ben Aarons, who broke a date to play with her. How Ben was wrecking a long-time partnership with Sammy Rothberg just because, according to Mrs. Edmunds, Ben put winning the McKenney above friendship. How Mrs. Edmunds said she didn't think Vicky would work out as a companion on that round-the-world trip.

Jake didn't think that last item was worth crying about. As far as he could see, being a paid companion to Katy Edmunds would be like hiring out to a mastiff as a bone. Jake didn't make any comment about that, however, because he had more important things to do. Right now he was letting his hands do the talking. They were working very softly and skillfully, stroking her hair, caressing her soft wet cheek, and in various other small and unstartling ways telling her body that it was warm and desirable and had some rights of its own. In a little while her body began to get the word, and stirred sensuously in his arms even while she still wept. She lifted her face to him. Jake kissed her eyes, savoring the way her lashes fluttered like trapped things, and then bent to her lips. This time she didn't cry "Oh!" and jump up and run away. She began kissing him back.

Vicky knew that something was happening to her and that something more was likely to happen. Her senses were out prowling like avid little spies, collecting information on what it was like to be pressed closely against a man. The information they brought back didn't frighten her this time. She felt deliciously soft and boneless, and in an odd way rather triumphant. No, Mrs. Edmunds, she thought, I do *not* intend to spend the rest of my life playing Old Maid.

Jake was familiar with all the signs of a dame who was ready. He kissed her throat and explored her breasts—two of hers wouldn't make one of the manicure girl's—and then began removing her clothes with neat economical motions, like an expert husker of corn. As soon as she was naked he scooped her up in his arms and carried her into the bedroom and placed her on the bed. He turned on a small shaded lamp, because he liked a little light to work by, and sat on the bed and examined the always interesting ways in which a woman differed from a man. She was certainly very thin; it was going to be like lying on a xylophone, but the music might be good. He was, however, disappointed in her breasts: small erect nipples on a faint pink halo on a meager pad of flesh. On an impulse he reached into his pocket and brought out one of the special lipsticks, perhaps the very one he tried to give her at lunch yesterday, an amusing thought. He opened it and, with the care of an artist, improved the coloring of her nipples. Very nice, he thought.

Vicky lay quivering on the bed, and said weakly, "Is . . . is it going to hurt very much?"

Jake gave a start. *"What?"* he said.

"Is . . . is it going to hurt me?"

He frowned and stared down at her. "Listen," he said, "haven't you ever done this before?"

She shook her head sadly and apologetically.

"Well, Good God," Jake said, and stood up. He wasn't going to get into anything like this. A kid her age, the first time, you never knew what might happen afterward. She might figure this was love, stars above, all that crap. When he showed signs of walking out on her she might throw fits, have hysterics, shoot herself, shoot him, yell for lawyers, who knows? He was certainly playing in bad luck. A virgin, and in Miami Beach, of all places. "Let's get you dressed," he said irritably, and collected her clothes from the living room.

It was like dressing a rag doll, except that she cried and cried. He walked her out of his room and down the corridor and up two flights of stairs to her room and assured her she was a swell kid and left quickly. She was still weeping but he refused to let it get to him, what the hell, he'd already given to charity this year.

Vicky wept on her bed for a long time, and then got up and washed and undressed and started to put on her pajamas. For a moment she debated scrubbing her body to remove the lipstick that decorated her like shameful red medals. But in the end she did nothing and went to bed cold and trembling, hugging her thin arms around the gaudy decorations.

9

BEHIND THE SUNGLASSES Tony Manuto was a young man with old eyes. His eyes had looked old for thirty-three years, which was his present age. He had been born in the tough Red Hook section of Brooklyn in 1935. This was the wrong place and time for him. He should have been born in Renaissance Italy where, after learning the skills of the sword and dagger and pistol, he would have become a condottiere and practiced the art of changing sides, and might even have won passing mention in a book by Machiavelli. On the Brooklyn street where he grew up, there was some demand for skill in the use of the switchblade knife and zip gun, but the art of changing sides was not held in high esteem, and this limited the development of Tony Manuto's talents.

The youth movement on Tony's street was called the Scorpions. If you were a boy who did not want to keep looking over your shoulder when you walked down the street, you joined the Scorpions. You could become a member when you were about ten, and remain one until you were old enough to get a job or a term in Sing Sing. Tony was tough enough to be accepted by the Scorpions when he was eight. In time, he should have been elected their president or War Leader, but he was not interested in directing the lives of other people. His own life engaged his full interest and devotion. The Scorpions had an idea that he felt that way and so, when Tony was sixteen and the office of War Leader had to be filled, they elected another boy to the post.

Soon afterward the president and the new War Leader called a meeting in a vacant store. "Me and the president been talking," the new War Leader said. "We don't like the way those crummy Bombers been acting, like as if they want in on our street. We're gonna start sending them home with their asses in a sling. We start off real easy, see, just beating up that guy Ortiz that keeps cutting across our territory. They get the message, so all right, we leave them be. They don't get the message, we spell it out for them some more. The president gives me the green light to pick a guy, and I'm picking Tony. Work that guy Ortiz over for us, Tony."

"Why me?" Tony said.

"Why you? Because you ain't done nuttin for the Scorpions lately, that's why you."

Tony looked at him with disgust. He knew that wasn't it at all. This creep wanted to make a big deal out of being War Leader. The creep was new at the job and wouldn't feel it was really his until he proved he could push Tony around. "What's in it for me?" Tony said.

"Screw what's in it for you. This is for the Scorpions."

So he would give Ortiz a working over, and then the Bombers would start laying for him, and maybe that was what the creep wanted. "I don't feel like doing it alone," he said.

There was a rustle of shock among the Scorpions, and the War Leader looked at him coldly. "That makes you chicken," he said.

That was a very tough rap, and Tony now wished things hadn't gone so far. But when it came to the chicken stage, you'd had it. He shrugged and said, "Screw you."

The War Leader got up slowly, and put a hand in the pocket where he kept his brass knuckles. He was a square solid kid who could hit like the iron ball on a wrecking crane. "All right, chicken," he said. "You wanna take it standing up or sitting down?"

Tony moved his feet apart for balance and got up, watching the hand in the creep's pocket. The hand came out wearing the knuckles and started a swing that could leave you wearing your head on backwards. There was no percentage in trading punches; sooner or later one of those wrecking-crane swings would get through. Tony ducked the punch. His own hand moved in a blur and his switchblade knife flipped out its steel tongue and licked into the creep's arm just below the shoulder. The creep said "Hey!" and let his arm drop to his side and stared at the quick bloom of red on his sleeve.

Tony backed out of the store, his teeth a thin white slash across his face, the knife weaving in front of him like the tongue of a snake. Nobody moved or spoke. Outside the store Tony turned and walked down the street, not running, not looking back. They would have to talk it over before doing anything. They wouldn't understand this at all: why would Tony go chicken about a Bomber and then take on the War Leader? The answer was easy. What was in it for him if he worked over the Bomber? Nothing. What was in it for him when he took on the War Leader? Keeping his face so he recognized it in a mirror.

Now if he wanted to keep his face unscrambled he'd better move it out of Brooklyn. He walked to the subway and rode into Manhattan and went to his uncle's barbershop. His uncle gave him a place to sleep above the shop. He didn't have to go back to school; at sixteen he was over the compulsory age. He hung around the shop a few days, and then his uncle got him a job at a weirdo joint called the Stuyvessant Club where jerks sat around all afternoon and most of the night playing a game from dullsville called bridge. Only, after he had watched it for a year, it wasn't dullsville after all.

His main job was to clean the place every morning, but when the members were playing he wore a white mess jacket and had to empty ashtrays and get new decks of cards and take orders for coffee and sandwiches. When not running errands there was nothing to do but watch the play. Tony had a mind like a movie camera; it didn't create anything on its own but it made a complete and accurate record of what he saw and heard. In a year he understood the game. It was real cool. It reminded him of a rumble between gangs, only with rules, like it was okay to kick and gouge but no fair pulling a knife.

He took an old deck of cards to his room and dealt himself
hands and studied them. And he watched and listened. It was best
late at night when maybe just one or two tables were in play, because then he didn't have to run many errands and lose track of
what was happening. Although he didn't know it, he was getting
lessons from the top players in bridge. The Stuyvessant Club was
where they came to cut each other up at one to ten cents a point,
and where they sometimes brought a well-to-do outsider to show
him what bridge was like when you took it away from the children.
By the time he was twenty-one, Tony was as familiar with end
plays and Vienna coups and the Grand Slam Force as, under other
circumstances, he would have been with the technique of rolling a
drunk. But he had never been in a game.

Then one night four members were playing late and Member
#1 went down two tricks on a little slam and growled that Mem-
ber #3 shouldn't have put him in it, and happened to look up
and see a smile on Tony's face. "What the hell are you grinning
about?" he snapped.

"Sorry, sir," Tony said.

"I didn't ask you to be sorry, I asked what the hell you were
grinning about!"

Tony never liked being talked to in such a way, whether the
speaker was a War Leader or a jerk who thought writing articles
for *Bridge World* made him a good player. "Sir," Tony said (he
had learned a little polite language at the Stuyvessant, where
polite language was sometimes spoken), "I was smiling because
you could have made that bid. Strip East of hearts and clubs,
throw him in with your last diamond, and he's got to lead into
your tenace in spades or give you a slough and ruff."

"Why you impudent brat," Member #1 cried, "if you think you
can talk to members that way I'll—"

"Aw relax," his partner said. "You asked for it, and anyhow
Tony's right."

"Right?" Member #1 said. "What the hell does Tony know
about bridge?"

Member #2, realizing that this was an interesting question, looked at Tony and asked, "Yeah, what *do* you know about bridge?"

Tony said, with the modesty that was to mark his career, "Everything, I guess."

Even Member #3, who had been on Tony's side, found this hard to take. He said, "Partner, deal out that double-dummy problem you had in your last *Bridge World* article, and let's see Tony solve it."

This was an amusing idea, and Member #1 cheered up and arranged the cards and asked Tony how he would make four spades after the lead of the queen of hearts. Tony examined the hand briefly; what was tough about playing when you saw everybody's cards? This was just a little problem in transportation, involving the discard of an ace from dummy, and working a trump coup. He explained this patiently, and stepped back.

Member #1 said, "Figure out what I owe and tell me tomorrow. When the help starts showing me how to play bridge, I'm through." He walked out.

"How do you like that?" Member #2 complained. "We haven't finished the rubber."

"Wouldn't you know," said Member #4, "and nobody in the place to make a fourth."

"Except," said Member #3, "Tony."

"I couldn't, sir," Tony said.

"Of course he couldn't," said Member #2. "For all I know he's never been in a game. Have you, Tony?"

"No sir," Tony said. "But it's not that. The manager wouldn't like it."

"We'll square him," said Member #3. "Sit down, Tony. You're my partner. Do you know any bidding systems?"

This was in 1956, before the general introduction of the Roth-Stone, Kaplan-Sheinwold and Duke-Ashcraft systems. "A few," Tony said. "Culbertson and Goren and Acol and Canapé and the Vienna Club and—"

"I'll settle for Goren," Member #3 said. "Tony, it's a nickel a point and I'll pay your losses, on account of I don't think we're going to have any."

Member #3 was right, and in the next two hours he and Tony won three rubbers and eighteen hundred points and ninety dollars each, and Tony had a start on his profession. At first his progress was slow; a few members knew of his skill and sneaked him into games late at night. As more and more members heard about him, however, there was more demand for his services, and this created an awkward situation in which he was not quite an employee and not quite a member of the Stuyvessant. Eventually the club solved this by firing him as an employee and giving him a membership, with the understanding that he was to make himself available as a fourth whenever needed.

For several years he earned a living in this way, and won a reputation as one of the most dangerous rubber bridge players in the country. But it was only a fair living. Unlike duplicate, luck was involved in the deal in rubber bridge, and Tony never tried to control this; his fingers were not nimble enough for outright cheating, and in any case only a very reckless or very stupid mechanic would have tried his skill at the Stuyvessant. When the luck ran against Tony, he could not win against the expert players at the club. So, when he discovered tournament duplicate with its dogmeat players who yearned to be Live Masters, he found a better way to make a living.

On Monday at the Xanadu, between the afternoon and evening sessions of the Men's Teams and Women's Teams, Tony attended the cocktail party given by Bubba Worthington to celebrate the fact that Tony had made him a Life Master. Bubba did not look on it that way. At first Bubba had awarded Tony some credit, but gradually he took it back, and by the time of the party Bubba was sure he had won the Charity Pairs in spite of Tony's mistakes. He was circulating now among the guests in his suite, his crew-cut hair bristling with virility, his eyes bright with excitement and too many highballs, his full lips twitching like a rabbit eating lettuce.

"And so Tony made this wild bid of three spades," he chattered, "and I had to decide whether to rescue at four diamonds or hope Tony wouldn't get doubled. So fortunately I made the save and we got an average out of it."

Most of the people around Bubba listened politely, restraining urges to tell about *their* hands, because after all Bubba was throwing the party and had some rights. Tony lounged against a wall and wished he could kick the creep in the tail. So Bubba made the save at four diamonds and went down one, never knowing that three spades was cold and if it was doubled they had a top. He did not like the creep's face or voice or the way he was dressed. Bubba was wearing a white sharkskin suit and a pale blue necktie and three points of a pale blue handkerchief in his breast pocket, and constantly adjusted the set of the necktie and the length of the French cuffs of his shirt. There was a bit of envy in Tony's reaction to Bubba's clothes; Tony would have enjoyed wearing such an outfit but he was unsure of his taste. He knew that a black suit and white shirt and dark unpatterned tie was safe, and so he always wore that combination.

Bubba's triumphal progress around the room brought him close to Tony, and he paused and cried, "Admit it now, Tony. You didn't play very well that night."

"I brought you in, didn't I?" Tony said coldly.

"*You* brought *me* in? Why Tony! Don't you remember that five club contract you put me in, down two?"

"Sure," Tony said. "You had to play it carefully to keep from making six."

Bubba giggled and said, "Tony, you have the most *convenient* memory. Frankly, looking back on it, you should have paid me instead of me paying you."

"That'll be the day."

"Do you ever play rubber bridge?" Bubba asked. "How I'd love to take you on in a few rubbers at, let's say, ten cents a point!"

A small twitching started in Tony's muscles, as if he were

crouched by a game trail and saw a fawn come toddling along. "Any time," he said.

"Really? Oh Tony, that's lovely! I dare you to set up a game, just four of us, cut for partners after each rubber. Would you?"

"How's for tonight, up here, after the team session?"

"Oh, good!" Bubba cried. "Oh, I'll look forward to this." He moved away to tell people about some more hands on which he had rescued Tony.

Tony started drifting through the crowd looking for prospects for the game. He didn't waste time considering some of them: Sammy Rothberg, for example, didn't have the right temperament for high-stake rubber bridge. Tony stopped beside Jake Jacobs and said, "I got Bubba lined up for a few rubbers after tonight's session. You want a piece of the action?"

"For how much?" Jake asked.

"Ten cents a point."

"Guy's no good, is he?"

"A pigeon."

Winning fifty or a hundred dollars meant nothing to Jake, but he disliked Bubba, one of those upper-class queers whose listing in the Social Register ought to come under Unmarried Maidens. Jake disapproved of queers; their existence was an insult to real men. Also, since Jake had returned Vicky Summers to the nursery, he had no plans for his spare time. "Deal me in," he said.

Tony nodded. His next stop was beside Runa Montez. Usually he stayed out of Runa's way; he didn't care for broads who used their bodies on men like brass knuckles. But she'd be perfect for this. "Runa," he said, "you want to make some expenses, rubber bridge, ten cents a point? Jake and I are fixing to give Bubba some action after the session tonight."

Runa laughed. It was a soft sleepy laugh that sometimes made men think their manhood was being questioned. "That baby?" she said.

"He's a pigeon, isn't he? Can't you use some pigeon feathers?"

"No," she said. "All I do with pigeons is wring their necks." She turned away.

Tony shrugged and moved along. He spotted Katy Edmunds and drew her aside and put the deal to her. Katy was another person who, like Jake, might be interested for the fun of it rather than the money.

Katy let out her fire-gong laugh. "Always working the angles, aren't you?" she said approvingly. "Yes, I don't mind. It will be a treat to play for a little blood. I'm tired of skim milk."

"Okay. I'll pick you up after tonight's session. We'll be playing here."

"Good. By the way, Tony, do you ever get tired of all this?"

Tony said, "Tired?" That was a stupid question.

"Do you ever feel you'd like a change? Maybe do some traveling?"

"I travel all over the country."

"I'm talking about something else. A trip around the world."

"Nobody's gonna hire me as director on one of those bridge cruises."

"That's right," Katy said, smiling at him sweetly. "But a lonely old lady might. Tony, I'm planning to take a trip around the world. Maybe spend a year doing it. I've been thinking how nice it might be to have you along, to keep me company and play bridge and so on."

This would be very interesting, Tony thought, if it came from a silly old bat with a million bucks, because then a guy might fix himself for life by playing his cards right. However, Katy didn't fit that description. She was an old bat but not at all silly. Next question: did she have a million bucks? He studied her for a moment, starting at the purple hair and getting as far down as the ring on her right hand, a turquoise set in a big silver snake. It wouldn't get you ten bucks in a pawn shop.

Katy turned off the sweet smile and rang the fire gong. "Don't get discouraged," she said. "I don't wear expensive jewelry but I have it, Tony. I have money, too, but I don't carry it around either. Credit cards and traveler's checks and junk jewelry, that's for me. There are so many thieves in the world, aren't there?"

Sharp old bitch, Tony thought. "Yeah, you can't be too careful. What would you figure on paying me, Katy?"

"Oh, all expenses and a little spending money. Fifty a week, perhaps."

"Get with it, Katy. That man Lincoln freed the slaves."

Katy chuckled. "But my dear, think of the fun you'd have trying to get my money away from me. And think of the fun I'd have trying to keep you from doing it."

"Yeah? Maybe you'd have all the fun. What I'd want is my expenses and four hundred a week. A couple grand in advance for getaway dough, in case the four hundred starts slipping your mind."

She patted his cheek. "Now *you* want to have all the fun. Well, think it over, Tony. Meanwhile I'll see you after the team games tonight."

Tony nodded and went away. Think it over? Katy wanted to put him in a private zoo and throw him a hamburger when she felt like it and from time to time poke at him with sticks. He'd take her up on it just as soon as he could arrange to go crazy.

Late that night after the team session, Tony and Jake and Katy played rubber bridge for three hours with Bubba Worthington, a nice clean above-board game that Bubba might actually have won if the cards had been running strongly his way. The cards did not run his way, however; the luck of the deal divided the strength rather evenly throughout the session, and so Bubba had no chance. Tony was a magnificent rubber bridge player, and Jake and Katy were very good, and Bubba was rather bad. Except for one rubber when he held most of the high cards, Bubba lost every time no matter who partnered him. He dropped three hundred and ten dollars, of which Tony got one hundred and fifty, Jake ninety-five and Katy sixty-five. Bubba complained about his bad run of cards and said they had to give him a chance to get his money back the next night, and it was so arranged.

After the others left, Bubba flung himself angrily into bed and squirmed around for an hour hating Tony and inventing fantasies in which he wiped the smirk off Tony's face.

Bubba was not alone in having trouble getting to sleep. Sammy Rothberg had not done well in the first two sessions of the Men's Teams, and had to take three sleeping pills before they worked. Ace McKinley had done well with Tony and Jake and Phil Bundy, but not well enough to hope to win in the finals the next afternoon, and after the bar closed Ace went to his room and sat for a while drinking without being able to feel the liquor at all. Carola Clark sat up late reading a paperback novel and wondering what Ace McKinley was doing. Vicky Summers scrubbed her body hard in the shower, removing a couple of faded bits of color, and this sandpapered her nerves so that when she got into bed her body felt like a pincushion.

10

In its effect on men and women, bridge is not an erotic pastime. Compared to it, such activities as dancing the waltz, playing mixed doubles in tennis and holding hands during a walk must be rated as orgies. The late Ely Culbertson tried to remedy this defect by stressing the sex angles of various bridge terms: "approach forcing," "vulnerable," "I went to bed with a king," "I caught the bare queen," "one over one," and so on. His efforts were wasted; calling attention to double meanings could not alter the fact that bridge appeals to the upper end of the spine rather than the lower. A woman studying a handsome male across a table may only be hoping that the idiot will lead clubs. A man who feels the touch of a female knee under the table may simply become annoyed that women take up so much room. In the course of a serious bridge game, men and women excite each other sexually about as often as they hold a Yarborough, a hand in which no card is higher than a nine. The odds against a Yarborough are 1,827 to one.

However, any activity that brings the two sexes together is likely to produce at least some murmur of the flesh. If and when it occurs in bridge it happens after the game and at times is a sort of comment on it, like a postmortem on the bidding and playing. Thus a woman may go to bed with a man to thank him for helping her win 16.40 red points. A man may go to bed with a woman to regain a feeling of dominance that he lost when he went down at four spades doubled. Then of course a pairing may take place for ordinary reasons: the man and woman are bored, restless, tense, lonely or unhappy. Or, finally, a man such as Jake Jacobs will hunt the other sex as Mallory is said to have tried to climb Mount Everest, merely because it is there. The fact that important bridge tournaments are usually held in hotels, with bedrooms at hand and with an excuse for walking along corridors at odd hours, certainly provides an opportunity, and where an opportunity exists, some males and females will use it. All in all, however, among bridge players such activity is below the normal level. A major tournament is probably less spicy than a meeting of the African Violet Society of America (which, after all, does deal with propagation) although more so than the annual convention of the Daughters of the American Revolution.

There are exceptions to all rules, and the exception at the Spring Nationals at the Xanadu was Runa Montez.

Runa was thirty-six years old, and a Life Master with more than 2,000 points. She lived in Los Angeles, where she ran a duplicate club and gave expensive lessons. As a teacher she got results by terrorizing her pupils, who learned their lessons carefully in the hope of avoiding her acid comments. It was believed that there was a husband, or perhaps two, in her past; certainly there had been more than two men, and her scale of living was much higher than her bridge income warranted.

She was tall, but unlike many tall women she did not do penance for it with a stooped posture and low-heeled shoes. She stood straight as a lance on her three-inch spike heels. At the bridge table she sat erect, a hawk on a perch, black eyes glittering, her teeth making occasional little clicking noises. Her hair was a black helmet, crossing her forehead in bangs and falling in straight lines on each side of her face. Her skin looked tanned, but since she almost never exposed it to the sun it was probably a natural swarthiness: a heritage of Indian blood, if you believed her story that she was a descendant of an Aztec princess.

Her features were too sharp and bold to qualify her as a beauty, but the hint of maleness ended just below the shoulders in a spectacularly curved body. She always wore a dozen or so thin bracelets; each motion of her arms created jinglings and janglings and golden whisperings, like a Swiss music box gone out of tune. Some people who knew her treated these musical sounds with the respect they would have given to a hiss from inside a snake charmer's basket, and to these people Runa was known as the Nylon Cobra. The name was an overbid, but in bridge an overbid will sometimes make if an opponent commits an error, and it was not wise to make too many errors against Runa.

She was playing now, on Tuesday night, with Sammy Rothberg. It was the first qualifying round of the top event of the Spring Nationals: the Vanderbilt Cup Knockout Teams. Each team had four to six members, any above four being alternates. There were four on Runa's team. While Runa and Sammy played north-south against the east-west pair of another team, Tony Manuto and Jake Jacobs played the same boards against the north-south pair of that team. This would go on for two sessions, at the end of which the teams with the best records would go into the knockout matches, where the loss of a match eliminated a team. Nobody but experts understood the scoring and the way it affected the strategy of the play, because the scoring was not a simple matter of converting ordinary bridge points into match points. In the qualifying rounds of the Vanderbilt, the hand score was first converted into International Match Points, which are not the same as match points. These were next converted into things called Victory Points. Nobody had managed to invent a further step involving the conversion of Victory Points into something else, so the players made do with these for their final qualifying scores.

"Sammy," Runa said, as they waited for another pair to come to their table, "the way you're playing tonight, have you thought of asking Lost and Found if your copy of Bridge for Beginners has turned up?"

"I have a headache," Sammy muttered, which was true. The use of sleeping pills when he went to bed, and of Benzedrine when he got up, made his head feel as if someone were chopping logs inside it.

"Something must be bothering you, Sammy. I mean, besides your bad play. Ben Aarons, maybe?"

"I don't want to think about that louse."

"Well now let's see," Runa murmured. "He picked up ten points on you in the Men's Pairs, and half a dozen in the Men's Teams, so that gives him a good lead in the McKenney and maybe you ought to start thinking about him. But he isn't playing in the Vanderbilt, unless he gets in as an alternate, so this is your chance to catch up, isn't it?"

He was aware of that and wished she wouldn't remind him. "I'll do better from now on," he said.

"I'm sure you will, darling. Just remember that clubs are the lowest suit, then come diamonds, hearts and . . . why *hello* there," she cooed, greeting their next pair of opponents. One was a man and the other a woman, and Runa spoke to the man. She did not ordinarily waste words on women.

The man looked down and started to smile and then wished he had not looked down. Many women dressed elaborately for evening sessions at the Nationals but Runa tended to undress. She wore black satin toreador pants and a black satin blouse. The neckline of the blouse did more than merely plunge; it took what might be called a suicide leap, rescuing itself at the last possible moment by clutching a diamond barpin. Looking at the plunge made the man feel giddy and he said hello and sat down quickly, bothered by a suspicion that his smile had warped into a leer.

A bubble of amusement quivered inside Runa. She reached for her cards, the thin bracelets on her wrists playing an accompaniment. Under the table her knee prowled against the man's leg. She was expert at this, having spent a long-ago year as a manicure girl in Los Angeles learning how knees could talk under a table. At the manicure table an eloquent knee was often worth an extra tip. At the bridge table it was sometimes worth an extra trick. The knee finesse only worked under certain conditions. It was no good when both opponents were men, because the man was likely to enjoy it and might even play better than usual. To get results it must embarrass the man, and that meant he had to be playing with a woman, preferably his wife, whose presence made him feel guilty. Runa thought that it was probably working nicely this time and that some good scores were coming up.

The man sorted his cards, wondering if the warm pressure under the table was accidental or deliberate. The thought made his skin feel as if each hair were a pin sticking into it. He stared at his cards and had trouble deciding on a bid, this being partly due to the fact that he had his cards arranged in five suits.

"You're the dealer and it's your bid," his wife said.

"I'm thinking," he mumbled.

"I was afraid of that," she said.

He played the hand and committed a revoke because of the five suits, and that upset him further, so that he did badly in the rest of the bidding and play at this particular table. He left, finally, with the sound of golden bracelets jingling in his ears, a sound that did not completely muffle the crackle of his wife's comments.

Sammy took a deep relaxing breath and said, "We did better against those two."

Runa's eyes glittered at him through spiky lashes. "You had nothing to do with it," she said.

Sammy frowned, and wondered what she meant, and became tense again.

Runa had played with Sammy on other occasions without reacting to him strongly, but tonight she had started to detest him. With that blond hair and fair skin he looked like a baby. She did not care for babies, especially ones who looked ready to cry. Whenever she said something to him, he blushed. That set her teeth to making sharp little clicks and brought a burst of jangling from her bracelets. Men often stirred gusts of emotion in her, as toys had done when she was a child. In those days an attractive toy that could take rough handling would make her chortle in delight, and she would play with it for hours. On the other hand, a fragile toy that started coming apart sometimes brought howls of rage, and she would pound it on the floor to break it more quickly. Nowadays she no longer chortled or howled, and the emotions found release in other ways. She stared at Sammy now and despised him for being so fragile.

A new east-west pair came to the table and Runa recognized

Harvey and Miggsy Ashcraft. She looked up and cooed, "Why, *hello* there, Harvey."

Harvey looked down at the plunging neckline, and wondered what was wrong with women these days. Just the other morning, when he and Miggsy thought of inviting Hank and Olga in for breakfast, Miggsy decided to wear a negligee that covered her about as well as steam in a shower bath. "Hello, Runa," he said peevishly. "I see you didn't bother to dress after you got up today."

Runa gave a purring laugh, and Miggsy said, "Harvey, that wasn't very nice."

"Well, neither is what she's wearing," Harvey grumbled, and sat down. He and Miggsy were not having a good game; apparently she thought that winning the Women's Pairs made her an expert. He glanced at Sammy Rothberg and said, "Hello, Sammy. Sorry to sound rude, but it makes a man wonder if this is bridge or strip poker."

Runa laughed again and let her knee touch his leg. "Did you say a man?" she asked.

"Yes I said a man," Harvey snapped. "And please give me a little room under the table. Let's play bridge, shall we?"

Runa turned her attention back to Sammy, who was blushing. "Yes, let's," she said. "Although I'm not sure that what Sammy and I are playing could be called bridge, and I don't think he could take strip poker. I'm the dealer and I bid one club, Harvey, and I don't think you could take strip poker either."

"May I remind you," Harvey said, "that only sixteen words should be used in the course of the bidding. The words for the numbers one to seven, the names of the suits, no trump, double, redouble, and pass. I'll call the director if all this chatter keeps on."

"Yes, Harvey darling," Runa said in a mocking tone, although it was obvious that mockery or anything else was wasted on this little pink-and-white creature. "One club."

Across the table Sammy responded one diamond. Runa had enough strength to jump to three no trump but she didn't feel like making things easy for Sammy. They were playing a modified version of The Method that permitted such a jump to game but that also used many bids of a semi-forcing nature. When in the mood, Runa turned these semi-forcing bids into a sort of Chinese water torture, thinking a long time before each call and then making a bid that left her partner with an awkward and sometimes painful problem. So instead of bidding three no trump she bid one spade. Several bids later, Sammy had an agonizing debate with himself and passed out the bid below game level. Runa smiled and played the three-spade contract carefully and made five.

"We could also have made five no trump," she pointed out.

On the next board Sammy tried to redeem himself and overbid his hand and went down, and Runa gave him a pitying look. She continued with the Chinese water torture bidding system throughout the evening. It was quite effective, and by the end of the session Sammy was soaked with sweat.

"I'm sorry," he said. "I just couldn't get going tonight."

She touched his hand, using the tips of her fingers to draw soft patterns on his skin. "The evening isn't over yet," she said. "Maybe you can still get going." There were equal parts of mockery and invitation in her tone, which made her remark another type of semi-forcing bid.

He blushed. He was not sure what she meant, except that she couldn't mean bridge because they had finished for the evening. He said in an uncertain tone, "Uh, can I buy you a drink?"

"No thank you. I have no inhibitions that need to be drowned in alcohol. I think I'll go out for a bit of air and then go to my room. Why don't you wait for the scores and give me a call? Or—" she fanned her lashes slowly down and then halfway up "—drop by to tell me, if you like."

A pulse began a chunking beat in Sammy's throat and he sat tall in the chair. Runa wasn't such a cold frightening creature after all. That was a rather exciting thing she did with her eyelashes, lowering them like a girl pulling down a shade before undressing and then lifting them a bit, half shyly, half boldly. He didn't know whether or not it was an invitation, and perhaps she didn't know either. Well, he knew what to do about *that*. All it took was the right approach: confidence, determination, a touch of aggressiveness. It would be very satisfying to dominate Runa.

"Right," he said briskly. "I'll get the scores, and see you later." He gave her a brilliant overpowering male smile and left the table.

Runa laughed softly and went outside. A little later, Sammy was going to try to prove that he was a big boy now, and that would be amusing. She heard footsteps approaching across the patio and turned to see somebody who probably *was* a big boy and who might be rather interesting. "Why, *hello* there, Jake," she said.

Jake had been watching Runa tonight just as he had watched Vicky Summers the preceding two nights. He was always watching some woman or other, and rushing after the woman like a bird dog showing how well he could retrieve. He could have caught up to Runa before she reached the patio but he held back, fascinated by the motion of her hips and flanks inside the satin toreador pants. It was like watching water rippling in moonlight.

"Hello, Runa," he said. "Want to go over scores with me?"

Runa yawned and said, "What kind of scores, Jake?"

This he liked. This he liked very much. She already knew the score. "There's a good nightclub down the way. Want to try it?"

"No thanks. Anyway, aren't you giving Bubba Worthington another lesson tonight, in rubber bridge?"

"Not if I get a better offer."

"I'll look through my things some time and see if I can find an old offer I'm not using."

"No stuff, Runa. I got some ideas to talk over with you. Like, well, the boys at the ad agency are always looking for a dame with real high-class hands to use in my ads. I been noticing your hands. Beautiful, just beautiful. So I thought that—"

"Jake, I come from Los Angeles."

"So?"

"They make movies out there, Jake. The boys at the movie studios are always looking for a girl with a real high-class shape to use in pictures, and this talent scout has been noticing my shape, beautiful, just beautiful, and if I'll just take off my clothes for a screen test—"

"Come on," Jake protested. "I wasn't pulling anything like that."

Runa laughed deep in her throat. "You just wanted me to take off my gloves?" She moved close to him and stroked his cheek and said, "There you are, Jake. There's one of my beautiful hands. Go ahead, have an orgy with it, darling."

Yessir, Jake thought, this broad could give you the sweats. "Okay," he said. "I can read the scoreboard. You got a no-hitter going against me. You don't mind if I show up at the ball park again?"

"Oh, I don't mind. Just remember to buy a ticket on the way in."

"I'll think it over," he said, and walked away. He was starting to get an idea about Runa, annoying in one way, very interesting in another. Maybe she meant that about buying a ticket. He didn't like buying tickets for night games, except indirectly and at bargain prices. And he certainly didn't go for the idea of buying out the whole ball park, which was maybe what Runa had in mind. Of course it might also be worth it, who knew? He shrugged, and headed upstairs to play rubber bridge and to work off some of his frustration on Bubba Worthington, the Unmarried Maiden from the Social Register.

Runa watched him go, and smiled. Jake was a perfect example of his type: the male dog, running around the neighborhood with his tongue hanging out, chasing the scent of bitches or else barking furiously up a tree at a sleepy-eyed cat. Perhaps some night she might come down from the tree and try her claws on him, always provided that the price was right. After all, Jake, she told his departing back, I can't pay my bills just by giving lessons in *bridge*.

She went upstairs to her room, and washed and undressed and got into bed. She picked up the phone and asked that no calls be put through until ten o'clock the next morning. She wriggled luxuriously on the bed, and waited. Some time later footsteps sounded in the corridor and a hand rapped on her door with firm male confidence. She smiled, and waited. The knock came again, less confidently. "Runa?" Sammy called. And then once more, in a very uncertain tone, "Runa?" Runa laughed noiselessly. He knocked a few more times, vacillating between a sharp nervous knock and a soft apologetic one, and she could picture him peering up and down the corridor fearful that other doors would open and people would look out to snicker or sneer or scowl at him. Finally the knocking ended and he went away.

She would have to explain to him the next day that the thought of his visit had not quite been stimulating enough to keep her awake.

11

A LITTLE WAY down the corridor from Runa, two couples in ad-joining rooms heard Sammy's knocking, but did not peer out to see who was calling on whom at 1 a.m. The couples were the Dukes and Ashcrafts. They were not interested in what was happening in other bedrooms but in what was happening—or not happening —in their own.

Olga Duke, wearing men's pajamas, sat at a writing table study-ing her score card from the Vanderbilt. She had compared cards with Miggsy so she knew how their team had done against each opposing team, although she had not taken the trouble to con-vert the hand scores into International Match Points and then into Victory Points. She was unhappy, and as she sat there her thin taut body was in a state of constant vibration, like a struck tuning fork. If her body *had* been a tuning fork, the note it produced would have been A-flat.

"On Board Sixteen," she said.

"Umm?" Hank said. He wore shorts and a T-shirt, his usual sleeping attire, and had been considering stealing up behind Olga and nibbling the nape of her neck, which looked boyish and un-protected and appealing.

"Board Sixteen," she said sharply, turning to face him, which removed from view the boyish and unprotected and appealing nape of her neck. "Harvey's and Miggsy's opponents stopped at four hearts and made four, playing the north-south hands we held."

"Hah! Didn't I make five hearts on that hand?"

"Yes, dear. But unfortunately you had contracted to take six."

Her neck now appeared to Hank as something worth wringing. "You put me in that slam."

"I most certainly did not. After you coaxed me by bidding three hearts, all I did was cue bid my diamond ace."

"Under the Duke-Ashcraft method," he said coldly, "that can be regarded as a slam invitation. We *are* playing The Method, you recall, not your private go-for-broke system. All you had to do was simply bid four hearts."

"You're not supposed to accept slam invitations unless you have extra strength. All you had was an extra king. Now if I had been bidding that hand with a different partner—"

"Let me see the damn card," he growled, and took it away from her.

She jumped up irritably and went into the bathroom and brushed her teeth, which she had already done once. She did not feel like going to bed while he was still prowling around the room. Heavens, the man was a positive satyr when he saw her lying quietly in bed; only a month ago he'd leaped on her like a ravening beast. After brushing her teeth she did a few exercises, trying to get rid of an empty nagging sensation somewhere in her body. Finally she came out of the bathroom. Hank was sitting on his bed scowling at the score card, big shoulders hunched, bare toes curled awkwardly against each other. He looked boyish and un-protected and appealing, and she began to regret scolding him about Board Sixteen. She wandered over to her bureau and picked up the chiffon handkerchief she had carried that evening under her bracelet, and waved it a few times in the air. The motion of the chiffon reminded her of the capes in a bullfight she had seen, when they were in Mexico City for the Mexican Nationals. The matador used a cape to dominate the bull, moving or halting the animal at will, and it was beautiful to watch. She held the handkerchief by the upper corners and looked through the gossamer material and saw Hank as a soft blur with light glowing on his shoulders.

She dropped the handkerchief and wandered to the other side of his bed and peered at his back. If she reached out quietly and grabbed his shoulders she could pull him over backward onto the bed, and lean over him and say she was sorry and bend down to kiss him. It was a rather nice idea. She started reaching for him.

"About Board Sixteen," Hank said sharply, swinging around toward her.

She jerked back. "What about it?"

"What was it you started to say about bidding that hand with a different partner? What partner? Harvey?"

"Don't be ridiculous. I've never played with him. But I must say, he wouldn't have overbid."

"The coward probably wouldn't have bid at all. Well, if it wasn't Harvey, I suppose you had Miggsy in mind. Just because you two lucked out a championship—"

"I wish you'd turn out the light and let me go to bed."

"*I'm* not the one keeping us up," Hank growled, and flipped off the light switch before she could move, thus making her stumble to bed in the dark. He listened to her progress, but unfortunately she did not stub her toes.

In the adjoining bedroom, Harvey Ashcraft sat before a mirror brushing his hair. He wore white nylon pajamas buttoned neatly at the neck, and a blue brocade dressing gown ornamented with two small dragons. Miggsy had embroidered the dragons, which looked slightly wistful. He always brushed his hair before he went to bed, in the hope that it would get the habit of covering the thin place on top. His hair was fine and silky and hard to manage. In one way the thin place worried him, because he hated the idea of baldness. In another way it was a hopeful sign; there was a theory that baldness was a proof of male potency. A touch of baldness would not be too high a price to pay for that. Unfortunately there had been several occasions recently when he wondered if he was getting short-changed.

"Harvey," a plaintive voice said, "aren't you coming to bed soon?"

He could not repress a faint shiver. Of course Miggsy meant wasn't he going to *his* bed soon, not hers. Or did she? He turned and peered at Miggsy. She was propped up in bed looking like a frilly lace valentine. Her nightgown had slipped off a plump bare shoulder. It was annoying the way she rushed into bed each night and lay there looking timid and defenseless and as if she expected the worst. It was ridiculous; no woman need expect the worst from a gentleman.

"You'll catch cold, sitting up in bed half naked," he said irritably.

"Daddy Bear could keep Mommy Bear warm."

"Oh for God's sake! What is this thing you've always had about bears? I've asked you and asked you not to call me Daddy Bear."

"Mommy Bear likes having a Daddy Bear around."

"Well, I don't like bears. They are big ugly hairy smelly creatures. Like . . . well, like Hank Duke." As he said that, a suspicion began slithering into his thoughts. Was there any connection between Miggsy's thing about bears, and the bearlike creature named Hank Duke?

Miggsy's lower lip poked out and began to tremble. "It wouldn't hurt you to copy a few things from Hank," she said, sniffling.

"I regret," he said coldly, "that I cannot become big and ugly and hairy. Do you want me to take fewer showers and become smelly?"

"He took a shower every morning this week! I heard him!"

"Is that what takes you so long in the bathroom? Listening to him take a shower?"

"You were singing back and forth with Olga the other morning!"

"It was merely a little joke."

"A joke?" she cried. "What's funny about larking around in a bathroom with another woman?"

"What's funny about you taking a shower with Hank?"

"Harvey Ashcraft!" she said tearfully. "You horrible . . . horrible . . ." Her voice trailed off and her mind became confused. The thought of taking a shower with Hank began towering through her head like a mushroom cloud. She slid down from the pillow and burrowed under the covers to hide her burning face.

Harvey mumbled, "Well, I didn't really mean it that way." There was no answer, so either she didn't hear him or didn't want to speak to him. He sighed, and took off his robe and prepared to go to bed. He paused just before turning off the light between their beds, and looked at the mound of sheet and blanket hiding his wife. "Good night," he muttered, and turned out the light and climbed into bed. It would only be fair, he thought, if some night after a quarrel *she* took the initiative in making up with him, instead of leaving it to him. If she really cared for him, she would crawl into his bed right now and bend over him with a tear-wet face and kiss him. The idea began to seem rather exciting; there might really be something in that baldness theory. He heard her stir in bed, and held his breath.

Miggsy had been crouched under the covers fighting off various lurid ideas, and finally managed to coax the big hairy creature to leave her thoughts in favor of the smaller pink-and-white creature. She felt relieved when she accomplished this. Unfortunately, nothing interesting happened in her thoughts after Harvey began occupying them. At the very least, he might yank the covers off her and grab her in his arms and press her to his hairy chest and . . . and . . . oh *no,* she mourned, Harvey doesn't *have* a hairy chest. She said aloud, faintly and sadly, "Harvey?" The covers muffled her voice and he didn't hear. She waited for another minute and then decided to sit up and look at him and say she was sorry for calling him a horrible something. She sat up in bed.

The horrible something had turned out the light and gone to bed without even saying good night.

"Oh!" she cried. "I wish I had married a man!"

Harvey pretended to be asleep. There was only one proper reply to her statement. It was to roar, "You did, woman!" and leap at her and prove it. He didn't think he was up to making that reply. He swallowed a lump in his throat that felt as big and angular as a pack of cards. He was going to go bald and get absolutely nothing out of it.

12

AT 1 P.M. ON WEDNESDAY P. J. Hoffmeister walked into the ball-room of the Xanadu. He was going to play in the Individual and had thirty minutes of free time in which to spread the gospel of the Hoffmeister No Trump. His bulging eyes peered around, look-ing for somebody who might listen to him, and focused on Tony Manuto. He did not like the idea of trying to convert that young man. Not only had Tony Manuto won the Charity Pairs (Hoff-meister always felt uneasy about approaching such notables) but also Tony had taken a top board against an actual bid of the Hoffmeister No Trump. Hoffmeister reminded himself, however, that the young man might be going around saying bad things about the Hoffmeister No Trump. That could not be permitted, no mat-ter how painful an effort it took.

He walked up to Tony and said, "To you a very good after-noon. I am P. J. Hoffmeister, of the Hoffmeister No Trump, ap-proved as a Class Two convention."

"Yeah?" Tony said.

Hoffmeister studied the sunglasses and could not decide whether Tony was looking at him or not. "Before now I have not been hav-ing a chance to congratulate you for winning the Charity Pairs," he said. "Probably you are remembering how my partner and I gave you tops on the last two boards."

Tony did not remember. He never remembered unimportant people. At the moment he was considering the subject of taking money from Bubba Worthington. Last night, in a rubber bridge session that lasted from 1 a.m. to 5 a.m., Bubba went for five hundred bucks. That made eight hundred Bubba had dropped in two nights, and the creep was starting to act like he was being raped. Question: would it be best to take it easy and keep Bubba alive a few more sessions, or let nature take its course tonight?

He flicked a glance at the jerk who was busting into his thoughts, and said, "Yeah?"

"Such luck I had, I don't think, on that last board against you," Hoffmeister said. "I am bidding the Hoffmeister No Trump and my partner is forgetting what it is, so you shouldn't be thinking it is one of those nogoodnik conventions."

Better let nature take its course, Tony thought. Bubba was playing worse all the time and it would be hard to nurse him along. So tonight ought to end the rubber bridge sessions. Meanwhile, what was this jerk in front of him talking about? "Whatcha peddling, Mac?" he asked.

"I am hoping that with an open mind you are looking on the Hoffmeister No Trump," Hoffmeister said earnestly. "Such a good game you play, it could still be better. The Hoffmeister No Trump I am wanting to explain to you so it will get you lots more tops. How often do you hold a sixteen to eighteen point no trump hand over an opening bid by the right-hand opponent? So I'll tell you, I worked it out by mathematics—"

"Get lost," Tony said.

Hoffmeister did not hear the actual words Tony spoke. He was not aggressive, but often when he started talking about the Hoffmeister No Trump the glory of it entered into him and washed away doubts and fears, and he would keep talking even though the other person might look at a watch and try to sidle away. But in this case Tony's words had a jagged edge that cut through Hoffmeister's concentration.

"By mathematics," he said, like a stuck phonograph record. "I worked it out by mathematics, but there was something you were saying?"

"I said, get lost."

"Lost?" Hoffmeister said, peering at the sunglasses to see if it was a joke. The eyes behind the sunglasses looked like things lurking in the depths of a pool, waiting for a little creature to fall in. "You . . . you are not wanting to hear about the Hoffmeister No Trump?" he asked.

"Negative," Tony said.

Hoffmeister gulped and went away. Tony drew his attention inward again; he had settled the question of Bubba, and now he wanted to think about Ace McKinley. He and Ace had one more event to play, the Open Pairs at the end of the week. It didn't seem likely that Ace would play any better in the Open Pairs than in the Men's Pairs and Men's Teams. So something more was needed. Tony wondered how hard it might be to sneak into Waldo Starnes' room and see where the guy kept the sheets on which were printed the computer-dealt hands that would be used in the Open Pairs.

Hoffmeister crossed the room to get as far away as possible from the young man in the sunglasses. He hated himself for doing this, but the encounter had left him upset. He sat down heavily in a small gilt chair. Nobody had spoken to him so harshly since Reba told him she was going away with Herman, that bum, who was not even a very good client. He took off the large plastic badge that announced I PLAY THE HOFFMEISTER NO TRUMP and stared at it; the badge slipped through his fingers and dropped to the floor. He allowed it to lie there, wondering if dropping it was an omen.

"I beg your pardon," a voice said. "Didn't you drop this?"

A thin elderly man picked up the badge and handed it to him. The man had white hair through which his scalp showed, blue eyes and frail blue-white hands. He gave Hoffmeister a friendly smile.

"Thank you," Hoffmeister said. "This head I got, I don't know if I am dropping things or not."

"Please excuse me for reading it," the man said. "I thought it was a committee badge, wouldn't that seem likely? But I see it says: I Play The Hoffmeister No Trump. How Interesting! May I ask what it is?"

"It is a Class Two convention," Hoffmeister said dully. "For

years I am working it out but it don't catch on." He called up a
reserve of strength and added, "It don't catch on *yet*."

"Then you must be Mr. Hoffmeister? May I say I am honored
to meet somebody who is making a contribution to bridge? My
name is Alfred Jenks. May I shake your hand, sir?"

Hoffmeister grabbed the frail blue-white hand quickly. "To me
it gives the honor," he said. "Such a pleasure it is, meeting a man
that don't have a closed mind."

"A closed mind? Oh dear me no. Wouldn't you say that when
bridge no longer changes and develops, it may start to go down-
hill? I would certainly like to hear about the Hoffmeister No Trump,
but perhaps you are too busy to explain it?"

Hoffmeister took several deep gasping breaths. This, he thought,
might be the turning point. He could not recall a famous player
named Alfred Jenks, but any man who talked so intelligently of
the need for bridge to develop must be at least a Life Master,
maybe even with one or two thousand points. "Time I got lots of,
anyway until the Individual starts," he said eagerly. "We will go
at it like this. How often do you hold a sixteen to eighteen point
no trump over an opening bid by the right-hand opponent?"

"Well, let me see," Mr. Jenks said. "We would have to start
with the fact that second bidder can hold any one of 8,122,425,444
hands. Now if we allow opening bidder fourteen high-card points,
there are twenty-six other points to distribute among the other
three hands. The chance that second bidder might hold sixteen
to eighteen of these in a no trump distribution is . . . um . . . let
me work out the percentages . . ."

"You are knowing bridge percentages?"

"Oh, naturally. I don't believe that good bridge is possible without a knowledge of percentages, wouldn't you say? You see, as an
accountant—"

"An accountant! I wouldn't believe it if I didn't hear it from my
own ears! Mr. Jenks, *I am an accountant too*. A little business of
my own I got, in Newark yet, I don't claim no C.P.A., but it's a
good living. You got a business maybe like mine?"

"No. I'm retired, and never went out on my own. I worked

for The Telephone Company, in Buffalo, New York, and we Telephone people stick with the Company. Before retiring I was head
accountant of the office. Now you were saying about the Hoffmeister No Trump?"

Hoffmeister began explaining the convention. Usually this created problems of the sort involved in trying to get a shoe onto a
foot that is either too large or too small: either the shoe will not
go on at all, or it goes on too easily and falls off just as easily. But
with this wonderful man there were no problems. Mr. Jenks asked
good questions and nodded happily over the answers. At the end
of a five-minute session Mr. Jenks repeated the convention with
all its different bids accurately and completely, without a glance at
the printed convention card. It was like sighting the Promised
Land after years in the desert.

"Mr. Jenks," he said solemnly, "I don't ever meet a man that
takes in the Hoffmeister No Trump like you."

"It's just a matter of applying one's mind to it, wouldn't you
say?"

"Only most people, for a head they got a paper bag full of water. Mr. Jenks, I am asking if you are playing this afternoon in
the Individual?"

"Well, no. I just planned to watch."

"For the Individual I got a ticket," Hoffmeister said. "They
make me buy a ticket for both sessions when it starts last night,
but if you and me, we could go in the side game, I am gladly
tearing up my ticket for the Individual and forgetting the three
dollars. You and me, Mr. Jenks, we understand each other and are
killing them dead in the side game and I—" he struggled with himself for a moment, but could not let money prevent the full working
of this miracle "—I am even paying your entry fee if any difference
it makes. What are you saying to this?"

Alfred Jenks smiled with infinite sweetness. "Thank you so
much," he said. "I feel greatly honored. But you see, I don't play
bridge."

"You . . . don't . . . play . . . bridge?"

"No, not since Emmy died, my wife, you know. I never did play much, and now I just watch." He got up and said pleasantly, "It has been so good to talk to you, and do you mind if I say that your convention is remarkably useful? I believe I had better find a chair to watch the Individual now, and may I give you my best wishes for a nice game today?"

He bowed and moved off, and Hoffmeister sorted out his collection of old bones and creaking joints and aching muscles and went slowly to seek his own table. The man understood the Hoffmeister No Trump perfectly and thought it was wonderful so, naturally, the man did not play bridge. Even in the Book of Job there were no torments like that.

Alfred Jenks had given much thought to the matter before deciding to watch the second session of the Individual that afternoon. He had considered watching the Vanderbilt, which was in its second qualifying round, but decided against it on the basis that it would be too tense an experience. All the experts were playing as teams of four in the Vanderbilt and they worked so hard trying to win that it upset him to watch. He had debated following the side game, but that seemed a bit dull when there was an event as colorful as the Individual to watch. Since partners in the Individual only played one hand with each other and had no time to learn each other's game, anything could happen. He found an unused chair and sat in it off to one side until he saw Hoffmeister take his place at a table. Then Alfred Jenks carried his chair to another section, and asked permission of the four people at the table to watch their game. He had nothing against Hoffmeister—in fact he admired the man, and was impressed by the Hoffmeister No Trump—but he did not want to run the risk of getting personally involved with him. It was so easy to get emotionally involved with people, and so very tiring.

Three women and one man were at the table he had chosen. Two of the women, and the man, merely glanced at him and gave a casual consent when he asked permission to watch. The third woman said, "Why, indeed you may! You just sit right here and bring little old me some luck," and pointed to the space beside her chair. He pulled up his chair and sat down, keeping well back from

the table to avoid interfering with them. The lady who invited
him to sit beside her was nice-looking. She had hair as white and
fluffy as candy made of spun sugar, and a thin sweet face on which
age had stitched many wrinkles. She sat perkily on her chair, like
the cardinals who came to the bird-feeder in his yard every morning. Yes, she was very nice. She was not careful, though. A careful woman—one like his late wife, for example—would not have
invited a stranger to sit beside her. Emmy always waited for people
to prove themselves before giving them any encouragement.

He watched the white-haired lady sort her first hand. She
showed it to him, and he decided that if he were playing he would
pass. She bid one spade and got the bid for two spades and with
the help of a defensive error made two. Her opponents could have
made three hearts, so that gave her an excellent board. She moved
around the table on the next two hands, playing in turn with each
of the others, and collected two more good boards.

When the change was called and she got up to move to another
table, he nodded to her and said, "Well, good luck."

"Mister Man," she said, "you're coming right with me. I declare, I never had such a good start. You brought me luck and I'm
not giving you up that easy." She had an accent that melted
words into a soft liquid.

"Oh I couldn't do that," he said. It was a mistake to follow one
person through a session, because you started to get emotionally
involved.

"Of course you can," she said, sweetly but firmly. "Sure as
my name is Mary Rose Rutledge, you're going to help me win
some points today, Mister Man. Like Bobby used to say—that was
my late husband, Robert Lee Rutledge, of Richmond, Virginia—
when you set your heart to a thing, Mary Rose, you about as easy
to budge as a ten-pound catfish on a ten-cent line. What's your
name, Mister Man?"

"Well, it's Alfred Jenks, but really I—"

"Jenks," she said, and her accent took the blunt name and
stretched it into a two-note song. "What a nice little old name. You
coming with me, Mister Jenks, or do I carry you?"

Before he quite knew what he was doing he said, "Well, for just one more round, then," and went with her to the next table. He didn't want to get involved any further but it was difficult not to do what she wanted. In a way she reminded him of Emmy, except that Emmy moved people around like a woman using a stiff broom while Mrs. Rutledge used a feather duster. He watched her play the next three boards, two good ones and one bad, and then said he had to leave and watch some friends in another section. This was not true and he disliked telling a lie, but their relationship had gone far enough.

Mary Rose took hold of the lapel of his coat and smiled up at him. He was a nice little old boy, and she was not about to turn him loose. For one thing, he was bringing her luck. For another, it was the first time in her life she had had a kibitzer of her very own. "You can't do that to me, Mr. Jenks," she said plaintively. "You brought me luck. And you've got to tell me what on earth I did wrong on that last hand to get that mean old bottom. I thought I was playing it real good. They haven't called the change yet and you have time to tell me."

"We-ell," he said doubtfully, and then could not resist explaining how the hand should have been played. This was a treat Emmy had never allowed him; the way to handle any mistake Emmy made was to pretend she hadn't made it. He knew all the rules of bidding and playing backwards and forwards, just the way a technician in The Telephone Company knew circuits, and it was gratifying to be asked to display his knowledge. By the time he finished his explanation, with Mrs. Rutledge uttering awed chirps, it was time for the next round and he found himself watching Mrs. Rutledge play three more hands.

After that there was no graceful way to leave and he watched her play throughout the afternoon. It was of course a tiring experience. His hands picked up a tremor and his blood pressure rose. He suffered through her bad hands and felt waves of excitement when she did well. Because of the way she played it was impossible to watch calmly. She went at bridge like a happy child skipping in and out of traffic on a busy street. Whenever she met disaster she bounced up gaily and skipped out ready for another accident. In general, however, she had good luck, and the disasters were infrequent.

"There!" she said when it was all over, her eyes as bright as those of a nesting bird. "We did it, didn't we, Mister Man? Didn't we come in somewhere?"

"Oh yes, yes, I think we did," he said, getting trapped into accepting the pronoun "we," a word that he had seldom used in the past except when talking about The Telephone Company. "My estimate is that we came in third or perhaps even second in section, but that we did not place in the overall standings."

"Second or third! Why, we might get a big old red point!"

"Yes, I think that's likely. I can't recall if the Individual has a sectional or regional rating in this tournament, but in either case it should be around a point for third and up to two points for second."

"Oh, how lovely! I declare, that gives me twenty-one points at least, five of them red, and this will be the first time I've scratched down here. Alfred, you and me have got to celebrate!"

The use of his first name made something inside him vibrate, as if a soft finger had plucked a harp string. "I—I really couldn't stay. I have to go home and, well—"

"Oh, I forgot, that nice Mrs. Jenks," Mary Rose said. "What a lucky woman she is."

"Um, well, it's not quite that," he said in confusion. "You see, Emmy died a year ago, only two years after we moved down here from Buffalo when I retired. So I live alone now and I have my dinner ready in the refrigerator and I shouldn't just leave the place untended, wouldn't you agree?"

A widower, Mary Rose thought, with a quiver of delight that she knew was shameful, probably Mrs. Jenks had been a real fine woman. A widower who brought her luck! No indeed, he wasn't going home to any old leftovers in a refrigerator. "Alfred," she said, "anything in the refrigerator will keep. We're going out to dinner and celebrate! There's the nicest place down the street, real good portions and they don't charge a fortune, and we're going to eat there and then come back and see how we did." She hoped he would offer to take her, but they were going anyway, and she could skip some event later in the week and save three dollars.

To Alfred Jenks this was both disturbing and fascinating. He couldn't remember when he had gone out to dinner with a woman other than Emmy, and he wondered what Emmy would say if she could look down on him and see. She really wouldn't have much right to complain; after all, he hadn't invited Mrs. Rutledge to dinner, she had told him to take her out to dinner, which was exactly what Emmy used to do. But of course the matter had to be put on the proper basis. "Very well," he said. "But naturally, you must be my guest." He had spent very little money in the last year and could easily afford it, and it was a nice feeling to be firm and masculine.

At dinner Mary Rose ordered the Yankee pot roast, because she was not one of those southerners who were still fighting the War Between the States. She knew it would be tasty and filling; it was also the least expensive entree, and she did not intend to alarm Alfred by throwing his money away wildly. "You been down here three years, Alfred?" she asked, chewing carefully so that her dental plates would not make clicking noises at him.

"Three years lacking a month," he said. "I would just as soon have stayed in Buffalo after I retired but Emmy, she was always a bit adventuresome, wanted to live in Miami. So we bought a house and, well, I don't quite know what to do with it now that she's gone. There are so many problems involved, selling it and all, and then I'd have to take an apartment or room, and the question is, where?"

"You and me, we've had the same mean old problems," Mary Rose said. "Bobby, that was my late husband, Robert Lee Rutledge, passed on eight years ago, and I've been at loose ends ever since. I got a married daughter up in Baltimore, but she's real busy and can't find time to write much. You got children, Alfred?"

"Oh yes, two grown boys up north. Both married. One of them

works for The Telephone Company just like I did and, my goodness, he'll be there twenty-five years in June and can join The Telephone Pioneers of America. Time flies, doesn't it?"

"It surely does. Alfred, how come you don't play bridge when you're so good at it?"

"Do you really think I am?"

"I declare, I learned more from you this afternoon than I learned for years."

"Well," he said, feeling both happy at her praise and slightly embarrassed by the confession he had to make, "it's a matter of temperament. I believe I do know bridge, but applying the knowledge in a game is something else. For example, if the opponent on my right makes a foolish bid, I just can't bring myself to double. People always look so hurt or angry when you set them. And that's the way it goes in every phase of the game."

Mary Rose sighed. "Just fancy knowing when to double, and not doing it. My trouble is I usually can't figure when to double. But Alfred, if you don't play bridge, what do you do with your time? A tournament like this doesn't come along often."

"Oh, I take the entry fees in a local bridge club and do the scoring. I read. I watch the birds at my backyard feeder. I used to play bridge with Emmy because she insisted on it. It wasn't much of a strain being her partner—you know, she always got in the no trump bid first so she could play the hand—but I haven't played since her last illness."

"Alfred, you and me are going to play in the side game tomorrow."

"Oh now really! I don't think I could bring myself to it, Mary Rose, and—" He stopped. The soft vibration as of a harp string thrummed in his body, and he realized that he had called her by her first name.

"It would be a sure enough treat for me."

"I—I wouldn't play nearly as well as you might expect."

"I'd love it just any old way you played."

She had fascinating eyes, he thought. They were bright and lively and, well, even a trifle bold, but in a nice way, like the eyes of the special cardinal that visited his backyard feeder every morning and then came to the window and rapped sharply on it with his beak, ordering him to put out more sunflower seeds. He always complied. "Well," he said, "perhaps just once . . ."

13

WEDNESDAY AT THE Spring Nationals was passing into history. Its major battles would be reported as solemnly as if Xenophon and Froissart were the chroniclers, and the play of leading contenders would be analyzed like the tactics followed at Waterloo. That marvel of modern science—the electronic computer—would be called onto memorize what had happened, so that such achievements as that of Mary Rose Rutledge, in winning 1.40 red points for coming in second in section in the Individual, would not be forgotten.

Lesser events of Wednesday would not be recorded, and there were many of these. Ace McKinley, who was not playing, wrote several newspaper columns, painfully conscious of his inability to spice them with hands that had helped him win a championship. Bubba Worthington played in a side game and scored poorly, thinking of what he was going to do to those vultures in the rubber bridge session later on. Katy Edmunds took the day off to go shopping, hoping to find a few salesgirls who would put up a fight, as a change from that tearful Vicky Summers. Vicky went by bus to the Seaquarium, and had a nice outing until she saw a shark whose mouth reminded her of Mrs. Edmunds.

Carola Clark played in two side games with Babs Hartley; the fact that they won 5.62 master points would be duly noted by the computers, but it would not be recorded that Carola's body went rigid when Babs hugged her after seeing their scores. Ben Aarons, who was not playing, felt an illogical relief when he noted that his former partner, Sammy Rothberg, not only qualified in the

Vanderbilt but also won in the first knockout match. Mary Rose Rutledge and Alfred Jenks returned from dinner and exulted over the 1.40 red points. They talked for a while before Alfred went home, and somehow it came out that Mary Rose had a monthly income of $278.40 from Social Security and an annuity, while Alfred had an income of $365.31 from Social Security, investments and a Telephone Company pension. Each of them privately added these figures and arrived at the rather exciting total of $643.71.

Sammy Rothberg completed the first knockout round of the Vanderbilt that evening with his blond hair damp and matted and with patches of sweat darkening his seersucker coat. Now and then a chill glided through his body. He did not feel well, and noticed that he tired quickly, his muscles losing their snap and hanging on his bones like strips of uncooked dough. He knew he must stop taking sleeping pills to knock himself out and bennies to get going. The trouble was, the tension never let up. Like this afternoon and tonight, how could he relax across the table from Runa, trying to decode her complicated bids? For that matter, how could he relax with a woman who practically invited him to her bedroom and then didn't open the door when he knocked? It was humiliating if she had gone to sleep. It was worse if she hadn't.

He stared at her now across the table and said, "We did better tonight, didn't we?" If she would just give him a smile and a reassuring answer, he could start to relax.

"Oh, maybe," Runa said, yawning. "But you still play as if you're seeing ghosts instead of cards."

"No, but seriously, Runa, don't you think that, if Tony and Jake did as well as we did, we won our match?"

"I'm not waiting around to see."

"I could phone you the results in your room."

She tilted her head to one side and looked at him, her eyes thin black glints. "How brazen of you," she said lightly. "Phoning a woman in her bedroom."

"Or . . . or I could drop by to tell you."

"Are you sure you won't lose your way, Sammy darling? Like last night?"

"No, really, I came by," he said earnestly. "I'll drop around tonight if . . . if it won't disturb you."

Runa got up from the table and stretched slowly, and the thin bracelets on her arms tinkled softly. "It takes a man to disturb me," she said. "Do you think you can?" She smiled and left the room.

Sammy watched her go. She had a slow walk that gave an insolent sideways thrust to her hips. What she just said was another maddeningly obscure bid that he was expected to decode. Well damn it, he was going to bid his own hand this time and not worry about hers. As soon as he checked scores with Jake and Tony to see if they won the match, he was going to her room and barge right in and bid the grand slam. If that was on her mind too, all right, fine, that body of hers would be a gorgeous dummy. If it was merely a tease and she went all shocked and proper on him, that was fine too and he could laugh and tell her to go back to her dolls, and walk out.

Beside him a voice said, "Where's Runa?"

Sammy gave a little jump, and looked up at Jake Jacobs. He didn't like Jake; the guy was as phony as a deck with five aces. Tonight Jake was wearing a maroon sports jacket with matching shoes in rough suede, and cream-colored slacks with matching necktie. Something had gone wrong with Jake's wardrobe and his shirt was plain old white. "What do you want Runa for?" Sammy asked irritably.

"What the hell, is it a secret where she went? We're on the same team, ain't we?"

"Well, she was tired and went to her room. You want to check our scores and see how we did?"

"Can't stop," Jake said. "Got another rubber bridge match coming up. Tony and I did all right. How about you and Runa?"

"All right, I guess."

"Here's my score card, Sammy. You check how our team did. See you tomorrow."

He dropped the card on the table, sure that he had nailed Sammy down for a while, and left the ballroom and headed for a house phone and called Runa's number.

"Hello," Runa said. Her voice sounded lazy and bored and slightly mocking, and stirred vibrations deep in Jake's body.

"Hi, Runa," he said. "This is your old teammate Jake."

"Well, imagine that. What's on your mind, old teammate Jake? Did you play a hand beautifully and decide to give me a thrill by telling me about it?"

"I wish I knew how to give you a thrill, baby."

"Oh but you do! Why last night you took my breath away by offering to star my lovely provocative hands in one of your ads. It simply made the day for me."

"All right, I goofed on that, baby. Put away the needle. I got a different idea."

"Now he's going to work up to my lovely provocative wrists. At this rate it's going to take you a long time to get around to the rest of me."

Jeez, Jake thought, going to bed with this broad would be something. Probably like wrestling her on a pile of old razor blades. "I wondered if you and me could play together in the Open Pairs. You dated up for them?"

"Now you're starting to interest me," Runa cooed. "I like a man who talks business. You are talking business, aren't you, old teammate Jake?"

"Yeah. What's the tax, Runa?"

"How much are you paying Tony to partner you in the Vanderbilt?"

"Fifty bucks a session, I pay the entry fees."

"Oh dear," Runa said lightly. "I didn't realize Tony came so cheaply. But of course he doesn't have lovely provocative hands and wrists, like me. For the Open Pairs I might settle for, oh, a thousand dollars."

"A thousand bucks! Who charges dough like that? Who pays it? Don't tell me Sammy Rothberg. He don't have that kind of scratch."

"Sammy isn't paying off in money. Just in amusement. Besides, you'd want to spend a lot of time going over your system with me, wouldn't you?"

Jake licked his lips and noted that they tasted like hunks of inner tube. "Yeah," he said thickly. "Some of my bids are a little complicated."

"Uh-hmm. And I'm a slow learner." She let a laugh ripple out, and Jake felt it down to his toes. "You might want to spend a lot of time teaching me."

He shuffled the idea around in his mind and dealt himself a few thoughts. He didn't object to paying if he had to, but a thousand bucks was shocking and in fact damn near immoral. He checked his reactions to see if he felt outraged but instead discovered a rising excitement. It could be worth it, and at least there wouldn't be any messy sentimental fallout, the way there would have been with that kid Vicky. However, he wanted more than the Open Pairs for all that scratch. "Look," he said, "it's a deal if you'll make it the Open Pairs plus the Mixed Pairs. That's if we get knocked out of the Vanderbilt tomorrow."

Runa laughed again. "I bet you won't play well in the Vanderbilt tomorrow," she said. "All right, it's a deal. By the way, a little something in advance would be nice. Five hundred, perhaps?"

"O.K. Uh, maybe we could get together now, and I'll ditch this rubber bridge I'm in?"

"No, darling. Go make yourself a few dollars. You might want something extra to buy me an ice cream cone. Maybe tomorrow night, we'll see. Good night, old teammate Jake."

"See you," he said, and hung up. He debated checking out of the rubber bridge session, because it would keep him up till all hours and a guy ought to be in top shape when he called on Runa. But hell, he could sleep late, and anyway he wouldn't mind making Bubba Worthington share the expense with him, probably the closest that queer would ever get to sleeping with a broad.

Upstairs in her room, Runa sat by the phone for a few minutes after hanging up, stroking it lightly with her fingertips and smiling to herself. Yes, she had handled old teammate Jake very well; she doubted that, in the past, Jake ever thought in terms of anything more than a cheap gift or a twenty-dollar bill. It was smart to make him pay a lot because no doubt he judged value by the price tag. She expected to enjoy Jake; he wouldn't be trying to prove anything with her, no more than a bull or a stallion. She hated men who tried to prove that they were irresistible, or that they were men, or that they could make her crawl. In a little while Sammy Rothberg would come along, and Sammy wanted to prove he was a man, and it would be amusing to prove that he wasn't.

She took off her clothes, and washed, and sprayed her body with perfume. Her nose wrinkled in distaste; the smell was like plunging her face into a jasmine bush on a night when all the flowers were opening. Ordinarily she used little perfume, but this was for Sammy because it would upset him. She put on her thin gold bracelets one at a time, smiling at the sleek coppery figure posing before her in the mirror, and turned out the light and stretched her naked body on the bed. The bracelets whispered softly whenever she moved and small puffs of air examined her body. She remembered those other nights when she lay in darkness like this, on the ship, the cabin stinking with that cheap perfume José made her use, waiting for the stealthy shuffle of feet and the click of the doorknob that meant José had arrived, smiling and sure of himself. José was a room steward on the ship, a young man with black hair and white teeth and the body and instincts of a puma. José had a hobby; he liked to make his girls crawl. She caught her breath sharply at the memory and her fingernails hissed over the tight sheet . . .

The matter of José had started very quietly and indirectly back in Los Angeles when she was nineteen years old. A customer came to her table in the barbershop for a manicure. He was nice-looking but old, fifty-five or sixty, with silvery hair and soft white skin. He had to be an easterner; you couldn't live on the West Coast without getting a tan. He was polite and didn't try to rub knees or get fresh, and while that was a pleasant change it was also a bit annoying, and she went to work to chip the ice off him. She gave him the premium-in-every-package treatment: the flashing eyes, the quick smile that lighted her face, the extra pats of the hand, the sleepy laugh. That got her a big zero. He answered questions vaguely and courteously, and asked none of his own. At the end of the manicure he handed her a dollar tip and started to leave.

Then he stopped and looked down at her, a tiny frown on his face. "Really," he said, as if puzzled at himself, "you're quite an interesting girl." He turned away and left.

Two days later he came back. This time she added the knee bit to the treatment. Double zero. Grandpop didn't have kneecaps, he had ice caps. Two days later, back again. This time she threw in some fortune-telling, tracing the lines on his palm with a fingernail (usually this was real pressure-cooker stuff) and telling him in a purring voice that romance was coming into his life. That was sensational; it actually won her another puzzled frown. But then he began coming in every day.

After the sixth visit she trailed him upstairs to ask the bell captain who he was. He had to be staying at the hotel or he wouldn't have come to the barbershop. But when he reached the lobby Grandpop went outside and took a cab. The bell captain said Grandpop wasn't a guest now but maybe had stayed there in the past. Grandpop came back each day the next week and she did everything but a striptease trying to get a raised eyebrow. She had never been so insulted in her life.

Finally, after more than two weeks, he got personal with her in a very odd way. He said, "On a trip I took to Mexico, I saw a profile like yours. A bit of late Aztec sculpture, probably of one of Montezuma's court ladies."

That annoyed her. When she finally dug a reaction out of him she couldn't understand what he meant. "For crying out loud," she said. "Am I supposed to know about late Aztec sculpture and Monty somebody-or-other?"

He seemed to wince, and said, "The Aztecs ruled Mexico before the white man came, and Montezuma was their last king. Of course some authorities claim he was not a king in our sense of the word, but rather a religious and political symbol who helped hold together a rather loose confederation of city-states."

She jabbed his cuticle with the orangewood stick. "I don't like guys who talk over my head."

He said politely, "I understand and sympathize with your reaction, including the jab from the cuticle stick. It is a pity that anyone is able to talk over that magnificent head of yours."

"I don't know what for God's sake you're yacking about!"

"For one thing, my dear, I'm talking about your brain, which is too good to contain so little knowledge. For another, I'm talking about your face. You have the same high cheekbones, the slanted eyes, the hawklike nose, that I saw in that piece of Aztec sculpture. No doubt your coppery skin would have matched up, too. What I'm saying is that you remind me of an Aztec princess."

"Oh, lay off! You come here all the time and I can't get a rise out of you and all of a sudden you start giving me a snow job about princesses."

"I'm sorry," he murmured. "I'm being very awkward about this, because I've never found myself in a situation like it before."

Probably he was making fun of her in some odd high-toned way. "The only situation you're in is sitting at my table and I won't stop you from walking out."

"No doubt I should," he said with a small sigh. "Let me ask just one thing. The Aztec matter interests me. Did your parents come from Mexico?"

"One of them did, and so what? My old man was a greaser, and what a jerk he was, leaving Mom as soon as he knocked her up. But don't give me any Aztec junk about him. He was a lousy bracero who came up every year to pick crops, and Mom was a stupid waitress who thought he looked like a movie star, and don't try to make with the princess bit out of that. Aren't you ready to beat it yet?"

"I've never even asked your name."

"It's Runa Herrero. Now—"

"Runa," he said softly. "That's lovely. But Herrero doesn't go with it. The name Herrero means blacksmith in Spanish. Very ordinary, very common. Your name ought to suggest some of the things that your face does. It shouldn't be Runa Montezuma, that's too obvious, and furthermore it's bad poetry. But Montez, there would be the right touch. Runa Montez."

"Listen," she said. "A couple months ago I smacked a guy who thought buying a manicure gave him a ticket to talk dirty. They told me the next time I got mad, I'm fired. Grandpop, the next time's coming up."

He smiled and rose and put the usual tip on the table. "You've been very patient with me," he said. "My name is Mark Heatherford and I'm at the Beverly Hills Hotel and I'd be honored if you would have dinner with me there tonight. Seven-thirty, and just wear something plain and quiet. I'll be waiting in the lobby."

That almost flushed her down the john. "What for crying out loud makes you think I'd come?" she asked in amazement.

"I'm not sure you will. But I'll be waiting there at seven-thirty anyway. And, by the way, I won't be coming back here again to bother you. Goodby, Runa."

Well, of course she *was* there at seven-thirty, tense and angry and confused, wearing the wrong clothes and too much makeup.

Dinner was served by a waiter who acted as if she had a right to eat at the Beverly Hills Hotel. Grandpop ordered stuff with crazy names like Tournedos Rossini and Mateus Rosé; the first turned out to be delicious beef and the second red wine that danced all the way down her throat. Grandpop talked easily about books she had never read and plays she had never seen, and somehow made them interesting. Not that she was taken in by any of that. Grandpop was working up to making a pass at her, just like other old goats had done, except that his offer was trimmed in mink. There was, however, a difference. The idea of mink in her life was attractive, and she couldn't dig up a feeling of disgust about Grandpop. A lot of other emotions, but not disgust.

"Runa," he said at last, "I find myself in a very odd position.

I've seen other men get in it, and felt sorry for them, and was sure it couldn't happen to me. But now it has."

"For crying out loud," she said irritably, "don't you ever say things straight out instead of playing word games?"

"That's the trouble with being a lawyer. Often the law is vague and so we get in the habit of being vague."

That was the first personal fact he'd ever dropped, and she grabbed it. "You're a lawyer, huh? One of my girl friends went with one. She called him an ambulance chaser and it made him sore. You that kind of a lawyer?"

"Not exactly. I'm a corporation lawyer, in Chicago. My firm does legal work for big companies. I came out here to handle some details on a merger of two companies. I should have returned to Chicago ten days ago, because my work here was finished."

"Yeah? What kept you?"

"I'm afraid," he said with a shrug, "you did."

There it was, out in the open. This was the time to tell Grandpop where he could get off. But instead she grumbled, "You took your own sweet time letting me in on the secret."

"I'm very slow and cautious, Runa. And, frankly, I was hoping that either I would lose interest in you, or that you would stop making what I believe is called a play for me. You really have, you know."

"I put on an act for all the customers."

"Like the one for me?"

"Well, maybe not. But don't let that give you any ideas. You just got me curious, that was all."

He sighed. "Runa," he said, "you attract me more than any woman I've ever met. Does that satisfy your curiosity? Shall we drop everything right there?"

Of course they ought to drop everything right there. She scowled at him, and said sullenly, "No."

"Very well. Then let me proceed. I am fifty-six years old. Recently I have considered withdrawing from corporation law work, which no longer stimulates me. For several years I have been telling people I wanted to get away and plan a history of the

Federal Trade Commission, so I have a fine excuse for a long vacation. I am considering sailing next Monday from San Francisco for a three-month cruise of the South Pacific on the *Calpurnia*."

He stopped, and looked keenly at her, and she had to work to get enough air in her lungs. Her skin felt tight as a drum and her blood thudded against it. This wasn't adding up to something quick and cheap, like sneaking up to his room. "Go on," she said huskily.

"Are you sure you want me to?"

"You're driving me nuts!"

"Very well," he said. "Will you come with me?"

"For crying out loud," she said helplessly.

"Your first thought," he murmured, "is that this is the usual proposition, and that I want to sleep with you. I won't deny the urge. But I can also promise that I won't touch you unless you want it." He gave her a wistful smile and said, "Frankly, I find that hard to imagine."

That killed her. Most guys pictured her simply gasping to go to bed with them. "For crying out loud," she said. "Then what would be in it for you?"

"Oh, a great deal. I would enjoy your youth and vitality. I would enjoy talking to you about literature and the arts and history. I would enjoy teaching you an amusing mental exercise called bridge. I—"

"What's bridge?"

"A card game, my dear."

"Like Spit-in-the-ocean?"

"Not exactly. Also I would like very much to give you hints about how to dress and talk and—"

She had been looking for something she could get sore about. "What for crying out loud is wrong with how I talk?"

He smiled and said, "For crying out loud."

"I don't get it. I—" She stopped, and felt her face getting barbecued. When he said *For crying out loud* he was answering her question. *That* was one of the things wrong.

This was some years before a writer named Bernard Shaw contributed incidental dialogue to a film called *My Fair Lady,* but Hollywood had discovered the Pygmalion-Galatea story soon after it discovered Cinderella, and Runa had followed the adventures of Galatea under various names in various films. "Go peddle it to the movies," she said. "They use it all the time. Rich guy takes on dumb broad, teaches her the right fork to use. Listen, I like me the way I am, so go jump in a lake."

"My dear, you're wonderful the way you are. I'm sorry if I sound superior, because I don't feel that way. If I saw dust on a work of art I'd want to brush it off. That's all I suggest."

"For crying—" She stopped, and then said weakly, "Now I'm all confused."

"No more so," he said in a resigned tone, "than I."

"How could you explain me on the ship? What if you bumped into somebody from Chicago?"

"You're my niece."

"What! Me with my Mexican color and you with that pale skin and . . . and . . ." She peered at him and noticed something startling. "How long have you had that tan?"

"I've been using a sun lamp for the last week. Silly, wasn't it? I didn't really think I'd ask you to go, and I was fairly sure you'd refuse."

"How many other little tricks did you figure out?"

"Quite a few. I must admit preparing this as carefully as that merger I came here to work on. As to bumping into somebody from Chicago, I had the passenger list of the *Calpurnia* checked. I recognize no names on it, and corporation lawyers are not widely known. I'm afraid I also had you checked, Runa."

"You got your nerve! What—"

"I couldn't take a chance. My dear, I had to find out if you were married, or if this might harm your prospects in any way. I had to find out if it might harm *me.* There's an age of consent in California and I wanted to know if you are what they call San

Quentin quail. You're not. You are nineteen. I had to find out, and I'll use the blunt word, if you were a prostitute."

A jerk of a detective poking into her life asking questions . . . what if the jerk found out she'd gone to a motel with that guy a couple months ago? She didn't do it for pay, only for fun, but what would it look like? "And what was the answer?" she said grimly.

"You came out very well. Lively, warm-blooded, quite normal. All I can do now is apologize."

She was still looking for something to stay mad about. "Hey!" she cried. "And all that crap earlier today about not knowing my name, you knew all along and—"

"No, my dear. I didn't read the report until late this afternoon. I wanted to make an independent decision."

"Oh *hell*," she muttered.

"We would not need passports," he said, ticking off points on his soft graceful fingers. "A simple landing pass provided by the ship will take care of stops at ports. The ship sails at 2 p.m. Monday, which would give us Monday morning in San Francisco to buy your wardrobe. You could tell the girls you room with that, well, the simplest thing is the truth, that you're taking a trip with a man, without mentioning who or where. All your expenses, and of course pocket money, would be provided. And at the end of the trip, to help you make a new start, I would be prepared to give you five thousand dollars. Well, there it is, my dear. I fear that it's the longest and dullest proposition you will ever hear in your life."

She hated his calmness and the way her stomach was churning. At least she wasn't going to let him think she was hooked on him. For crying out loud, he was *ancient*. She was going to make this a straight business deal. "And what if," she said, "we get back from the trip and you say goodby, Runa, ha-ha-ha, and walk off without giving me five grand? What do I do, yell for the cops? They'd laugh too."

"I see your point."

"You could give me the dough now."

"This is awkward," he murmured. "Then you might walk off laughing. Runa, I already know I'm half a fool. I'd hate to spend the rest of my life knowing I'd been a complete fool."

"No money, no trip," she muttered. And if he shrugged and walked off, she'd be the complete fool.

He sent the waiter for more coffee, and took a thin white envelope and a pair of scissors from his pocket. He cut the envelope and handed one half to her. She looked inside and gasped. The envelope had contained five one-thousand-dollar bills. "My God," she whispered. "You cut them in half!"

"They'll be quite acceptable at a bank when taped together. Separated, they're worthless. I'm sorry we can't trust each other."

"You think of everything, don't you? Having the money on you, the scissors—"

"The legal mind, my dear, trying to cover all the problems that might arise. I try to be thorough. Are you coming with me?"

She stuffed the half-envelope into her handbag, and made her body quit shaking. "All right," she said. "You made a buy."

After the first week aboard ship she almost gave him back her half of the envelope to prove she trusted him. After the second week she marched into his cabin one night and said irritably, "Do you have to be a gentleman all the damn time?" For six weeks after that she could hardly let him out of her sight. The other passengers accepted her as his niece, and nobody recognized him even though it turned out there were several couples on the cruise from his hometown of Chicago. She and Mark had long fascinating talks and she learned about clothes and grammar. He taught her bridge. She was hot stuff at it—no, *skillful* at it—and it was a game educated people played and it was wonderful to be able to do something better than they did. The whole cruise was a technicolor dream until, with a month to go, José declared himself in on it, and the colors went muddy.

José was the room steward who took care of the cabins in their corridor. She had been vaguely aware of him: hot black eyes, a smirk, a swaggering walk. He came from the Mexican section of L.A. She'd gone to school with jerks like José. There was a knock on her door late one night, and when she opened it José was standing outside, grinning.

"What is it?" she said. "I didn't ring."

"That's good, baby," he said. "I don't like dames ringing for me."

"Are you drunk? I'm not baby to you. I'm Miss Heatherford."

She started to close the door but he put a foot against it and slipped into the room. "*Miss* Heatherford," he said. "What a laugh."

"Listen, either you get out or I'll—"

"You'll call Uncle? That's another laugh. Baby, I've seen you sneak into his room a dozen times at night. An old guy like that, jeez, you must be ready for a live one by now. Right?"

She swung a hand with clawed fingernails at his face, but he was waiting for that. He grabbed her wrist and growled, "Don't get tough with me. You little Mexican bitch, I know all about you."

"Who's Mexican?" she cried. "I'm—"

"You are, baby. I'd of known it anyway, your looks and skin, but that old bastard has a full report on you in his cabin. Guy didn't take no chances, I'll give him that. Now are you and me gonna play nice or do I start telling everybody what gives with you and Uncle?"

She broke away from him, and gasped, "You're going to end up fired, breaking into my room like this."

"You invited me in, and when I finish spilling the garbanzo beans, everybody's gonna believe it."

"There's not a thing you can do to either of us. Those people on board from Chicago don't know him, so nothing you said could get back to his people. Beat it!"

"Why give me this Chicago crap? Think I'm a dope? I told you I been all through his stuff."

"What do you mean, Chicago crap? He's from Chicago."

"My God," he said, and sat on the bed and stared up at her. Then he grinned. "Man," he said, "this makes it real juicy. He ain't Mark Heatherford from Chicago. His name is Martin Hume and he's a big shot from New York. And guess what, baby? He's got a letter in his cabin saying it looks like maybe he's gonna get made a federal judge."

He might just as well have kicked her in the stomach.

"You're lying," she said faintly.

"Look for yourself when you get time, baby. But I don't feel like waiting. You gonna be nice, or does the stuff hit the fan right now?"

"It can't be true," she gasped. "He couldn't have distrusted me that much. Give me a little time to look for myself. Give me until tomorrow night."

He got up from the bed and said lazily, "You don't need a little time, baby, you need a little attention," and began taking off her clothes.

The next afternoon, while Grandpop took his usual nap in a deck chair, José let her into the cabin and showed her what he'd found. Mark Heatherford of Chicago was without doubt Martin Hume of New York. She found another sidelight on his nature: the letter mentioning his probable appointment as a federal judge was addressed to him at the hotel where she had worked. It seemed likely that, after getting interested in her, he moved to the Beverly Hills Hotel under the fake name as a safety measure. A very cautious man.

After that, the final month of the voyage was like a fever or headache that had to be endured until it went away. She tried not to let Grandpop notice any change. They hadn't trusted each other, and there was no use getting upset over proof of extra distrust. And, to his credit, Grandpop was taking a greater risk than she had known; probably he wanted very much to be a federal judge. She did a good acting job with him.

She didn't have to act with José. He liked her to show disgust and fury. No doubt he would have liked her to cry, too, but she wouldn't give him that pleasure. He got enough as it was, thinking up interesting ways to make her crawl. He enjoyed bringing her cheap perfume and making her drench herself in it. He liked making her parade around wearing nothing but junk jewelry. In the early morning hours he would sleep in her bed, ordering her to stay up and call him before it was time to go on duty. Of course, being a man, he figured she was learning to like this, and started suggesting ways they could blackmail Grandpop when the cruise ended. She pretended to go along on this. She wasn't going to do it, though: Grandpop was paying for his fun, and she was paying for hers, and the only person getting a free ride so far was José. He was going to pay too.

Two nights before the end of the cruise, while José slept in her bed, she borrowed his passkey and let herself into a cabin down the corridor. Mrs. T. Harry Jones, a nice old lady who wore magnificent diamonds, was snoring peacefully in the cabin. Runa took two of her best diamond rings. She crept back to her own cabin, cut a section from the rubber heel of one of José's shoes, cut out a hollow for the rings and put them in it, and cemented the cutout piece back in place. The next day the ship was in an uproar over the theft. José, as the room steward, was of course questioned, and reported it to her very resentfully. She gave him a lot of sympathy. On the final morning, a few hours before docking, she left a crudely printed note in the purser's office when nobody was looking. It said: "About them rings. I seen José putting something in the heel of his right shoe."

José wasn't around to say goodby when they docked, or to collect his tips, and there were ugly reports about the finding of the rings. Some of José's passengers found this a good excuse not to leave a tip. Runa considered that a nice fringe benefit. The real payoff, of course, was that José would know exactly who to blame.

After landing, Grandpop gave her the other half of the money envelope. He was in a wistful mood and didn't want to give her up, at least not yet, not abruptly, but she cut things short. What the hell, it couldn't have worked out in any case, José or no José. She went alone to a hotel and stayed overnight and got all the crying out of her system. She didn't plan to cry over any more men. The next morning she returned to L.A. with some knowledge of how to talk and dress and with a passion for bridge and with five one-thousand-dollar bills pasted together.

She had a vague idea of going to night school, but she started playing duplicate around L.A. and gave up the notion of school, and in a few months met Howie at a duplicate club. He had a used car lot with a big sign that said: HAPPY HOWIE'S CAR MART. Smaller signs explained that Howie was Happy because he liked getting licked on car deals. After he offered a number of deals to her that didn't involve cars, and found she wasn't interested in making him happy that way, he got around to the last-ditch, rock-bottom, take-it-or-leave-it offer: marriage. This was a novelty to Runa and she accepted, although she suspected it was a mistake to marry a man who played such lousy bridge. She was right. After a few months Howie started coming home from work and kicking her around, not angrily or viciously, but in the same thoughtful appraising spirit in which his customers kicked the tires of his used cars. The marriage didn't last long, and Howie wasn't so Happy when he had to pay off in the divorce settlement.

Runa didn't marry again for three years. This time she accepted a young lawyer she met at a regional tournament. Thinking about it later, she suspected that marrying him had something to do with Grandpop being a lawyer. It turned out that he wasn't a younger edition of Grandpop, though, and furthermore he never could get the hang of weak two bids. They broke up after a couple of years and she didn't try marriage again. By that time she was fairly well fixed. She started her own bridge club and, what with giving lessons of one kind or another, made out nicely.

She never saw Grandpop again. At least, not in person. Once in *Time* magazine she saw a picture of Federal Judge Martin Hume and read about an important decision he had made. And once he read about her, probably when the ACBL Bulletin wrote her up as one of the top players on the West Coast, because a heavily insured package arrived from Mark Heatherford, whose address was a post office box in New York City. The package contained a small terra cotta figure. It was of a woman with high cheekbones and slanted eyes and a hawk nose, wearing a robe that the potter had incised to represent feathers. Runa broke

mering was his pulse. No, he didn't want to turn on the light and have everything sort of jump at him before he was ready for it. "I could turn my back and you could slip on a robe," he mumbled. She would look great in, say, a black robe that maybe revealed a bare shoulder and a length of slim leg.

"Oh I don't think so," she said. "If I give in to you on this I may end up fully dressed."

The mocking tone in her voice made his face hot. He hated the way he blushed so easily, but at least in the dark she couldn't see his face. The darkness had a tinge of violet in it, perhaps from the blood swirling around his eyes. He couldn't tell where she was in the room; the laugh and the jingle of bracelets seemed to come from everywhere at once. If she would just come up to him and maybe take his hand . . . "We won our first match," he said hoarsely. "I think our team plays the Duke-Ashcraft bunch tomorrow. Sixty-four boards, all afternoon and evening."

There was no answer but the thin flat chiming of bracelets. The sound might be coming from the bed. He took quick shallow gulps of air that left his lungs starved. The gulps brought something else to his attention. Perfume. It was thick and sweet and choking, and reminded him of the time when as a sophomore at college he went with a couple of guys to a cat house. Not with Ben Aarons, though; Ben had said no thanks, not as if he was scared or a Boy Scout but merely as if the idea didn't interest him. There was perfume like this in the cat house and the girls sat around in panties and bras. They had heavy faces and makeup put on with a trowel. They looked at you with bored eyes, waiting for you to take them upstairs and get on with the job. He went upstairs with one of them and thought of disease, so he paid her and said he was writing a theme about sex for college and merely wanted to get some information from her. It was all right with her just to talk, except there wasn't much to talk about, and thank God the guys who went with him never suspected.

"Runa?" he said faintly.

"I think," Runa murmured, "she got bored and went to bed."

"Yeah, well, it is kind of late," he said, trying not to stammer. "So I won't keep you up and that's all I had to report and I'll see you in the afternoon, right?" He fumbled behind him for the doorknob and found it and slipped out, but not quickly enough to stay ahead of the sound of the lazy laugh.

14

THE ONLY THING WRONG with bridge, Bubba Worthington thought angrily, was the people who played it. And of the players, certainly three of the most unpleasant sat at the card table in the living room of his suite at the Xanadu. Take Mrs. Edmunds, for example, with her purple hair and the metallic laugh he could feel in the roots of his teeth. Didn't she know that women her age shouldn't wear big gaudy rings, like the turquoise set in a silver snake, that called attention to their wrinkled hands? How different from Mother, who had soft white velvety hands and never wore more than a single small diamond. Next there was Jake Jacobs and his revolting clothes; imagine anyone wearing a maroon sports jacket, cream-colored slacks and maroon suede shoes. Jake always reeked of lotions and powders, but perhaps that was preferable to his natural odor, which was probably goat-like. Bubba told himself not to dislike Jake additionally for being a Jew; nowadays one must be tolerant, especially after what Hitler had done to the race, and it was rather touching the way little Israel stood up to all those noisy Arab countries.

Jake finished counting the score, and said, "You sure butchered that rubber, Bubba. You cost me eighty bucks."

No, Bubba told himself firmly, he was not going to be anti-semitic, no matter what the provocation. He rose and said, "Before we start the next rubber I want to change my shirt. Excuse me, please."

"Hah," Jake said. "He wants to lose a fresh one when he plays with you, Katy."

Bubba ignored the remark. "Please help yourselves to drinks," he said, showing them that a host was always courteous no matter how rude a guest might be.

He went into the bedroom and closed the door. It was too much to hope that Tony would take a couple of drinks and get careless during the next rubber. The fellow never took a friendly drink while playing, and of course that was one of the differences between a gentleman and a cad. Tony made a vulgar commercial thing out of a social game. Why, the fellow wasn't even a very good player. It was Bubba's own fine play that had brought them the win in the Charity Pairs and erected the big red 1 beside their names. In these sessions of rubber bridge Tony had merely been lucky, that was all.

Or, Bubba wondered, was it all luck? Wasn't it possible, and indeed likely considering Tony's lack of real skill, that the fellow was cheating?

He stripped to the waist and looked with displeasure at the damp patches of sweat on shirt and undershirt. He sponged under his arms and used powder sparingly, and stood before the mirror for a minute doing isometric exercises. He pressed the tips of the fingers of one hand against the fingers of the other, pushing with one hand and resisting with the other, while breathing deeply. The muscles of his shoulders and chest made nice ripples under his skin. Obviously he hadn't lost the strength he had developed at crew in prep school and college. He would of course have made the varsity at Harvard if he had stayed beyond freshman year, but he couldn't stand the school, all those Back Bay fellows with codfish faces, and those greasy radicals. Then when he went to Oxford he would undoubtedly have rowed against Cambridge and made his Blue, but he didn't want to stay in such a messy town, where so many undergraduates had voices like girls and hair like sheep dogs.

He put on fresh clothing, knotted his tie carefully and fixed the collar pin to hold it in place, put on his jacket and adjusted the three points of the white handkerchief in the breast pocket, and went back to the living room. Now he was ready to play the next rubber with Mrs. Edmunds. He really had to do better to-night; Mother had been fretful when he telephoned to ask her to fatten his checking account a trifle. The last two nights had cost him more than eight hundred dollars. Tonight was a slight improvement; he dropped only forty dollars playing with Tony and eighty while playing with Jake. A good rubber would wipe that out. It would also leave Tony in the hole for the session, a pleasant result.

The first hand was a lovely cold three no trump his way. One more like that would blitz Jake and Tony and take a 900 or 1,000 rubber, almost enough to get even, at ten cents a point. The next hand was even better, and almost immediately Bubba knew it must be a little slam in hearts. He bid it confidently. On his right, Tony doubled. Bubba gave him a pitying look, and redoubled. Unfortunately, it turned out that Jake and Tony were playing Lightner Doubles, a convention that called for an unusual lead against a slam contract. Jake found the killing lead, the deuce from a long topless club suit. Tony trumped. The deuce called for a return lead from Tony's lower side suit, and he returned a diamond. Jake took the trick with the ace, the only missing high card, and shot back another club to be trumped. Down two, vulnerable, doubled and redoubled. One thousand points on one lousy hand! The worst thing about it was that four hearts was cold even with the club lead, and would have wrapped up the rubber.

"That's my money you're throwing away, too," Mrs. Edmunds said irritably.

After that, as so often happens, the rubber turned into a long bitter seesaw. Nobody held a big hand. Jake and Tony put to-gether a couple of part scores to make game, wiping out an op-posing part score, and Bubba ran into several sets ranging from two hundred to five hundred points. Across the table from him, Katy Edmunds played in grim silence. She wanted to get the rub-ber finished no matter who won; Bubba was pushing too hard, try-ing to get more from his cards than was in them, or at least more than he could get out of them, and that was the road to big sets.

She also noticed that Jake and Tony were playing really vicious bridge, tempting Bubba to climb out on limbs and then kicking him off. She wondered what had got into the pair of them tonight; on other evenings they hadn't cut Bubba's throat so coldly. They were also, and incidentally, cutting her throat too, damn it.

Tony was living up to his reputation as one of the most dangerous rubber bridge players in the country. He was tuned to exactly the right pitch, like a fine violin, and his senses reached out to pick up and analyze everything that Bubba did. His eyes were busy at work behind the dark glasses. He did not watch Katy, knowing that she frequently changed the pattern in which she sorted the cards in her hand. He watched Bubba's cards and fingers. Bubba was a pattern sorter. Spades went all the way to the left, sorted in order of ranking, and then hearts, diamonds and clubs. If Bubba pulled the second card from his left and it was the queen of spades, the first card had to be the king or ace of spades. Usually, partway through each hand, Tony knew how many cards Bubba held in each suit, and whether he had higher or lower cards in a suit than whatever card or cards he had played. In doing this, Tony was violating one of the proprieties of both contract and duplicate bridge: "A player should refrain from looking intently at any other player during the auction or play periods, or at another player's hand as for the purpose of observing the place from which he draws a card." Tony knew this law perfectly and often did very well by breaking it.

Another deal was made, and Jake and Tony bid a little slam in spades. Bubba trembled with eagerness. This looked exactly like the heart slam on which he'd dropped a thousand points; he was blank in clubs and could trump an opening club lead, and from the bidding Katy must have an ace. He doubled. On his right, Tony redoubled. Bubba prayed that Katy would read his double as Lightner, asking for an unusual lead. Good old Katy did. She led a club. Then Tony's hand came down; it held no clubs, and Jake ruffed high from dummy and Bubba could not beat the card. Jake pulled trumps and ran clubs and hearts and discarded two low diamonds and Katy never made her diamond ace. A little slam in spades, vulnerable, doubled and redoubled, with an over-trick. Counting the slam bonus and the 500 for rubber, 2,420.

Jake began adding the scores, and for a few moments there was no sound but the rattle of Katy's fingernails as she drummed on the table. The sound drilled into Bubba's nerves and he saw that the woman was glaring at him. "All right," he cried, "how should I have played that hand?"

Katy said, "With another partner."

"There's nothing wrong with my double of that bid," Bubba said, trying to think of a reason to explain the horrible result. "What do you expect when . . . when Tony cheats all the time?" His voice went skirling up on the final words.

On his right, the black sunglasses swiveled toward him like shotgun barrels, aimed at him for a second and turned away. Tony said nothing.

"Aah, don't be a bad sport," Jake growled.

Katy said, "You don't even know enough about the game to know if somebody's cheating."

"But he does cheat!" Bubba cried. When he first made the accusation, his stomach had squeezed together in a sickish way, but now a surge of excitement gripped him. It was true, and Tony didn't dare deny it, and it accounted for all the bad scores he had been getting. "He leans over and peeks in my hand! I know he does! Why else would he redouble, unless he knew I was blank in clubs and that his hand could ruff too high for me?"

Tony said in a flat voice, "I often redouble dogmeat."

"Let's stop it right there," Katy said sharply. "I'm not going to sit around while you two fight. I'm through. How much do I owe, Jake?"

"You're minus three hundred and five bucks for the evening, Katy. Bubba's down five hundred and forty-five. I get three hundred eighty-five and Tony collects four hundred sixty-five. Anybody want to check my figures?"

"It can't be that much," Bubba complained.

"No?" Jake said. "You just lost a four thousand two hundred and fifty point rubber. See for yourself."

While Bubba stared at the figures, Katy ripped traveler's checks from a booklet, signed them and threw a five-dollar bill on the table. "Couple of buzzards," she said angrily, and walked out. Of course, she thought, Tony peeked when he got a chance, why not? People ought to hold their cards up, and not keep them in a fixed order. She marched out of the room, thinking again what fun she could have with Tony on the world cruise.

Bubba began writing a check. The figure was really shocking and Mother would be upset and wonder how a Life Master could lose so much. But what good was bridge skill against a crook? "This is the last money you'll ever cheat me out of," he said.

The black sunglasses glittered at him again. "Cool it, man," Tony said.

"Yeah," Jake said. "Let's not have any fights."

Bubba's muscles felt cold and hard and deadly. A few minutes ago his muscles had trembled, but now he knew there wouldn't be any fight unless he pushed it because it turned out Tony was a coward along with being a cheat. Maybe he *ought* to push things. "Don't worry," he said. "Tony doesn't fight, he just cheats. He's scared of fighting. Want me to prove it? You want to step outside and settle things, Tony?"

Tony gave a disgusted grunt. He went to the door leading onto the tiny balcony and opened it. "You step outside first," he said. "It's only a three-story drop."

"Very funny," Bubba said. "*Very* funny." He rose and moved lightly toward Tony, balancing carefully. There was the most delightful tingle in his body.

Tony took off his sunglasses and put them in his pocket. His cold dark eyes examined Bubba with distaste. "Don't bug me," he said.

Bubba grinned at him. Bubba had taken boxing lessons and knew how to handle a fighter like Tony, if indeed Tony would fight at all. Tony would make a wild swinging rush. Years ago in freshman days at Harvard Bubba had had a fight with Billy Three-Eyes—that was S. William Harbison III—who rowed on the 150-pound crew. All Billy Three-Eyes did was make wild rushes, and Bubba kept him off with left jabs and cut him up badly. He stared at Tony now and willed him to make such a rush. "You going to fight," he asked softly, "or chicken out?"

Tony said wearily, "I'm gonna take my dough and go to bed."

Bubba set his feet and flicked two left jabs at Tony's face and followed with a right cross. Tony jerked his head back and the jabs missed. He stepped smoothly inside the right cross and brought up his knee in a little twisting jolt into Bubba's groin. Bubba's mouth flew open in a soundless scream and he slid limply down the knee and onto the floor. Tony stepped back and put on his sunglasses and studied the writhing body at his feet.

"Jeez!" Jake gasped. "Whatcha do to the guy?"

"I gave him the knee. It's quiet, and there's nothing like it for taking the juice out of a guy."

Down on the floor, Bubba was starting to retch. "Get a doctor," he moaned. "I want a doctor."

"You don't need a doctor," Tony said. "That was just a nudge. You wouldn't be talking if I really gave it to you."

Bubba gulped back waves of nausea and stared up at him. All he could see was a blurred figure, tall and straight as the big red 1 that had once lifted proudly beside his name on the Recap sheet of the Charity Pairs. "You ruined me," he moaned.

"What the hell," Tony said. "There wasn't much to ruin." He collected his winnings and walked out with Jake.

15

BEFORE THE START of the Spring Nationals J. B. Rothman, assistant manager of the Xanadu, had had no experience with bridge tournaments. He expected that it would be like any big convention, but in fact it was very different. Ordinarily at a convention people left the meetings with an air of duty done and a holiday earned, and hurried off to play golf and shop and fish and swim and visit night clubs. But when bridge players finished a meeting they hurried off to play more bridge, or at least to talk about it. They talked bridge in the lobby and corridors and restaurants and bedrooms. If you passed two bridge players, one was sure to be saying something like: ". . . I had four diamonds to the queen-ten, and when he led the nine I . . ."

Rothman was a student of human nature, and began trying to figure out the reasons for the way bridge affected those who played it. The game, he decided, had many of the trademarks of a disease. It was rather like malaria with its alternating periods of high fever and relatively normal health. (He assumed that bridge players *did* have periods of normal health, because it seemed improbable that they could survive if they always ran such high temperatures.) It was also possible that, as in the case of malaria, there was some kind of carrier like the anopheles mosquito that transmitted the disease from avid bridge players to healthy individuals.

Certain facts, however, did not fit the disease theory. If bridge was a disease, why didn't some lucky victims develop an immunity to it? And why couldn't it be cured by putting the victims in isolation wards, while their cards and bridge books were burned by doctors wearing antiseptic masks and biteproof clothing? To the best of his knowledge, however, no bridge player had ever developed an immunity or had been cured, nor did any of them seek a cure. This did not fit the picture of a disease. Furthermore, where had the virus of bridge been lurking in the ages before making its first appearance? No, bridge in itself could not be a disease. It must be the symptom of one.

After long and careful observation Rothman decided that bridge was a symptom of that deep-seated human ailment: the urge to blame things on a partner.

Of course the institution of marriage might seem to provide an outlet for this urge, but actually it did so in a most imperfect way. Could a wife blame her husband if a soufflé fell or her child got the flu or she could no longer get into a size twelve dress? It was not impossible, because the human mind was capable of great ingenuity, but it was difficult. In the same way, could a husband blame his wife if his boss snarled at him or That Man in the White House did something unusually idiotic or a two-foot putt failed to drop? Very difficult. In marriage there was also the problem that constant blaming of the partner could break up the marriage, and it was costly in time and money to replace a husband or wife.

Seemingly bridge had none of these defects. As the tournament progressed Rothman overheard many bridge conversations dealing with partners. In the first place, of course, there were no excellent partners. At best, a partner was barely adequate. At worst, the partner was an ogre or witch out of folklore, lurking across the table and waiting for a chance to butcher a hand. The in-between partner merely had spells of insanity. The partner could always be blamed for everything that went wrong. And fortunately, unlike the marriage partner, the bridge partner could easily be replaced if the need arose.

Rothman was pleased with his theory and wanted to test it by questioning the bridge players. His first chance to do so came on Thursday morning.

One of the clerks reported to him, "Suite 300, a Mr. Ensley Worthington, is checking out. He was paying the tournament rate and had it reserved through Sunday night. Shall I put it back on the regular rate?"

"No, no," Rothman said. "We promised four hundred rooms. We'll have a dozen bridge people asking for rooms before evening. Mr. Worthington is leaving early? I'll make sure he isn't dissatisfied with the Xanadu." He went up to the guest who was leaving and said, "I hope you enjoyed your stay with us, Mr. Worthington."

Bubba looked at him suspiciously. It seemed odd that, after the most distressing experience of his life, this hotelman wanted to know if he enjoyed himself. "Very much, thank you," he said stiffly.

Rothman studied the full lips that drooped at the corners, the crew-cut hair that somehow seemed limp, and the yellow-green tinge of Mr. Worthington's skin. The young man hadn't enjoyed something. "I hope you had good partners and won a lot of points?"

There must be a reason for this, Bubba thought. Perhaps some sniggering tale had been spread about the fight, and the hotelman wanted more details. "I had excellent partners," he said coldly. "Thank you for your interest, and goodby."

Very annoying, Rothman thought. Was there, after all, something wrong with his theory?

Bubba walked toward the lobby doorway with head up, a cavalier retiring from a lost field with flying colors. For a moment he felt keen and healthy and virile. But then, unfortunately, he saw Tony. The fellow was lounging against a wall near the doorway, looking like an undertaker in his black suit and white shirt and dark tie. The black sunglasses glittered at Bubba in an evil way and caused a dull ache to creep up through his body. When Bubba examined himself that morning he had found there was still tenderness and swelling left from the attack on him last night. It was slight, but one couldn't be sure what might happen. He would have to consult a doctor and didn't know how to go about it. After all, he couldn't ask Mother. As for Father—he shuddered—Father was a *surgeon*, and surgeons always thought in terms of whipping out a knife, horrible thought.

He walked past Tony trying to hold himself straight and proudly, but aware that he was starting to shuffle and bend over. Perhaps he would recover physically, perhaps as Tony claimed it was merely a nudge, but psychologically he would never get over it. He went through the doorway like an old woman hobbling to market with a basket of slightly cracked eggs.

Tony watched him go and felt relieved, because Bubba had given no sign of intending to make a fuss over what had happened. Tony did not like fights; they could get you in trouble. He especially disliked a fight that grew out of a charge of cheating. He knew that from time to time there had been annoyed comments about him at ACBL meetings, and that he couldn't afford to get involved in any public scandal. Doris kept him informed of things like that. Doris was on the ACBL staff at the headquarters in Greenwich, Connecticut, and went out with him whenever he got up that way. She was unmarried, and at the age when broads were grateful for attention. It took an effort to give her the attention, because she was as plain and solid as a side of beef, but it was worthwhile to have a pipeline into the ACBL office.

He continued lounging near a lobby doorway, keeping track of interesting little events. Waldo Starnes, the Chief Tournament Director, came skipping and hopping through the lobby and carried a briefcase into the office of the hotel manager and later emerged, giggling over some secret joke. The Dukes and Ashcrafts entered the lobby from opposite directions, each wife walking a little ahead of her husband as if she didn't know him or want to know him. Miggsy Ashcraft wore a dress of white ruffles that resembled detergents foaming out of an automatic washer. She saw Hank Duke and gave a squeak of delight and stopped to talk to him, her hands fluttering around his chest in patting motions. Harvey Ashcraft looked at Hank as if studying cards that a partner had overbid. Olga Duke walked up to Harvey, waving her gauze handkerchief like a magician about to produce a rabbit; this was a waste of time, Tony thought, because the rabbit was already standing in front of her. However, her sleight-of-hand was good enough to make a smile materialize on Harvey's face. Something was going on with the Dukes and Ashcrafts. Tony's team would be playing the Duke-Ashcraft team in the afternoon and evening, and he thought maybe it might be easy to take them. At this moment Sammy Rothberg stumbled through the lobby, his eyes like heavy weights in their hammocks of dark flesh. Tony shrugged; there went a quarter of his team, and maybe it wasn't going to be easy to take the Dukes and Ashcrafts after all. What was Runa doing with Sammy: keeping him up too late, or not late enough?

"Hello, you buzzard," a voice said to him.

He turned and saw Katy Edmunds, trailed as usual by that pale thin girl. "Hi, Katy," he said. "Thanks for the contribution last night."

"Don't thank me. That Bubba ought to be back in diapers. Did you have to slug him after I left?"

"Nah. He'd lost enough blood as it was."

"Oh," Katy said in a disappointed tone. "Well anyway, count me out from now on. I'm not going to play innocent bystander and get shot by accident again. I see you meet the Duke-Ashcraft team in the knockout round today. Going to take them?"

"I got my doubts."

"Well, if you lose, how about playing with me in the Mixed Pairs tomorrow?"

"Fifty a session, you pay the entry fees, and if we come in first, second or third I get a bonus of—"

"Just forget that part of it," Katy said cheerily. "You buzzard, you got the bonus from me last night."

Maybe he did owe her something. "All right," he said.

"And Tony, keep my offer of that cruise in mind. I haven't given up on you yet. Well, Vicky and I are going to lunch and play in side games today, and maybe she'll remember that aces take kings. I'll see you later. Come along, Vicky, and kindly stop acting as if I'm leading you in chains."

Tony watched them leave. The thin girl really did drag along as if carrying chains. Stupid kid; what did she expect from Katy? He thought about that round-the-world trip and gave a little shiver, a very unusual reaction for him. It would be a cold day when he joined Katy's chain gang.

He nodded to Jake Jacobs, who came upstairs from the barbershop looking as polished as an apple for teacher. Tony thought: Jake wouldn't play apple for anybody but a broad, and I wonder who she is? He saw P. J. Hoffmeister cross the lobby, staring into the distance, and bump into Ben Aarons, who seemed to be staring into himself. Ben apologized, and Hoffmeister lit up like a juke box and apparently started a sales talk. Ben walked on as if he didn't hear a word, which probably meant he didn't, Ben ordinarily being a very polite character. Ben had a nice lead in the McKenney but the way he acted you might think all his finesses were offside, so what gave with him? He watched a wren-size woman swoop on an old guy like he was birdseed, and chirp at him, "Alfred, how wonderful!" Both of them looked dead enough to blow off the tree in the next breeze, so what could be wonderful in their lives? He saw Carola Clark sweep across the lobby playing First Lady while Babs Hartley strode beside her playing Secret Service agent, very cold and suspicious. He saw Ace McKinley stop and watch the royal procession and frown, and then go mail a fat letter.

Ace turned away from the mail slot and spotted him and came over. "Howdy, son," Ace said boomingly, as if to make himself heard over the noise of a cattle drive. "How's every little thing?"

"This joint is Deadsburg," Tony said.

"Too bad. Me, I just branded a few columns and sent them off to my syndicate. Don't forget, son, I'm counting on you and me taking the Open Pairs so I can brag on us in my column."

"Yeah," Tony said. He wondered how far Ace was willing to go to win the Open Pairs. There was a nice simple system that would do it, if Ace would buy the idea. Of course the guy always acted like your friendly neighborhood bartender, full measure, folks, and no sneaking cheap brands into expensive bottles.

But under the right conditions would he water the stuff a bit? Tony decided to hand his idea to Ace in a plain wrapper, so that if necessary he could pretend he didn't know what was inside. "You asked once if I had any stuff you could use," he said. "Ever thought of writing about cheating at bridge?"

"Whoa there, son. That's dynamite."

"You chicken about handling dynamite?"

"Kinda gives bridge a bad name to write about cheating. I know there's always talk about it at tournaments. You seen any here?"

"Only the usual. The slow pass to tell partner you almost have a bid, the quick one to say you're sitting this one out, stuff like that. Lot of people do it without meaning to cheat. That wasn't what I had in mind."

"You mean like those finger signals they claimed a couple guys used in the World Championships a while back?"

"A finger signal is for squares, account of it's too easy to spot. I ran into a cool system once in a high stake game of rubber bridge. Guys used the corners of the table for signals. One corner meant lead clubs, another meant lead diamonds, another hearts and the fourth corner spades. No pointing or anything stupid like that. Guy who was signaling just looked at one of the corners."

"That's right cute. But if you spotted it you must have caught on. What happened?"

"Yeah, I spotted it. I wait till one guy stares at the club corner and his partner wriggles and don't lead, and I say, Hey, man, no use you staring at that corner because your partner hasn't got a club. They gape at me and I give them a hard look and say, That's a two thousand rubber for us, right? They didn't say a word, just paid up and got out."

"Shoot, what a yarn!"

"Of course," Tony said casually, "they were dopes. Two guys staring at corners of the table all evening and always making the killing lead, it makes you wonder. But I'd hate to run up against that stunt in a big-time tournament where just one guy was signaling his partner. It only takes a little edge to bring a good pair in on top."

"Reckon you're right," Ace said, peering intently at Tony.

"Like, say, the partner giving the signals uses the near left-hand corner for clubs, the far lefthand corner for diamonds, the far righthand corner for hearts and the near righthand corner for spades. The other guy don't give signals, just reads his partner's. And, let's say, the guy reading the signals wears dark glasses so nobody can tell he's watching close when his partner is on lead. It'd work good, wouldn't it, Ace? An edge like that could give a good pair the championship."

Damn those black sunglasses, Ace thought. You couldn't ever figure what Tony had in mind. He swallowed twice, a feeling like gulping broken glass, and said, "I hope you're not hinting at anything."

All right, Tony thought, Ace wasn't buying. "Me?" he said. "We're talking about you writing a column, aren't we?"

"Yeah, sure," Ace said, gulping once more. "Trouble with writing stuff like that is you make some folks suspicious and maybe give other folks ideas. I wouldn't touch it. Well, I got to run. See you at the Open Pairs." He turned and hurried off.

Tony shrugged. That knocked the easy system on the head. Now he'd have to try another idea, one that would be a lot harder to arrange.

He went down to the coffee shop and ate a ham on rye and drank black coffee, and headed upstairs for the first thirty-two boards of the knockout round. He and Jake were playing against the Ashcrafts, while Sammy and Runa took on the Dukes. Just as Tony figured after watching the scene in the lobby, Miggsy and Harvey didn't play very good bridge. They listened pityingly to each other's bids and looked on any card the other led as if it were a mistake the puppy made on the rug. He and Jake should have gobbled the Ashcrafts raw. Funny thing, though; Jake was playing worse than the Ashcrafts. A couple of times Tony even thought Jake threw a hand deliberately.

At the break before dinner Tony said, "I figured we were gonna get knocked out today, but I was betting on Sammy to louse things up. I should have bet on you."

"Aah, it's only a game," Jake said easily.

"When you say bridge is only a game, you got to be working on some broad."

Jake laughed. "Any objections?"

"Not if you're happy," Tony said, and went off as usual to have dinner alone. The guy was paying fifty bucks a session, and that bought him a license to act stupid. Tony didn't understand it. There was more satisfaction in making a tough bid than in making a dame. Lots of hands were real tricky, but the average dame was a laydown.

The woman on Jake's mind was of course Runa, and she was aware of it. During the afternoon session she sat fifty feet away from Jake, facing him, and from time to time saw him staring at her. He seemed to like the way her white jersey pullover kept track of her breathing. She paid more attention to Jake than to the jittery creature who sat opposite her. She was through with Sammy Rothberg now. He had wanted to prove he was a man, and she had proved he wasn't, and that was the end of it. The only man at the table was Hank Duke. She made various casual tries at annoying Hank but without success; apparently Hank had a limited emotional capacity and could only get annoyed with one woman at a time, and his wife had natural advantages in that respect over other women. The Dukes threw bids at each other as if they were kids in a rock fight. It didn't hurt their score, however, because Runa carefully threw away points faster than they did. She wanted to get rid of Sammy as soon as possible.

Sammy knew that everybody was playing bad bridge, including himself, and the knowledge made him try harder and play worse. At the dinner break he went to his room and took aspirin and slumped in a chair. His head felt like a huge bell in which his blood was clanging. There was a bell in London called Big Ben. He didn't know why so many things had to be called Ben: Big

Ben, Ben Aarons, and Benzedrine or bennies. He wondered if he was losing more ground to Ben in the McKenney race; qualifying in the Vanderbilt and then winning their first knockout match was worth some master points, he couldn't recall how many, and Ben hadn't been playing in the Vanderbilt, but Ben had been in side games picking up a point here and a point there. The guy would be playing with Carola Clark in the Mixed Pairs tomorrow and the Open Pairs Saturday and Sunday, and the Ben-Carola combine could be murder. Ben might come out of the tournament with a lead of fifty points or more.

He skipped dinner and took a couple of bennies—that damn name again—and went to the evening session of the knockout round with his head like a balloon instead of a bell. At the very least he had to do something tonight to redeem himself with Runa. At the table he saw that Runa had changed from the white jersey outfit to hostess pajamas in red lamé. They left her forearms bare, and her gold bracelets kept up a steady whispering. He remembered how those bracelets had jingled in the dark last night.

The bennies seemed to be having a queer effect on him. Half the time he felt as if he were floating a foot above the chair, and the rest of the time he weighed a ton and it was a miracle that the chair didn't break. He heard the flick of cards at tables across the ballroom and had to strain to hear bids at his own table. Sometimes the cards blurred and sometimes the pips started growing out of the cards on stalks, very sharply and clearly. He didn't know how he managed to get through the evening, except that tonight Runa made no comments, good or bad, about his play. She acted as if he weren't there.

When the last board had been played he wrapped his tongue and lips carefully around some words, and said, "How do you think we did?"

"Are you kidding?" Runa said.

"Absolutely the worst bridge I've ever seen," Olga said. "We should all be ashamed. But I'm afraid you two handed us gifts faster than we could return them. Of course I don't know how Harvey and Miggsy did against the other half of your team."

Sammy mumbled, "I'll go over and check with them."

Runa yawned and said, "You look awful. You'd better go to bed."

He looked across the table at her, and somehow the big room and other people vanished, and nothing was left in the world but a shimmering creature in red. "You mean," he said thickly, "with you?" Suddenly everything came back into sharp focus, like the way the pips on the cards had grown toward him on stalks, and he saw Hank and Olga and Runa staring at him. No, he thought, he hadn't said it aloud. He couldn't have.

"My God," Runa said. "What makes you think I go to bed with boys?" She got up and left the table.

Hank and Olga gazed at him in disgust. After what had happened recently in their own lives, the subject of going to bed with a person of the opposite sex was painful, and they did not care to hear it mentioned in public. Without a word, they gathered their things and departed.

Sammy sat for a few minutes trying to understand what had occurred and why he had done it. It was hard to think, because now his head was playing another trick on him. His head was no longer a bell or balloon but an empty plain over which the wind howled, blowing away thoughts faster than he could catch them. Finally he rose and walked as if on stilts into the bar and downed a few drinks. A spark of an idea started growing in his head and grew, fanned by the wind, into a big warm blaze. Runa said he was a boy and he really had been acting like one. But now he was going to show her he was a man. He left the bar and went to the fourth floor and felt his way along the corridor walls until he reached her room. This time he wasn't going to knock politely.

He pounded on the door and called loudly, "Runa! open up. It's Sammy." He thought he heard a rustling inside, but she didn't open the door or answer. He pounded again and shouted, "Hey, Runa!"

Two nights earlier his softer knocking had not been heard by the Dukes and Ashcrafts, a few rooms away. Tonight they heard him, and two doors popped open and Harvey Ashcraft and Hank Duke looked out. "You must be drunk," Hank growled. "Why don't you beat it, Sammy?" From the other doorway Harvey complained, "You'll have the house detective up here in a minute if you keep on."

"Shut up," Sammy cried. Hank and Harvey frowned at him and went inside their rooms and closed their doors. Sammy lifted his fist to pound again on Runa's door. As he did so, the door jerked open. Sammy's knock hit emptiness and he staggered forward off balance into the room. A hand gripped the lapels of his jacket and held him up, and he found himself staring into Jake's face. Jake had fine white teeth that he often boasted cost him $1,800 for the recapping job, and that he liked to display in smiles. The teeth were in evidence now but not in a smile. Above Jake's pants his chest was bare and sweaty and ridged with muscles, and scratches cut red lines across it. Light from the corridor washed over the bed where Runa sat, a sheet pulled up to her shoulders.

"You son of a bitch, get out," Jake whispered. He held Sammy with his left hand and slapped him with his right hand. "And if you come back I'll break your goddam neck," Jake growled, and shoved him out through the doorway.

Sammy fell on the floor and heard the door slam shut. He got up painfully and crept back downstairs to his own room. The big warm blaze in his head had been snuffed out by the gale, and he was alone in a screeching void. He staggered into the bathroom and got the bottle of sleeping pills and a glass of water and began taking pills. After a while he couldn't remember whether he had taken any or not, and gulped more of them. Then he went to his bed and stretched out and waited to see what would happen.

Slowly he began to realize that things were going to come out all right. The wind stopped screeching. The sun came out, and it was not an empty plain after all but a gorgeous room with red lamé draperies and with a small gilt chair, like the ones in the ballroom of the Xanadu, set on a dais for him. He sat on the chair, and presently Ben Aarons entered and bowed and placed a large

16

ALFRED JENKS AWOKE at nine o'clock on Friday morning, far past his usual rising time. For a moment he felt guilty, knowing that he would be late for work at The Telephone Company, but at last he remembered that he was retired and lived in Miami instead of Buffalo. Even so, however, a strange feeling of guilt remained. Finally he managed to track down the cause. Good heavens, the birds! He took the sunflower seeds and hurried outside, hoping none of the neighbors would see him in his bathrobe. His favorite cardinal, the one that often pecked at the window in a demand for extra seeds, was perched in the bougainvillea bush uttering complaints, and several other birds were fluttering around anxiously.

"Yes, yes," he told them. "You're all annoyed with me, I know. But it was tiring yesterday afternoon, playing all that bridge, not that it wasn't enjoyable, and then we had dinner and it was late when I got back. There!" He stocked the feeder and returned to the house.

By the time he washed and brought his bowl of cornflakes and milk to the table, quite a show was going on at the feeder. Two cardinals were visiting it, and sparrows were darting in like rude small boys, and the dab of sunlight in a tree was a goldfinch. And yes, there was the painted bunting, an explosion of red and blue and green. It was so lively it reminded him of Mary Rose Rutledge, although of course this was a male painted bunting, the female not being so showy. Down on the lawn a purple grackle walked along looking for bugs, very solemn and intent, like a

man pacing a room with hands clasped behind his back, in fact
like the manager of the Buffalo business office of The Telephone
Company, Mr. Arbuthnot. However, Mr. Arbuthnot had not liked
bugs, and used to say at meetings, "We simply have to get these
bugs out of our operation."

Outside the window, wings buffeted the air and the cardinals
squalled and a pair of blackbirds began their morning raid. Alfred Jenks cranked open the window and rattled the screen and
said sharply, "Go away! Shoo!" The blackbirds cocked their heads
to one side and gave him hard bright stares, and gobbled seeds.
Alfred sighed and gave up. The blackbirds were more than he
could handle.

After breakfast he washed the dishes and made his bed and
cleaned the living room, remembering to use the carpet sweeper
rather than the vacuum cleaner on the rug. Emmy used to say
the constant use of the vacuum cleaner was bad for rugs with a
soft heavy pile. He debated changing the placing of the furniture
but finally decided not to move anything, although he did not like
the arrangement. He was not sure it would look better if he made
changes. Besides, there had been talk about Mary Rose coming to
see his house on Sunday afternoon, and perhaps she would have
ideas about moving the furniture, as women often did. She might
even think that the furniture was not suitable for the Florida
climate and suggest that he get lighter and cooler furniture.

The thought made him frown, and he looked at his blue-plush
overstuffed chair and stroked a shiny spot where the nap was
worn. The one thing he had insisted on, when Emmy made that
adventuresome decision about moving to Florida, was bringing
their furniture from Buffalo. Perhaps the heavy fumed-oak pieces
were too big for the living room, and the overstuffed chairs too
hot, and the blue velvet drapes too dark, but he was used to them.
It was good to have a familiar oasis in this strange garish land. He
certainly hoped Mary Rose wouldn't suggest any changes. She was
an adventuresome person, even more so than Emmy.

He went into the bedroom and studied his three suits. Two had
been for business wear in Buffalo and the other his Sunday suit.

Any of them would be uncomfortably warm on the bus trip to Miami Beach, but the Xanadu was air-conditioned so it would be all right once he reached the hotel. He really must hurry. It was after eleven o'clock. The bus trip would take more than an hour and the afternoon game started at one-thirty. Perhaps he and Mary Rose would come in above average today; yesterday their score had been below average. It was odd that, when he merely watched others play, he knew exactly what to do, whereas when he took part in the game he became confused and uncertain. Mary Rose, of course, doted on the excitements of playing. It was quite stimulating to watch her. She was a charming woman, and he would miss her when the tournament ended and she went back north.

He paused, and his heart began fluttering like wings at the yard feeder. Just suppose that, this afternoon or tomorrow or when she visited his house on Sunday, he said quietly to her, "Mary Rose, do we have to say goodby?"

Or suppose, as was perhaps more likely, *she* said, "Alfred, do we have to say goodby?"

He contemplated that, and found his thoughts becoming as confused and uncertain as they did when he played bridge. He tried to marshal arguments for and against. That was like holding a bridge hand and trying to decide if it should be played at three no trump or four of a major, always very upsetting. He wandered out to the kitchen, leaving the matter of which suit to wear for later consideration, and looked at the telephone on the wall. Miami was served by Southern Bell Telephone Company, a subsidiary of American Telephone & Telegraph Company. It was reassuring to be in territory served by The Telephone Company rather than by one of those independents. Perhaps he should call and leave a message for Mary Rose not to worry if he was slightly delayed in arriving.

He dialed the number, listening with pleasure to the firm efficient clicks. A voice said, "Good morning, the Xanadu Hotel."

"I am calling Mrs. Robert Lee Rutledge," he said.

"Thank you. I will ring her room."

"No, no," he said hastily. Good heavens, he never quite knew what was going to happen when he talked to her; perhaps he would end up calling a taxi and taking her to lunch. "I merely wish to leave a message."

"Thank you, sir. I will take the message."

"Ah, this is Mr. Alfred Jenks."

"Yes, Mr. Jenks?"

Now what was he going to say? He thought for a second, and at that moment his favorite cardinal swooped onto the ledge outside the window and rapped sharply with its beak on the glass. "Yes, yes," he called to the cardinal. "I'll be there right away . . . I'm sorry," he told the girl at the Xanadu, "I was talking to somebody else. Will you tell Mrs. Rutledge that something has come up and Mr. Jenks will be busy the rest of the week?"

"Thank you," the voice said impersonally.

"And . . . and give her my best wishes."

"Thank you," the voice said with finality, and the receiver clicked in his ear.

Alfred Jenks replaced the phone in its wall holder and hurried outside, eager and trembling, to feed the cardinal.

Mary Rose Rutledge received the message from Alfred Jenks at twelve forty-five, when she came up from lunch in the coffee shop. She went to the main desk and peered at the honeycomb of boxes in which room keys were filed and letters placed, and saw an envelope in hers. A letter from Barbara in Baltimore, she told herself happily, and edged along the counter until she got the attention of J. B. Rothman, who was helping out on the desk, this being the busiest time of day.

"I see a letter for me, Room 286," she told him. "And I just know it's good news, maybe my daughter wanting me to visit her in Baltimore. Could you get it for me, please?"

"Certainly, Mrs. Rutledge," he said, giving it to her.

"Mercy me, you remember my name!"

"Indeed I do," he said a bit sadly, thinking of how the auditor was going to find that special rate he gave her, and report it to the manager.

"So nice to be in a friendly hotel," Mary Rose said. "I . . . why, it's a telephone message, not a letter. I wonder who—"

"Telephone, Mr. Rothman," a clerk said, passing the desk phone to him.

"I hope it's good news anyway," Rothman told Mary Rose, and lifted the desk phone and said, "Rothman speaking."

"Housekeeper, Third Floor," a brisk voice said. "Room Three One Zero, a Double-X."

Rothman kept his voice calm. Double-X meant that a guest seemed to be dead in his room. It was a private code used to keep unpleasant things quiet. Single-X was serious illness, Triple-X was suicide and Four-X was murder. He had never, Thank God, heard the Four-X signal. "You've been in there yourself?" he asked.

"Of course. I wouldn't take a chambermaid's word for it."

"I'll be right up," he said, and replaced the phone. Somebody across the desk was trying to catch his attention, and he recalled that it was a Mrs. Rutledge, who was hoping for good news. He wished he could borrow some from her. "I beg your pardon," he said. "I've been called away." He went to the files and riffled the cards until he reached Room 310. Mr. Samuel Rothberg, New York City, Tournament rate. He picked up another phone and called the house doctor and asked him to come to Room Three One Zero at once, a Double-X.

Mary Rose turned away from the desk feeling as if somebody had tied a knot in her throat. Alfred wasn't coming. He wasn't coming today or tomorrow or at all. He was so final about it! Something has come up and Mr. Jenks will be busy the rest of the week. Not ill, not away, just busy. What could Alfred find to keep him busy? Could one of his sons from up north have arrived for an unexpected visit? No. Children might not be faithful about writing letters but at least they would let you know before coming to visit you. She wondered if it could possibly be a woman, perhaps some widow who lived down the street from Alfred. For a moment the idea was annoying, but then the annoyance passed and she hoped it *was* a woman. A nice lively woman. Like, well *yes*, like herself. Alfred did need a woman.

She took a deep breath and packed Alfred carefully away in her memory along with Bobby—that was Robert Lee Rutledge—and all the other nice people who had gone out of her life. She said to herself cheerfully: Mary Rose, go get yourself a partner for this afternoon. She lifted her head and noticed a young man looking at her; in spite of his dark sunglasses she saw his eyes distinctly, and he was definitely studying her with interest. She had played against him in the Charity Pairs, which he won. He was Mr. Tony Manuto, a Life Master. Was he actually considering asking her to be his partner? The eyes behind the glasses flickered and looked away. If he had considered it, he changed his mind. She smiled at him wistfully and went on her way to the Partnership Desk.

Of course Tony had not been considering anything of the sort. He had merely been fascinated by the thought of what you could get away with if you looked like that old bag. You could walk up to the desk and go into a fluttering act and ask for the key to another person's room, and the clerk would give it to you without hesitation and probably wouldn't even remember you afterward. It was going to be harder for him to get away with it but he had to take the chance. At the worst, he could always claim he make a mistake. He walked to the desk, relieved to note that the assistant manager had gone somewhere else. The clerks wouldn't be as alert as the assistant manager.

"Room 340," he said casually. "Key please."

"Yes sir," the clerk said, and got it and slid it across the counter and turned to another guest.

Tony took the key and sauntered away, enjoying the tingle in his body. It felt as good as getting away with a risky pre-empt. Back in the ballroom, Chief Tournament Director Waldo Starnes was starting work on today's event, the Mixed Pairs, and Tony was going up to Waldo's room and start work on Saturday's and Sunday's event, the Open Pairs. The printed sheets of computer-dealt hands for the Open Pairs ought to be in Waldo's room, and an advance look at them would guarantee a win. He knew from careful observation during the tournament that each set of hands came in a large manila ACBL envelope carrying the name of the event in which the hands were to be used. Thus there would be four envelopes for the Open Pairs, two for the qualifying rounds and two for the final rounds. The flap of each envelope was sealed with pressure tape, and each envelope had to be opened in the presence of members of the Tournament Committee.

It would be almost impossible to remove the pressure tape without damaging the flap underneath, and you couldn't steam off pressure tape. However—and this was rather amusing, Tony thought—the envelopes had bottom flaps that were sealed in the course of manufacture, and nobody had thought of reinforcing these with pressure tape. He had experimented with similar envelopes and learned how to steam open the bottom flap. There was a handy gadget for doing this, a nasal inhalator used to treat colds with medicated steam. You plugged it into an electrical outlet. It had a long spout, very convenient for aiming the steam. At the moment the inhalator was steaming away in his bathroom, ready for use. A bottle of quick-acting glue was also ready so that he could reseal the envelopes. He had very little time, no more than half an hour before he had to show up for the Mixed Pairs, and he couldn't afford to waste a minute.

He took the elevator to his own floor, the fifth, so nobody would see him getting off at the third, and then walked down two flights. He passed Suite 300, where he had given Bubba lessons in rubber bridge and in the use of the knee to end a fight, and turned a corner and saw three people clustered around a nearby door: a chambermaid, a housekeeper, the assistant manager. That was no good. He didn't know what they were doing but housekeepers and assistant managers had sharp eyes and long memories. He ducked back around the corner. Fortunately the corridors ran all the way around this wing, and he reversed his route and reached Room 340 from the other direction. This corridor was empty. He unlocked the door and slipped into Waldo's room and put on the safety latch.

No sealed ACBL envelopes were lying on the bed or table or bureau. He opened drawers and checked the contents, discovering nothing but the fact that Waldo liked polka-dot shorts. The closet was the only other possibility. He hoped to find it locked, which would be encouraging and which would not create a problem, since the room key ought to open it, but the door was unlocked. There were no envelopes on the closet shelf. He pulled out Waldo's two suitcases and opened them, and for a moment thought he had scored all the points, because one suitcase was half full of ACBL envelopes. When he picked up the first envelope, however, he knew his top had just turned into a bottom. The envelope had already been opened; it was for an event already held. All the envelopes were for past events, and you could buy a set of the sheets for twenty-five cents downstairs at the Hospitality Center.

He opened one envelope and riffled through the printed sheets just to make sure. They were from the Men's Pairs, held six days ago. Somebody, no doubt Waldo, had gone through one set of the sheets marking down how he would have bid each hand. Tony jammed the sheets irritably back into the envelope. It was absolutely no comfort to him to see that Waldo got all the bids wrong, even when looking at all four hands.

How could a guy as stupid as that, Tony thought, be bright enough to put the unused envelopes in a place, probably the hotel safe, from which they couldn't be borrowed? Tony did not know that he himself had been responsible. A week earlier he had made Waldo suspicious by asking questions about the computer-dealt hands, doing this merely to create a smoke screen around the subject that really interested him, the subject being how badly Ace McKinley needed a big win.

Tony replaced the suitcases and shut the closet door and left the room. Now two ideas had flopped: the hint to Ace McKinley about using the corners of the table for lead signals, and the hope of finding the computer-dealt hands in Waldo's room. He still hadn't run out of ideas, but they got tougher to work out as he neared the bottom of the list. He returned to his room and shut off the steaming inhalator. He looked at his room phone. It would be convenient to make a certain call from here but he didn't want it on his bill. He went downstairs and dropped Waldo's key on the counter and went to a pay telephone booth and called the Greenwich, Connecticut, office of the ACBL. No, it wouldn't be nice to have this charged to his room.

When the call went through he asked to speak to Doris, and presently her firm businesslike voice came on the line. He said, "Hello, kid. This is Tony."

The firm voice went soft and frilly. "Why Tony, how wonderful! Are you calling from New York? I thought you were in Miami at the Nationals."

"I'm in Miami, all right. How's my best girl?"

"I'm fine," Doris said. Then she sighed and added, "But I don't know how your best girl is. What's her name?"

"Come on, kid. Don't I always call you soon as I hit town?"

"Well, you say you do, but . . . oh, it's silly of me to act like this! I'm sorry. How are things going? I saw you won the Charity Pairs."

"Things are lousy. I'm in a jam."

"Oh Tony! That play-for-pay trouble again? I haven't heard any complaints about you lately."

"Nah. I'm not pulling that skull again. The dogmeat wants me, they come to me. This is different. Look. I'm playing in the Open Pairs this weekend with Ace McKinley. And goddam it, like a fool I let a jerk down here needle me into a bet, a few days ago, that he and his partner would wind up higher in the Open Pairs than Ace and me."

"And somebody reported you for making the bet? Tony, you must have seen those notices posted all around, telling people they mustn't bet on any of the matches. The ACBL is getting very strict about that. You see—"

"Hold on, kid. Nobody reported it. What I'm worried about is losing the bet, because it's for a bundle. Ace McKinley is playing bridge like it's pinocle."

"How much did you bet? I could lend you a hundred or so."

He chopped out a laugh. "I'm on the hook for one thousand bucks."

"Tony!"

"Nice round figure, huh?"

"Couldn't you cancel the bet and tell him you simply can't pay?"

"I already get called a lot of nasty names. If they add welsher to them, I'm dead."

"Tony, I'd do just anything to help if I could, but—"

"You can do everything, kid."

"I . . . I can?" She sounded uncertain and troubled, as if suspecting what was coming.

"Yeah. Tip me off about a few of the pre-dealt hands. You have copies in your office."

"Tony! You don't know what you're asking! It's cheating! You could be barred for life, and I could be fired and—"

"Nobody will know," he said gently. "It's not really cheating, either, not as if I wanted all the hands so I could win the thing. This jerk already cheated me, see, needling me into a bet before I knew how badly Ace is playing. So this just evens the score. All I need is about ten hands from the final two rounds. You call me at six tonight and just read the hands over the phone. I don't even copy them down, so there won't be anything on paper to get anybody in trouble. All I do is memorize them as you read them. Just ten hands, that's all."

There was a long pause, and Doris said weakly, "I can't."

"Listen, if I lose this bet, I'll be broke for months. I wouldn't even be able to take you to the automat. If I win the grand, we can have ourselves a time, kid."

Another long pause. "It's no use, Tony. I can't."

He thought about the tone of her voice. Faint, but too goddam firm. Okay, scratch another angle. Now he'd better jam the gears into reverse. "Well," he said, "I guess you're right. I shouldn't have asked, just taken my medicine. Sorry, kid."

"Tony," she said, taking a deep breath, "I ought to do more than just say no. I ought to report this."

Jeez, he thought disgustedly, women and their ideas. They'd wear girdles and uplift bras and God knows what to cheat a guy, and then go honest about doing a little favor like this. "Kid," he said, "I already feel bad about asking you to do it, so what's the good of trying to cut my throat too? Anyway I'd have to say I never made the call. This is a pay phone, so the call can't be traced to me. You report it and they start wondering about you. They want to know how come a girl in the ACBL office let herself get so chummy with a guy like me. Maybe they even wonder if you made it up, to get back at me for something. Lot of angles to watch, kid."

"Tony, you're a son of a bitch!"

"Yeah, but don't forget I'm your son of a bitch. And I already said I wished I hadn't asked you."

She sighed. "All right, Tony. I'll forget it."

"That's my girl. And maybe I'll have luck in the Open Pairs anyway."

"Tony," she said, with the weakness back in her tone, "will I see you when you get up here again? Or will you be mad at me?"

"You're a swell kid. I'll call you first thing."

"All right, Tony. And . . . and good luck."

"See you," he said, and hung up the phone. Believe it or not, he would call her, account of he still needed that pipeline into the ACBL office. It might be nice to find out, after the Open Pairs, if there was any nasty talk about him. All his good ideas for winning had been knocked in the head, so he was going to have to try risky stuff. If people got a hint of what he was doing, they'd start talking. Of course if they really caught him at it they wouldn't stop with talk, and his pipeline into the ACBL wouldn't be of much use, except to let him know what the vote had been on barring him from big-time bridge. He shrugged. For five grand, it was worth taking a serious risk. He put the matter out of his mind temporarily, and headed for the ballroom to play with Katy Edmunds in the Mixed Pairs.

17

WHILE THE AFTERNOON ROUND of the Mixed Pairs was being played, the Dukes and Ashcrafts were playing the first thirty-two boards of a knockout match in the Vanderbilt. The day before, they had survived a knockout match only because three of their opponents—Runa and Sammy and Jake—were thinking of subjects other than bridge. Today they were playing a good Canadian team and the situation was different. The Canadians went to work as if their cards were scalpels, and the Duke-Ashcraft team bled International Match Points all afternoon. When the session ended, the Dukes and Ashcrafts left their tables and approached each other with no more spirit than people opening a tax bill. After a team game in bridge, when a pair has unhappy results to report, it is sometimes difficult to decide what attitude to take. Is it better to hope that the other pair has played brilliantly and won victory for the team (the other pair may be insufferable about this) or to hope that the other pair has done worse? Neither the Dukes nor Ashcrafts could decide which attitude to take, and so for a few moments nobody spoke.

Finally Hank Duke said, "How did you make out, Miggsy?"

Harvey Ashcraft had found the session an uncomfortable experience, like a tight pair of undershorts, and the question irritated him further. "Why do you ask how Miggsy made out?" he said. "I had the impression that I also was playing. Is there some reason for overlooking me?"

"I didn't overlook you," Hank said coldly. "I ignored you."

"Oh please let's not fight," Miggsy said, giving Hank little anxious pats on the chest, and adjusting the collar of his open sports shirt, which allowed a fascinating tuft of black hair to peep above the V neck. "Let's go up and have a drink and be friendly."

"Or anyway," Olga said, "let's go up and have a drink."

They went silently upstairs to the Dukes' room, where Harvey and Olga began preparing drinks. Miggsy stood in front of Hank and stared up at him, like a child staring at its first skyscraper, and said softly, "Will you compare scores with me, Daddy Bear?"

Hank Duke smiled down at her. Daddy Bear. He rather liked that name. Harvey Ashcraft scowled; it was becoming more and more obvious that there was a connection between Miggsy's thing about bears and the bearlike creature named Hank Duke. At the table where she was mixing drinks, Olga Duke bit her lip and put two jiggers of bourbon in Miggsy's glass, it being well known that Miggsy liked three-quarters of a jigger. Then she put half a jigger in her husband's glass, it being well known that Hank liked a jigger and a half.

"I'll be glad to compare scores," Hank said, "but I don't think we're going to like the results."

"Harvey and I were very bad," Miggsy said, "but maybe you pulled us through, do you think?"

"I doubt it. Of course we have another chance at them tonight. Here's my score card."

Miggsy and Hank sat on the bed, and Miggsy began comparing the two private score cards, and cried, "Ooh! How beautifully you played that first board! You actually made a slam, and our opponents didn't get to it. You must have won us eleven IMPs right there. Oh, you play so well!"

"Revolting," Harvey muttered to Olga.

"A child could have made that slam," Olga murmured. "In fact, a child did."

Hank Duke moved closer to Miggsy on the bed, and said, "Well, I did play that rather nicely. And on the next board we should have made a good score, but Olga booted it away."

"He doesn't appreciate you," Harvey said to Olga. "Good heavens, doesn't the man remember you won the Women's Pairs?"

"No," Olga said. "He only remembers what he wins."

"I can't take much of this," Harvey said. "I'll give them their drinks and let's go in the other room."

He took the drinks to Miggsy and Hank, and waited in front of them trying to get their attention. They were bent over the score cards and Miggsy was giggling and Hank was letting out buzzsaw chuckles. Their shoulders rubbed together and Miggsy's soft hair touched Hank's cheek as they peered at a score. It was disgraceful, Harvey thought, to put on such an erotic display right before his eyes. He resisted an urge to pour Hank's drink down inside his sports shirt.

"Here are your drinks," he said stiffly, and shoved the glasses into their hands and joined Olga in the next room.

For several minutes Miggsy and Hank sat together on the bed, checking scores. As experienced bridge players, they had no trouble proving that all bad scores were the fault of their partners and all good scores the result of their own brilliance. This made the checking a pleasant experience.

"Harvey's game has gone all to pot these days," Hank said. "In fact he's gone sour as a person, too. Back when we were bachelors he was such a sweet guy. I took care of him in a lot of ways, back then, because he always seemed so helpless."

"It must be nice," Miggsy sighed, "to have someone take care of you."

"And you're just the sort of sweet kid who needs taking care of," Hank said warmly. "I—" Then he stopped, realizing that he was getting on dangerous ground. He was a strong-principled man who did not approve of making unconventional bids either in bridge or private life. "Hm, well," he said. "Let's check Board Seven. You and Harvey let your opponents make four hearts when they should be held to three. What happened?"

"Oh, Harvey did the most awful thing. His opening lead was the seven of clubs, and I . . . umm . . . let me see."

"I can tell you the hands if you've forgotten."

"No, no, I can remember all the cards, Hank. It's just that I can never picture everything in my head all at once. Let me write down the hands, and look them over." She took paper and pencil from the night table between the beds, and jotted down the holdings on Board Seven. She circled the seven of clubs that Harvey led, and the king of clubs that she played, which held the trick. Then she circled her return lead, a brilliant switch to the jack of diamonds. She studied the hands for a moment. "Oh!" she exclaimed.

"What is it?" Hank asked, leaning over to peer at her notes.

Miggsy moved the paper away so he couldn't see it. She had just discovered something awful: her brilliant switch to the jack of diamonds had given the opponents their extra trick. "I decided not to show you," she said.

"Oh, come on, Miggsy!"

"No. It . . . it wouldn't be fair to Harvey."

"Oh, the hell with Harvey," Hank said, reaching across her for the paper.

"No," Miggsy cried. "No, Daddy Bear. You mustn't! I—"

She leaned away to keep the paper as far from him as possible, and Hank leaned over her to try to reach it, and finally the force of gravity took charge and Miggsy fell backward on the bed with the weight of Hank on top of her. "Oh!" she cried, the exclamation coming out of her like the last plaintive note squeezed from a bagpipe. . . .

In the adjoining room, Harvey and Olga had been discussing two problems, one named Hank and the other Miggsy. After some moments of being very fair in talking about their mates, which made for dull conversation, they relaxed and began treating themselves to a bit of unfairness.

"He was never right for you," Harvey said. "You have very fine sensibilities, and Hank bulldozes them out of his way."

"As for Miggsy," Olga said, "fond as I am of the girl, there are times when she needs a good shaking, and you're just too nice to do it."

Harvey said sadly, "It's been odd, the change in Hank. Back when we were bachelors he was such a sweet guy. But after marrying you he started wanting his own way in everything. Take the way he named our system the Duke-Ashcraft Method. He wanted his name first. Actually our names should have been used in alphabetical order, like Kaplan-Sheinwold and Roth-Stone. But no, he insisted on Duke-Ashcraft."

Olga gave him a long dark smouldering look over the top of her highball glass, and said softly, "Ashcraft-Duke. I like that. You come first with me, Harvey."

"You're a very understanding girl, and if I weren't so loyal to Hank I'd—" Then he stopped, realizing that he was getting on dangerous ground. He was a cautious man who did not approve of extramarital adventures or the Gambling Three No Trump. "Hm, well," he said. "Shall I freshen our drinks, Olga? They—"

At this moment, through the open door into the next room, came the little scream from Miggsy as she discovered that she rather than Harvey had booted Board Seven.

All week, in Harvey's mind, a suspicion had been growing like crabgrass on a neat suburban lawn. "What's that!" he whispered. "Did Miggsy scream?"

"More of a gasp, I think," Olga said, frowning.

"Maybe that's worse," Harvey said, moving toward the doorway. He missed hearing the next two remarks from the adjoining room, reaching the doorway as Hank said, "Oh, come on, Miggsy!"

Harvey winced.

In the next room, his wife said, "No. It . . . it wouldn't be fair to Harvey."

Harvey thought in mounting horror: *What wouldn't be fair?*

Hank's voice said firmly, "Oh, the hell with Harvey."

Harvey gulped.

His wife cried, "No. No, Daddy Bear. You mustn't! I—"

There was a moment of silence that might suitably have been called pregnant. To Harvey it was not a moment but endless time in which he stood frozen while unthinkable acts took place beyond the open door. Finally he heard the faint "Oh!" that was squeezed from Miggsy like the last plaintive note from a bagpipe.

The sound flipped a switch from Off to On in Harvey's body. "God!" he cried, and rushed into the next room. What he saw was, in general terms, no worse than he expected, but in details it was far worse, because his imagination was not accustomed to dealing with subjects more lurid than the tables of probability in bridge. He saw such awful things as his wife's limp white outflung arm, and her legs dangling like those of a rag doll over the side of the bed. All the rest of her body lay smothered and hidden and crushed under a huge male beast.

"You beast!" Harvey cried, grabbing one big shoulder and tugging at it. "Get up!"

All this came as a shock to Hank Duke. He had merely fallen clumsily over Miggsy, while trying to reach the paper on which she had marked the hands of Board Seven, but he had a normal earthy male imagination and knew immediately how things must look. At the tug of Harvey's hand, Hank exploded up and off the bed, twisting around as he did so, rather like a reversed film of a diver doing a half gainer. In a way his explosive action was unfortunate, because it gave Harvey the idea that he had jerked Hank up from the bed one-handed. He had not realized he was so enormously strong. His body tingled to an electric surge of adrenalin and his muscles felt as if they were ballooning to great size and he pushed Hank back against the wall, which was easy to do because Hank was off-balance and not expecting it.

"You beast!" Harvey cried, realizing that he was repeating himself but being unable to think of a better word. "I'm going to take you apart."

Hank's body tingled to an electric surge of adrenalin and his muscles felt as if they were ballooning to great size, and in his case his muscles were not giving him courage under false pretenses. His muscles really were large. His arms and shoulders and body made a slight twitch, and suddenly, horrifyingly, Harvey found himself swung around and pinned against the wall. One big hand gripped his shoulder and the other hand drew back and clenched into a fist that looked like a basketball. The fist was obviously going to smash into his face. The adrenalin gurgled out of Harvey like water from a bathtub. He looked at the fist and uttered a weak "Oh," like the last plaintive note squeezed from a bagpipe, and melted down onto the floor. It was a fine defensive action. As Harvey sagged, the fist whooshed over his head, disarranging one lock of his pale silky thinning hair and then hitting the wall. This happened so quickly and with such exquisite timing that nobody realized Harvey had not been hit, least of all Harvey, who had fainted.

Harvey groped his way slowly back to life, testing it on the way to see if he could endure it, like a bather trying out cold water. Oddly enough, life seemed not only bearable but even pleasant. He did not hurt anywhere. He was comfortable and the air was filled with soothing sounds. He opened his eyes cautiously and found that his head was cradled against Olga's chest, that Hank was touching his face gently, and that Miggsy was patting any part of him she could reach.

"Speak to me, Harvey," Hank pleaded. "Is anything broken? God, I'll never forgive myself, the best friend I have, the sweetest guy in the world, and I have to slug him. Harvey, can you ever forgive me?"

"You poor poor Harvey," Olga murmured. "Just lie there quietly and let Olga smooth away the bad old hurt."

"Are . . . are you going to live?" Miggsy asked mournfully.

"Yes, I think so," Harvey said. It felt luxurious to lie there being stroked and petted. It was wonderful to have good old Hank, the sweetest guy in the world, take care of him the way Hank used to in their bachelor days. It was exciting to have his head cradled against Olga's chest, which although thin felt as alive and vibrant as a violin playing a gypsy tune. Good heavens, he thought, noting his physical reaction to Olga's nearness, perhaps the thinning of his hair *was* a sign of virility, after all.

Hank said, "I can't find any lumps on your head. I don't under-stand it, because I hit you awfully hard."

Miggsy said, "Your poor hand is all swollen and bleeding, Hank." She took his right hand and snuggled it against her soft plump bosom.

"A mere nothing," Hank muttered, but did not pull his hand away. Good Lord, he thought, noting his physical reaction to the touch of Miggsy's breasts, Harvey had not been far off in his sus-picions.

Harvey said, "My head must be surprisingly hard. I don't even have a headache."

"That's wonderful, Harvey old boy," Hank said. "And I want you to know it was all a misunderstanding. Miggsy and I were comparing scores, and she wrote out the hands on Board Seven and suddenly decided not to show me how you two played it, and—"

"I didn't want him to see," Miggsy said sadly, "because I found that I made the mistake, not Harvey."

"So I was leaning over her trying to grab the paper," Hank said, "and I lost my balance and fell. And that's when you came in. So it was all completely innocent and there's nothing more between Miggsy and me than between you and Olga. Does that clear things up?"

Harvey paused thoughtfully before answering, and during the pause noted a change in the vibrations reaching his ear from Olga's chest. It was as if the violinist had switched from bowing his instru-ment to plucking the strings in pizzicato. At the same time Hank noted that his bruised right hand, snuggled against Miggsy's breasts, rose and fell several times like a skiff riding ocean waves.

"I have sometimes thought," Harvey said, slowly and carefully, "that all the trouble we four experience has come from a failure to arrange our partnerships correctly." Under his ear, a couple of violin strings seemed to snap; in front of him, Hank's face turned as red as a holding of thirteen hearts. "Naturally," Harvey said even more slowly and carefully, "I refer only to our partnerships in bridge."

"Naturally," Hank said solemnly. "And speaking of partner-ships, Harvey, would you like it better if we changed the name of our system to the Ashcraft-Duke Method?"

"That is not necessary," Harvey said. "I will be proud to play the Duke-Ashcraft Method . . . with Olga."

"Oh my goodness!" Miggsy cried. "You mean I can play to-night with Hank? And that you and Olga will play as partners? Oh what fun! And if things go well, we can go on as partners?"

"We are of course speaking just of bridge," Harvey said.

"We are?" Miggsy said.

"Naturally," Harvey said, listening to the violins of a full sym-phony orchestra playing beneath his ear, and smiling.

What happened that night, in the second half of the knockout match against the Canadians, became a legend in bridge. The Duke-Ashcraft team was down by fifty International Match Points, an almost hopeless position with only thirty-two boards to play. The Canadians shrugged when they saw that Miggsy Ash-craft was playing with Hank Duke, and Olga with Harvey; obvi-ously the switch to untested partnerships was an act of despair. It turned out, however, to be an act of genius. Hank Duke played even more aggressively than usual, now that he did not have to worry about a partner who was also aggressive. He waded into his opponents like an armored knight swinging a mace, while be-hind him Miggsy came skipping like a gay young squire, dispatch-ing the fallen with a dagger. Harvey Ashcraft played an even finer defensive game than usual, now that he did not have to worry about an overly defensive partner. He held off opponents with Fabian skill, while from the protection of his defenses Olga swooped out in deadly raids. The Canadians first lost twenty In-ternational Match Points and their confidence. Then they lost twenty points and their tempers. Then they lost twenty points and their lead. Finally it was no longer a game of bridge but simply hot-blooded joyous massacre.

Commentators were later to describe the Duke-Ashcraft play that evening as perhaps the finest bridge ever seen at a Nationals. They agreed it was superior to the play by which in following matches the Duke-Ashcraft team went on to win the Vanderbilt, and even to play by which in future years the Dukes and Ashcrafts took many more team championships. Commentators often pointed out, in future years, that Hank and Harvey were lucky to have found such perfect partners as Miggsy Duke (the former Miggsy Ashcraft) and Olga Ashcraft (the former Olga Duke).

18

ON FRIDAY NIGHT, while the Dukes and Ashcrafts tried out new partnerships in the Vanderbilt, the final session of the Mixed Pairs took place. Experts often refer to this event as the Mixed-Up Pairs, because of the odd results both in scoring and human relations that can happen when men and women play as partners. A good mixed pair may be very good indeed, but a few mistakes may cause a mixed pair to go to pieces rapidly. This is because the sex element is present. It is frequently impossible for a man to criticize a woman's bidding or play without also making her feel that he detests her hairdo, clothes and figure. A woman's criticism of a man's bidding or play may be taken as a slur on his virility. Such reactions do not produce fine bridge.

On Friday night, however, half a dozen mixed pairs avoided these problems and played well. Among them were Katy Edmunds and Tony Manuto, who were going to come in sixth overall, Runa and Jake Jacobs, who were going to be fourth overall, and Carola Clark and Ben Aarons, who were about to become the Mixed Pairs Champions. As the last card was played, Katy reached across the table and patted Tony's cheek and said, clanging her fire-gong laugh, "Nice going, you bum." Runa Montez gave her body a little ecstatic shake, which set her thin gold bracelets to chiming, and said, "Maybe I'll keep you a while longer, Jake." The tinkle of her bracelets and purr of her voice set up quivers of anticipation in her partner. Carola reached across the table to touch Ben's hand, and said, "I think we won it, Ben. A few more like this, and you'll have the McKenney nailed down." Ben's solemn face almost pro-

duced a smile, and he felt a glow of pleasure that temporarily
wiped out a thought that had nagged him all day: *Where was
Sammy Rothberg keeping himself?* Sitting beside the table, where
she had been kibitzing all evening, Vicky Summers tensed at the
sight of Carola's slim fingers touching Ben's hand.

At that moment the public address system began its warm-up
procedure, clacking and hissing like a flock of geese, and produced
the voice of the president of the American Contract Bridge League.
"Ladies and gentlemen," he said, "may I have your attention for
a minute? I have been called on to make a sad announcement.
Your attention, please."

The reference to a sad announcement silenced the crowd more
quickly than is usual at a bridge tournament. Several dozen people
wriggled uneasily in their chairs, wondering if they had been reported for making slow passes to tell their partners they almost had
a bid, and a surprising number of people had a momentary and
horrifying and illogical thought that the ACBL was going to announce it had run out of master points.

"I regret to inform you," the voice said, "that one of our finest
young players died here today as the result of an overdose of
sleeping pills. It was of course an accident. I have delayed making
the announcement until the end of this session so that the news
would not, as it well might, affect the play of some contestants."

Among those listening in the ballroom, many nodded their heads
in approval: *Very thoughtful of the president.* An equal number
shrugged: *So who was going to let it spoil a bridge game?*

"In fact," the president said, "no announcement at all would
ordinarily have been made. But because of the prominence of our
departed friend in the world of bridge, the officers of the ACBL
agree with me that the announcement should be made. We have
decided that the Open Pairs Championship tomorrow and Sunday will be held in honor of a fine young player who came here to
the Spring Nationals tied for the lead in the McKenney race. I
deeply regret to announce the passing of Mr. Samuel Rothberg
of New York City."

In the hum and clatter that followed the announcement several noises went generally unremarked. One was a sharp clinking of bracelets as Runa jerked her hand up to her mouth. Another was a crack as a pencil broke in Jake's fingers. Then Jake set his jaw and stared across the table at Runa, and shook his head warningly. Runa took a deep breath and let it out slowly, and shrugged. And so Jake and Runa, the last two people to see Sammy alive, faced an unpleasant test with courage and came through it unscathed.

At the north position at Table 1 Section 1 the noise was a crash as Ben Aarons jumped up and knocked over his chair. Behind the black-framed glasses his eyes looked like erasures on a score card. He stood there opening and closing his mouth soundlessly for a few moments, tall and gawky, like a heron trying to swallow an oversize fish. The three players at the table and the six kibitzers stared up at him silently, willing him to get the words out but shrinking from the thought of hearing them. Ben was not aware of their presence. Finally he managed to force a sound from his throat. "Sammy," he said in a flat toneless heron croak. "Sammy." He turned and started out through the ballroom, bumping into chairs and tripping over feet and walking blindly into people.

"Oh my God," Carola cried, jumping up. "I've got to go after him! Heaven knows what he might do."

A hand gripped her arm with surprising strength and a voice said, "No. I'll take care of this."

Carola stared at the speaker. There were always kibitzers at any table where she played, and tonight Babs and several friends and several strangers had been watching. This was one of the strangers. During the evening Carola had become casually aware of her presence, noting that some thin plain girl was sitting near Ben, forever blinking and forever disarranging her hair with frantic little clutchings and rumplings. "Who on earth are you?" Carola said.

"I'm nobody," Vicky said. "But I can take care of this." She did not recognize herself in what she was doing and saying. All she knew was that she and not this cool lovely perfect woman was going after Ben.

Carola said uncertainly, "You know Ben? You know what's happened?"

"Of course I do," Vicky said. "I will handle it. Please wait here." She walked away from the table, head up, thin shoulders squared, leaving behind such an impression of authority and confidence that Carola said helplessly, "Oh well," and sat down, which she would not have done if she had known that never before in the twenty-nine years of her life had Vicky Summers acted with authority and confidence.

Vicky did not catch up to Ben in the ballroom. People were standing up and moving around, and Vicky was not the sort of person for whom people made room. Ordinarily it would have taken her five minutes to reach the doorway, because she would have stood patiently on one foot waiting for people to move aside. Tonight she tapped people on the shoulder and said briskly "Pardon me" and even elbowed past them when they did not give way. She did not take time to analyze the strange and icy creature who had taken charge of her mind. There was nothing in her thoughts but the tall young man who caromed through the crowd ahead of her. She reached the doorway of the ballroom as Ben was walking out onto the beachfront patio. She caught him on the far side of the patio, where he had paused to stare blindly at the ocean. He was swinging a fist slowly and methodically into the trunk of a coconut palm.

She grabbed his arm and said sharply, "Don't be stupid. Stop that!"

He stared down at her, his head tilting from one side to the other to get her into focus. "You're, uh, Vicky," he said at last. "Get the hell away from me."

"I don't intend to. I want to talk to you."

"I don't want sympathy."

"I didn't come to give you sympathy. What makes you think you deserve any?"

He grabbed her arms and sunk his fingers into them. "Damn right I don't," he said hoarsely. "You know why I don't? Because

I killed Sammy. I killed him, goddam it! Anybody deserves sympathy he's the guy only he's dead. You understand? Dead!"

Under any normal circumstances she would have cried out from the hurt of his fingers, but now she gave herself an impatient shake and broke his grip and said, "Don't be such an idiot."

"Who's an idiot?" he shouted. "We were partners, see? From way back in college. I'm tied with him in the McKenney, see? Only that's not good enough. I got to be first. So I gave him the knife and bust the partnership. It's called psyching a guy, but it turns out like murder. I start beating him and he gets rattled and starts on the pill deal and gets more rattled and takes more pills and now I really got him licked, don't I? I got the lead in the McKenney, right? Sammy isn't coming out of any coffin to louse me up, right?"

"Don't give yourself so much credit," Vicky said. "What makes you think you control other people's lives? You can't even run your own very well. And stop grabbing my arms. You're getting blood from your silly hand on my dress."

He looked at his right fist and saw the torn knuckles, and lifted the fist and licked it. "How did I do that?" he muttered.

"Hitting the tree with it. I can't afford to throw dresses away, so please stop acting so ridiculous."

This stupid annoying girl was messing up his thoughts; he wanted to think about Sammy, but she kept making remarks that distracted him. Like that remark about not running his own life very well. He growled, "What do you mean, I can't even run my own life very well?"

"Well for one thing," she said with great seriousness, "you don't eat properly or you wouldn't be so thin."

He shook his head to get rid of a dizzy feeling. Maybe he was going crazy. He wanted to try himself on a charge of manslaughter but instead found himself accused of not eating properly. "Anything else?" he said, trying not to shout at her.

"Of course. Among other things you don't take care of your clothes. I noticed way back in Boston that you had lost a button from the sleeve of your jacket. Well, you're still wearing the same suit and the same button is still missing."

He peered down at her through the black-framed glasses, tilting his head from side to side again. She was in focus now. She was thin, plain and unbelievable. "A button is missing, big deal," he said. "What of it?"

"It ought to be replaced."

"Great. I'll ask the first person I meet to sew one on."

"You could ask me," she said briskly. "I have a needle and thread in my handbag. And I have a little packet of men's buttons in black, gray and brown, in four sizes."

"You . . . you always carry them around?"

"Ever since Boston, when I saw you were missing one."

He said helplessly, "You can't be for real." He didn't expect any results from the remark—nothing else he said had got through to her—but for some reason this did.

"You think I'm not for real?" she said, her eyelashes fluttering like trapped moths. "Well of course you're right. They don't make real girls like me. Real girls are bright and attractive and don't make fools of themselves the way I always do." She was losing the odd assurance that had carried her from the bridge table out to the patio and through the last few minutes. Her knees were starting to tremble, and her words came out in little roller-coaster swoops. "Imagine carrying buttons all the way here hoping I could sew one on for you," she chattered. "Of course I'm not real. I'm just a bad dream. Or maybe a quick dull one. I don't know what got into me these last few minutes. I wanted so awfully to help you and all I can think of is sewing on a button. Oh, I wish I were dead. I—" She tried to go on talking but the words came out like squeaks from a rusty hinge, and she began to cry.

"Now, now," Ben muttered. "Now, now." He put an arm around her thin shoulders.

At first it was awkward holding her, because they both seemed to be composed of angles and knobs that refused to fit, but as time went on the angles and knobs smoothed out, and he began experimenting with words that fit the situation better than "Now, now."

The cleverest thing he found to say was that he really would like to have the button sewed onto the sleeve of his jacket. That cheered her up, and in some odd way cheered him up. And so, in talk of buttons and other important subjects, the thought of Sammy Rothberg retreated to the back of Ben's mind. It would always remain there, but it was already starting to become a small sad ghost out of the past. Later that evening Vicky sewed on his button, and proved herself quite good at mending things.

19

ON SATURDAY, in the qualifying rounds of the Open Pairs, Ace McKinley became very unhappy. It was not unusual for him to feel that way at the bridge table, because in recent years his game had been erratic and his scores disappointing. This time, however, he was unhappy for another reason. In spite of playing his usual erratic game he and Tony were getting tremendous scores. It did not make sense. Not unless . . . unless . . .

His thoughts kept going back to that cheating story Tony had told him a few days ago. He hadn't liked the sound of that story when he heard it, but when he asked if Tony was hinting at anything, Tony had said they were just talking about stories Ace might use in his newspaper column, weren't they?

It took a partner to help Tony cheat with signals, if indeed cheating was taking place. He was Tony's partner. I am not cheating, he told himself nervously. That story of Tony's did *not* work on my mind, so that I'm unconsciously giving those corner-of-the-table signals. Tony isn't a hypnotist. And he can't read my mind, he couldn't possibly count on that story affecting my actions at the table. I want him to lead a club now, because I can trump it, and I am *absolutely not* staring at the near lefthand corner of the table.

Across the table, Tony led a club.

Ace thought miserably: I didn't really stare at that corner, did I? Couldn't it just be that Tony figured out the right lead all by himself? Ace trumped the club to set the contract and rack up another good board. Right now a bad board would have made him happier.

At the end of the afternoon session he tried to see if Tony would admit anything. "We had a real big game, don't you reckon?" he asked.

"Yeah," Tony said. "We made the scene."

"You're getting off some sweet leads."

"Why not?" Tony said.

That wasn't very revealing, Ace thought. He said carefully, "You seem to be reading my signals real good." Tony might say, "Yeah, I'm glad you got the word about working those corners." Or Tony might say, "What signals?" The second answer would be as much a giveaway as the first answer, because there were legal methods of calling for leads, and any honest player would assume they were talking about the legal ones. Ace waited for the guy's reaction.

"I got eyes," Tony said. "Why wouldn't I read your signals?"

Tony walked away to have one of his lonely meals, and Ace went to the bar to see if a couple of drinks would make him feel better. The more he thought about it, the less he liked Tony's reply. It could be taken in two ways, and he didn't care for one of them. He decided to control his actions rigidly that evening and to look only at his own cards.

Unfortunately that turned out to be impossible. When he tried to stare at his cards his eyes got as twitchy as if someone were poking a needle at them. He rubbed them, and blinked, and squeezed them shut, but they kept acting like eggs frying in a hot pan. His eyes wanted to look at corners of the table. They were going to do it anyway so at last he gave up and let his eyes play their guilty games. Maybe, he thought miserably, he really wanted to cheat. In any case he was almost certain that cheating was going on. Two bits of evidence pointed to it. One was the remarkable score they were making. The other was the way Tony behaved. Ordinarily Tony sat at a bridge table like a carved idol with empty eye sockets, moving only to play a card. Tonight, however, Tony squirmed, and got up and stretched, and made frequent trips to the refreshment table for orange juice. Perhaps Tony was jittery over cheating.

In the next section of the Open Pairs Katy Edmunds was playing with Vicky Summers, and Katy could have explained that cheating did not make Tony nervous. She had played enough with Tony to know that he had no more nerves than a loaded pair of dice. Thus she was very interested in the fact that she saw Tony making so many trips for refreshments. There had to be a reason for the trips other than orange juice; if Tony was hooked on orange juice then she, Katy Edmunds, was going to be elected Miss America. She spent a lot of time watching him because it amused her more than events at her own table. Vicky was a disappointing partner today. Not only was the girl playing better than usual but also she refused to get upset. The sharpest remark merely brought a faint smile to the girl's face, very dull of her.

I think, Katy told herself as she watched Tony's fourth trip to the orange juice fountain, he's doing it to get a peek at boards he hasn't played yet. A bit reckless of you, isn't it, Tony, even with those dark glasses? Somebody might get suspicious and warn the director.

She smiled at the thought, and waited for a chance to test her theory. Two trips later, Tony's course through the tables started to bring him close to Katy's chair. Katy, sitting East, had just finished making a little slam in hearts. "Probably a good board for us," she said loudly, spreading out her hand. "A lot of East-Wests won't be in it, although the slam can't lose unless South leads away from his diamond king." The North-South pair at her table growled at her for talking loudly, and a shadow flitted across the table as Tony went by. Katy didn't look at him; what was the use? Nobody could tell whether, behind those dark glasses, Tony peeked at her cards. That is, nobody could tell by watching Tony. But if you really knew him, you knew Tony had peeked. Also there had been a tiny break in his step, a slight hesitation as he passed the table. Katy gave a pleased wriggle and memorized the board number, sixteen, so that she could check it when the scores were posted.

Some time later Board Sixteen reached Tony and Ace McKinley. The East-West pair bid a little slam in hearts. They were missing the ace and king of diamonds but that was not evident from their bidding, because East had cue-bid diamonds on the way to the slam for the sole purpose of heading off a diamond lead. Ace McKinley knew the opponents lacked the ace of diamonds because, sitting North, he was looking at it in his hand. He did not, however, have the opening lead. He sat waiting for Tony's lead against the slam, ordering himself not to stare at the far lefthand corner of the table. Tony waited for a few moments, and led a low diamond. Ace McKinley took the trick. It was probably useless to return a diamond, because Tony would not have risked the underlead of a king, but no other return looked promising so Ace led back a diamond. The king came from Tony's hand, and the slam went down.

At the end of the session Ace got up, shaking, and went to the bar for a drink, knowing that he and Tony had qualified very high, maybe top overall, and that they had done it by cheating. The Recap sheets were posted at 12:45 a.m. but Ace could not force himself to go up immediately to see how they had done. By the time he approached the sheet for his section, the crowd was thinning. One of those leaving was Katy Edmunds. She looked pleased, having just learned that on Board Sixteen Tony and Ace set the little slam in hearts and earned a top.

Somebody touched Ace's arm, and he looked at the cool slender woman who for so many years had sat across from him at bridge and breakfast tables. "Howdy, Carola," he said. "You make out good?"

"Ben and I didn't qualify," she said. "That news about poor Sammy upset Ben. Actually he took it better than I expected, but his mind wasn't on the game today. How about you and Tony?"

"Haven't looked yet," Ace said.

"I'll take a peek," Carola said, going up to the Recap sheet. Then she turned and gave him one of her rare smiles. "Oh Ace!"

she cried. "You're top overall! You and Tony have the best carry-over into the finals!"

"Great," Ace muttered.

"You act as if it were a bottom."

Ace took a breath of air that felt like ground glass blown into his lungs. He had to talk to somebody about his problem. In one way Carola was the last person he would have picked; what man wanted to look bad in front of an ex-wife? On the other hand she was smart, and might still like him enough to try to help, and she was on the Tournament Committee. He drew her aside and said grimly, "The trouble is, I think we did it by cheating."

"Oh, Ace!"

She must still like him, he thought, because in the course of one minute she had first smiled and now looked ready to cry. For Carola, that was a hurricane of emotions. If she hadn't been deeply stirred she would merely have looked faintly interested. "Can we sit down somewhere and talk it over?" he said. "I need help." They went to a table in a corner and Ace told her the anecdote about the two guys who used the lead signals, and about the perfect leads Tony had been making.

Carola said, "But why would Tony suggest cheating to you? He'd be taking an awful risk. Couldn't he have told you the story just for the obvious reason, for use in your column? What would make the risk worthwhile to him?"

"It's called money."

"How much are you paying him?"

When he started talking to Carola he hadn't realized it might go this far. He hadn't figured on broadcasting the bad news about his column and lecture dates and all that. "Fifty a session, and entry fees," he said, hoping that would head off the questions. It didn't, though. Carola had a mind like a computer, and only needed an instant to compare the risk for Tony against fifty bucks a session, and get the answer.

"Tony wouldn't take a chance for fifty a session. That's his regular price. What else is he working for?"

Here it goes, Ace thought. That champion cowhand, Ace Mc-Kinley, is about to fall off his horse. "Five thousand bucks if we win it," he said.

"You offered that creature *five thousand dollars?*"

"I didn't make the offer, but shoot, it amounts to the same thing. He set the price and I agreed to it. Carola, I couldn't get anybody but Tony to play with me. It's not a secret that I haven't won in a long time."

"But Ace, if you'd only asked me to play!"

He levered a grin onto his face, and said, "I hinted about it, early in the tournament, but the idea went over like a bouquet of cactus."

"Oh, yes, I remember. I didn't know how serious you were, and I hesitated, and then it slipped my mind. But let's get back to why you agreed to pay that much money if you won. Why would it be worth that to you?"

He wondered if he could make a better last stand than Custer did against the Sioux. "I wanted to show everybody I could still win a big one."

"That can't be the whole story. What's the rest of it?"

"I'd rather not go into it."

"Do you want me to start guessing?"

"Oh, shoot," he said, giving up the struggle. "Well, the truth is I'm not getting the lecture dates I used to. Papers are dropping my column, and the syndicate is unhappy. I need a big win. In this racket, when you stop winning you're in about as much demand as a deck of fifty-one cards. A while back I told you I made sixty-seven thousand bucks last year. That's a laugh. It was closer to thirty. Not bad for some guys, maybe, but you know me. Ace McKinley likes a fresh horse every day and a new saddle the moment he gets sweat on the old one."

"You idiot," she wailed. "I asked you if we shouldn't cut that alimony, and you offered to make it more."

"Us top cowhands got to do right by our gals."

"All right, we'll take that up later. Now let's see where we are. You think your score is due to cheating. We have a motive for

Tony cheating, and a motive for you. Right now we can't prove whether or not Tony cheated. But we can prove you didn't."

"Can we?"

"Certainly we can!"

He shook his head slowly. "No ma'am," he said. "I can't prove that. I wanted to win this real bad. One hunk of my mind could be robbing the bank and another hunk could be swearing I'm ten miles away attending church. So that's the problem. What do I do about it?"

"You don't make it easy for yourself, do you? Or for me."

"I tried riding easy and got bucked off."

Carola sighed. "All right, we'd better start by talking to Waldo. After all, he's chief director. He'll have to know."

They located Waldo in the bar, where he sat in a dark corner in the hope that nobody would find him and complain about the scoring, and gave him the full story. Waldo listened with great interest, bouncing up and down in his chair and uttering squeaks that might mean horror or glee.

"Oh how fantastic!" he cried finally. "How amazing! Oh how brave of you to tell me about it, Ace!"

"Brave, hell," Ace said. "I call it scared."

"I've never had such a remarkable problem," Waldo said. "For one thing, there's no real proof."

"Except how I feel."

"I could suggest that you withdraw from the Open Pairs," Waldo said. "I could move up the highest pair of nonqualifiers."

"That's ridiculous," Carola said. "It's an admission of guilt."

"I merely said I *could* suggest, I didn't actually make the suggestion. I wanted to get your reaction. What I really think is that we need an observer tomorrow afternoon to watch how Ace and Tony play. If nothing turns up, we forget the whole matter. If anything does turn up, the observer can signal to Ace at the end of the afternoon session, and Ace can say he's ill and can't play the evening session. That would head off gossip, and I could put in a substitute pair for the last session. Of course if anything turns up, we can't stop with a withdrawal and a substitution. The Tournament Committee would have to hear the case. You're on the Committee, Carola. How does that plan sound to you?"

"I'll go along with it," Carola said. "Who do we get as an observer?"

Waldo bounced four times in his chair. "You," he said happily.

"Me? You're actually asking me to spy on Ace?"

Waldo wrapped his arms around his elfin body and gave himself a hug. "It's not spying when Ace knows you're doing it," he argued. "Furthermore, it keeps the scandal all in the family, so to speak. Oh isn't that *good,* all in the family, ex-husband and ex-wife? If we bring in anybody else, the story gets more circulation, and I do think this should be kept as quiet as possible. Also, Carola, your presence as a kibitzer won't cause talk, at least not the kind of talk we're worried about. You failed to qualify for the finals. Isn't it natural for you to skip the consolation game in favor of watching your former husband? He'll have a gallery anyway, being in the lead. Oh, I think this will work out beautifully!"

"I detest the idea," Carola said. "What do you think, Ace?"

"I'll buy it."

"Ace, I'd have to report anything wrong that I saw."

"Good. I don't want favors."

Carola got up slowly and said, "All right. I'll be there tomorrow afternoon. Thanks, Waldo. Good night." She walked away as if the floor were glare ice.

"Sorry to cause so much trouble," Ace muttered, and left.

Waldo shivered with delight. How fabulous, he thought. How exhilarating! He took a note from his pocket and studied it again. The note said: "I wish to report Mr. Tony Manuto for unethical actions. During the afternoon and evening sessions of the Open Pairs he made many trips through the room, each time passing tables where boards that he had not yet seen were in play. In particular, during the evening session, he walked past my table and looked at my cards, which I had just spread after playing Board Sixteen. Later, when I checked the Recap sheet, I saw he made a top on Board Sixteen. While this is not absolute proof of cheating,

I feel obligated to report it." The note was signed: Mrs. W. B. Edmunds.

Lovely, lovely, lovely, Waldo thought. Mrs. Edmunds also had failed to qualify for the finals. Would it not be pleasant to ask Mrs. Edmunds to join the kibitzers at the McKinley-Manuto table? Yes, very pleasant. Mrs. Edmunds wanted, for unknown reasons, to get Tony in trouble. Carola wanted, for obvious reasons, to keep Ace out of trouble. So two pairs of very sharp and hostile eyes would be watching Tony in the finals of the Open Pairs. How super!

Carola went to her room and splashed cold water on her face, which felt like a Halloween mask. She took off her dress and sat in front of the mirror and began brushing her hair. Why, she thought angrily, hadn't she agreed to play with Ace when he suggested it early in the tournament? Or why, at least, hadn't she telephoned his syndicate to check on her suspicion that he wasn't doing very well lately? She remembered figuring out several reasons against making the call but they all boiled down to one: it was easier to do nothing.

Watching for signals the next afternoon would be unpleasant, although of course Ace was not cheating. People couldn't cheat when they didn't want to, could they? Of course not. She did a test to prove that. She held her hairbrush in front of her, like a hand of cards, and told herself: I am going to stare at this brush and not look at the near lefthand corner of the bureau. She began staring at the bristles. After some seconds an odd feeling gathered around her eyes. They started to feel large and bulgy, and began twitching. I will not look, she insisted. She was balanced on a ledge with a nasty drop to the left, and must not look down. But the drop to the left kept pulling at her, dragging her closer and closer . . .

"Oh damn it!" she cried, and gave up the test before proving she had gone crazy.

A knock sounded on the connecting door and Babs Hartley called, "Carola?"

"Yes?" Carola said wearily.

Babs opened the door, apparently taking *Yes?* as an invitation, and said, "I thought I heard you call."

"I hit a tangle in my hair."

"Such a bother, tangles. Were you having one with Ace tonight, that long talk you had with him?"

"I don't really want to discuss it."

"Of course you don't you poor thing," Babs said soothingly. "He's given you a headache again, so like a man. Would you like a back rub to relax you?"

"No thanks," Carola said, brushing her hair with quick angry strokes.

Babs moved over behind her and slid her hand up the back of Carola's head, letting the soft hair whisper through her fingers. "Such lovely hair," Babs said. "It feels like sunlight."

"Don't touch my hair!" Carola said, jerking away.

Babs put her hands on Carola's shoulders. "My," she said. "Aren't we edgy tonight."

Carola whirled around. "And don't touch me at all!" she cried. "I don't like it! And I don't like people coming into my room without an invitation. Is that clear?"

Babs tilted an eyebrow languidly. "Clear, but rather crude," she said. "I really thought better of you than that."

"Try thinking worse of me. I like it that way."

Babs shrugged. "So it appears," she said. "Well, have fun with your sweaty cowhand, my dear. And remember not to lead singleton kings to him." She went into her room and shut and locked the door.

Carola got up and locked the door on her side. It was about time she worked up enough courage to do that. Perhaps Babs thought her remark about a sweaty cowhand was devastating. On the contrary, after living so long in a women's world, the thought of a sweaty cowhand had considerable appeal. She hoped she could work up enough courage to do something about that, too.

20

As WALDO PREDICTED, Ace and Tony drew a sizable gallery Sunday afternoon at Table 1 Section 1 of the Open Pairs. Not all the spectators, however, stayed through all the play. Mary Rose Rutledge, who could not squeeze another entry fee for a side game out of her budget, watched for thirty minutes and then left, because the complicated bidding and play confused her. The Ashcrafts and Dukes looked in on the game; they had stayed out of the Open Pairs in order to rest for the Vanderbilt, which would resume on Monday. Also, in their new spirit of togetherness, they did not wish to compete against each other in a pairs game. After watching Ace and Tony for an hour, the Ashcrafts and Dukes left, because the bidding and play were not up to their own standards.

Ben Aarons sat down to watch and saw Vicky Summers in the gallery. He tried to catch her attention and succeeded easily, due to the fact that she was trying to catch his. He took her to one side, and said, "How come you're not playing?"

"Mrs. Edmunds and I didn't qualify," she said. "She wanted to watch here instead of playing in the consolation. I'm sorry you and Carola Clark didn't make it."

"Oh, that. Well, I'm kind of glad we didn't. I think Carola really wanted to do some cheering for Ace, and I can use a breather. Listen, did you bring a bathing suit? Why don't we take a swim in the pool?"

Vicky had not brought a bathing suit nor did she own one, because a bathing suit made her look like an unfinished game of jackstraws. She fought down an urge to refuse the invitation with some miserable squirming excuse, and said, "Why, I'd love to. I've been meaning to buy a suit in the shop downstairs. I could meet you at the pool in half an hour."

"Good," he said. "And by the way, what about tonight?"

"Tonight?"

"Now look, you're not going to pretend you forgot our arrangement back in Boston, are you? We were going to get in a game here at the Nationals. Well, the side game tonight is our last chance."

His face was very solemn and intent, and she realized that this was no time to show any emotion. With an effort, she even managed not to blink rapidly. "Oh yes, I do remember," she said gravely. "I'll be glad to play tonight. See you at the pool in half an hour, right?"

"Right," he said, and walked away bumping into a few more chairs and people than usual.

P. J. Hoffmeister sat on the outskirts of the gallery for a time, holding himself erect to give full visibility to the large plastic badge on his coat that announced: I PLAY THE HOFFMEISTER NO TRUMP. He hoped that somebody important among the players or kibitzers might notice it, and later ask him to explain the convention. But nobody even noticed him, let alone the badge, and so finally he wandered away. J. B. Rothman, assistant manager of the Xanadu, paused beside the table, realizing from the number of spectators that it must be an important match. The scene reminded him of a George Bellows painting of an old-time prize fight, the crowd leaning forward intently, smoke coiling up into the lights, violence frozen in a taut pose in the ring. He shook his head in wonder, and went away. Juan Gomez, the bellboy, stopped to empty ashtrays and watched for a minute, his lips moving as he whispered to himself the names of the cards. Runa Montez and Jake Jacobs, who had qualified and were playing in Section 1, visited the table for fifteen minutes and a couple of bad scores. This did not disturb them. They were practical people, and knew that they could not always count on perfect moments in bridge and in bed.

Thus, in the course of the afternoon, Table 1 Section 1 drew attention from all but four of the people whose lives had brushed and become more or less entangled at the Spring Nationals. Babs Hartley was one of the four absentees, being upstairs packing. Alfred Jenks was home watching his birds. Bubba Worthington was forty miles north in Palm Beach, playing rubber bridge with his mother and two of her friends, soothed by the awe with which they looked on a living breathing Life Master. Much farther north the fourth absentee, Sammy Rothberg, was arriving in New York City in a quilted bronze container in a Railway Express car attached to the East Coast Champion.

Ace McKinley was not aware of the ebb and flow in the crowd. He was aware of nothing but his eyes, his cards, Tony, and Carola. His eyes were steel balls that wanted to roll to magnets at the corners of the table. His cards felt like the lids of hot pans; he supposed he was playing them no worse than usual but he had little knowledge of what he was doing. Tony, that glassy blank stare across the table, played like a machine and kept on making unbelievable leads. Carola seemed as remote as a cloud in a summer sky. She did not meet his glance or give him any hint of what, if anything, she was discovering.

He completed the last board of the afternoon session, and looked again at Carola, because now she had to give him a signal. For a moment nothing at all showed on her face. All right, he thought dully, you spotted something. Don't try to kid me about it. We were cheating, weren't we?

As if she had read his thoughts, Carola nodded slowly. Then she said clearly and calmly, "You don't look well, Ace. Are you sure you ought to play tonight?"

Although he knew it was coming, that did not make it easier to take. Well, Carola had done her job and now he had to do his, which was to try to keep a scandal from becoming public. "Yeah," he said thickly, "I feel lousy. Tony, I'm sorry, but I'm going to have to withdraw."

"You what!" Tony cried, leaning halfway across the table.

"I will have to withdraw," Ace said.

Tony started coming around the table like a big fast cat, but an even more nimble person popped up in his way. It was Waldo Starnes, Chief Tournament Director, materializing as if from a puff of smoke, hopping up and down excitedly.

"Oh how awful, I heard that," Waldo chattered. "Poor Ace isn't feeling well and has to withdraw. What a pity when you were having such a fine game, and now I'll have to dig up a substitute pair for tonight. Please don't be hard on poor Ace, Tony, I know it's a hideous disappointment, come here a moment and let me talk to you." He pulled at a sleeve of Tony's coat and tugged him off to one side and lowered his voice and whispered, "Let's keep things quiet, please. Tony, I'm sorry to tell you that charges of unethical conduct have been brought against you and Ace."

Tony put on a smile that looked like a knife scar. "You're kidding."

"No, no, Tony. If Ace had not withdrawn, I would have been obliged to call a meeting right now to hear the charges. As it is, we can postpone the meeting until tonight, after the evening session is under way, and avoid the talk that would start if you two were disqualified. The meeting will be in the room behind the directors' table, at nine-thirty. Please attend it."

"Who's bringing the charges?"

"Several people. I will see you at nine-thirty, Tony, and thank you for taking this quietly, like a gentleman." He smiled, and skipped away through the crowd.

What's this stuff, Tony thought, about taking it like a gentleman? He was taking it quietly because, at the moment, there was nothing else to do. He glanced back at the table and saw Ace McKinley starting to walk slowly toward the exit. There were a lot of questions in Tony's mind, such as who if anybody had told Ace of the charges, and what Ace was thinking, and what Ace knew, and so on. But it didn't seem likely that he could get the answers now, before the hearing. So he waited, as he had done years ago in Brooklyn, for the guy with the brass knuckles to make his move.

The hearing began at nine-thirty before the Tournament Committee. Waldo Starnes opened the hearing by reporting how Ace and Carola came to him the previous night with Ace's worries about corner-of-the-table signals. Ace was asked to confirm the report, and did so.

"You thought cheating was going on?" the chairman asked Ace.

Ace said, "I felt sure of it, what with me not playing well and our scores being so good."

"And you felt that, willingly or unwillingly, you might be giving those corner signals to Mr. Manuto to guide his leads?"

Ace nodded.

"And you admit agreeing to pay a bonus to Mr. Manuto of five thousand dollars if you won the Open Pairs?"

"That was the deal."

"A large sum of money, surely? Far greater than payments about which we sometimes hear rumors?"

"A hell of a wad," Ace said. "Craziest thing I ever did."

"Mr. Manuto," the chairman said, "do you confirm asking for such a bonus from Mr. McKinley?"

Tony had been staring at Ace, wondering why anybody would want to check if a gun is loaded by peering into the muzzle and yanking the trigger. He gave himself a little shake, and said, "No rule against it, is there? All the rule says is I can't make a big public show out of looking for business. The rule don't say how much I can charge, five bucks or five thousand."

"But the amount of five thousand dollars is correct?"

"Why not? The guy's been playing bad bridge, and wanted a big win, and maybe I could get it for him. He must have figured it was worth it if we won."

"Do you remember telling Mr. McKinley that story about the corner-of-the-table signals?"

"Sure. I thought it might juice up one of his columns. That's all there was to it. He didn't give me any signals like that, and I didn't expect any. The guy was imagining things."

"Thank you," the chairman said. "Waldo Starnes, please?"

Waldo said, "Since Mr. McKinley felt he might be giving those signals without wanting to, I asked Carola Clark to observe the play this afternoon and report what she saw. Carola?"

Carola got up and peered at a little pile of notes. "I saw no evidence of the use of corner signals," she said. "At certain times I tried to make notes of where Mr. McKinley looked, when he was waiting for a lead from Mr. Manuto, but I had to give up. I couldn't make notes quickly enough. He was very jumpy and his eyes were never still, and it would have been impossible for him to give those signals."

"You sure of that?" Ace asked.

"I am," Carola said firmly.

Ace took a deep breath and closed his eyes. For the first time in thirty hours they had stopped burning and twitching.

Tony said impatiently, "All right, then, what's the problem? Don't that settle everything?"

"Not quite," Waldo said. "We still have the question of whether there was unethical conduct of some other type. Mr. McKinley believed that only cheating could account for the scores he and his partner were making. Carola?"

Carola studied her notes again. "I thought that many of Mr. Manuto's actions this afternoon were, at the very least, highly questionable," she said. "He frequently leaned to one side or the other, which could have given him a chance to see cards held by an opponent. He was playing in the South position, next to the table from which his table was receiving the boards, and many times he leaned backward, as if to hear any talk about completed hands at the next table. On six occasions, when his table had finished before the call for the move, he got up and went to the refreshment table, each time walking past tables where boards he had not yet seen were in play."

"Mr. Manuto?" the chairman said.

"Now look," Tony said. "Has anybody here got any doubt Carola is still torching for Ace? The guy thinks cheating is going on and that he's in on it. She wants to prove he isn't, and the easy out is to prove I'm doing it by myself. I like her, and got nothing against her, she's just making like a dame, is all. Maybe I was wriggling around a lot, and getting up to walk off the jitters, but we were leading the Open Pairs and big dough was riding on it. It don't prove anything that I was jumpy."

"You have a point there," the chairman said.

"Indeed he does," Waldo said. "So perhaps I had better call in another witness." He went to the door and opened it and beckoned to somebody.

The person summoned was Katy Edmunds. She had dressed carefully for the event, wearing a mink stole over a gold brocade dress that looked as if it had been hacked from an old theater curtain. She nodded to the committee, and gave Tony a smile that twisted her mouth into a fish-hook shape.

"Mrs. Edmunds," Waldo said, "can you identify this note as the one you gave me last night?" Katy looked at the note, and identified it, and Waldo read it aloud to the committee.

Things were getting a little tight around the throat, Tony thought. He couldn't figure Katy's angle; what was it to her if he did some fancy footwork, as long as he didn't step on her toes?

The chairman said, "Mr. Manuto, do you recall passing Mrs. Edmunds' table last night just after she had played Board Sixteen?"

Tony thought: What a question! Guy hands me a switchblade knife and thinks I'm going to cut myself with it. "I don't remember passing her table or not passing her table," he said. "I never know whose table I'm passing or what boards they're playing, account of I don't look."

"But you do recall playing Board Sixteen, I assume? You made a top on it by setting a small slam in hearts. Do you remember how you did that?"

"Board Sixteen, hmm? Small slam in hearts . . . yeah, yeah, sure. That was a stupid bid the jerks playing against us made. I figured they were missing an ace and I didn't buy a cue bid they'd made in diamonds. I had the king of diamonds and figured my partner had the ace so I underled my king. Just good bridge, is all."

"Yes, no doubt," the chairman said. "Now I believe that Mrs. Edmunds also observed the game this afternoon. Did you notice anything questionable, Mrs. Edmunds?"

Katy reported observing the same things Carola had seen. No, she had not noticed any words or actions that indicated Ace and Tony were using illegal signals for leads.

"Mr. Manuto?" the chairman said.

"Well jeez," Tony said in an aggrieved tone. "It's the same stuff Carola talked about. All right, so I was jumpy and nervous and moved around a lot, what with all that dough on the line and us having a big game. I didn't peek at anybody's cards or try to pick up any talk from the table back of me or anything. I had enough to do thinking of our own game and the ape way Ace was playing. I hate to say it, but the guy really has cracked up."

"No personalities, please," the chairman said.

"Guy's got to keep his name clear," Tony said. "Where's the proof of any of this junk?"

"Perhaps I have it," Carola said icily, riffling through her notes. "I believe I overlooked this when I made my first report."

Tony studied her expression and decided that it had been a mistake to say Ace had cracked up. He should have laid off Ace, and maybe the dame would have laid off him.

"At four-twenty this afternoon," Carola said, "Mr. Manuto took one of his trips to the refreshment stand. He hesitated about one second in passing Table Three, where at that moment Board Twenty-six was being played. Mr. Manuto made his hesitation behind the North player at Table Three. Some time later, Board Twenty-six was in play at Table One, and Mr. Manuto and Mr. McKinley were defending against a bid of two spades. Halfway through the hand the declarer led a club and Mr. McKinley discarded a diamond. Mr. Manuto said to him sharply, 'No clubs, partner?' Mr. McKinley mumbled, 'No clubs.' Mr. Manuto said even more sharply, 'You sure of that?' Then Mr. McKinley gave a jump and said, 'Oh shoot, I do have one,' and pulled out a club. If the revoke had become established, it would have cost Mr. McKinley and Mr. Manuto two of the tricks they won later in the hand. I have never heard of a player querying his partner *twice* about a possible revoke. I cannot understand such an action unless the player knew what cards his partner held. Mr. McKinley was playing North, of course. Half an hour earlier, on one of his trips, Mr. Manuto had paused behind the North player at Table Three, when the same board was being played."

"Nice going, Carola," Katy said. "I missed that."

"No comments, please," the chairman said. "Mr. Manuto, would you like to speak?"

"All I can say is, I knew he had to have a club," Tony said, wondering if this sounded as weak to everybody else as it did to him. "The bidding and distribution pointed to it."

Nobody said anything for a few moments, and people began wriggling uneasily on chairs, and finally the chairman cleared his throat and said, "Is there any more testimony? No? Then thank you all very much. Mrs. Edmunds, we will not require your further help. Mr. McKinley and Mr. Manuto, will you wait within call while the committee discusses this matter? And Waldo, may we see a copy of the sheet from which Board Twenty-six was duplicated? It may help us make a decision."

An hour later Ace and Tony were called back into the room. Ace studied the faces of the committee and obtained no more information than if he had been looking at the backs of cards. Tony, who was good at reading cards and faces, studied the committee and got a lot of information. He did not think he was going to take many tricks in this game.

"Mr. McKinley," the chairman said, "the committee has voted to censure you for agreeing to pay five thousand dollars to Mr. Manuto if you won the Open Pairs. Even though the ACBL has not banned playing for pay, and even though it is known that this practice exists, the sum involved here is so large that we cannot overlook it. In agreeing to pay such a bonus, your conduct was detrimental to the best interests of bridge. You may appeal the action of the committee if you wish."

"I don't plan to appeal," Ace said.

"Very well. Now, in regard to the corner signals that you suspected you might be giving to your partner, the committee has determined that no such signals were given. The committee has voted to commend you for bringing this matter to the attention of the director. In view of the fact that this commendation somewhat balances the vote of censure, the committee will recommend to the ACBL that no further action be taken in your case. Do you have any comment on this?"

"I have no comment," Ace said.

"Then, since you are not involved further in this hearing, we will excuse you."

Ace glanced at Carola, wondering if by chance he might see one of her rare smiles, but her face merely held an expression of faint interest. He turned and walked out of the room.

Tony remembered a distant afternoon when he faced a group called The Scorpions instead of the Tournament Committee. Groups were odd, he thought; they liked to make rules that, for example, you could only kick a guy's teeth in with your left foot, and if you used the right foot you broke the rules and made the group sore. He could feel the disapproval here in this room, just as he felt it that day in Brooklyn, like a weight coming down to mash you. This time, however, there was no use reaching into his pocket for a switchblade knife, because nobody was going to swing at him with brass knuckles. They had something better to use on him.

"Mr. Manuto," the chairman said, "the committee has studied Board Twenty-six, on which you made your double warning against a revoke. We have reconstructed the bidding and the play up to that point. We find nothing in the bidding or in the cards of which you properly had knowledge—that is, those in your hand, those in the dummy, and those previously played—that accounts for your accurate picture of the remaining cards in your partner's hand."

"Don't forget I'm a top player," Tony said. "I can figure more from the bidding and distribution and play than most clucks can." He didn't think that would do much good, but they weren't charging him by the word.

"We give you credit for being a top player, and we recognize that all top players are good at such deductions although," the chairman said drily, "not as good as they think. We have decided that the incident of the double warning against a revoke, and your conduct at other times, provide ground for disciplinary action. So—"

"Do I have a right to say anything more?" Tony asked.

"If you wish. But we are no longer hearing your case. We have reached our decision."

"Okay," Tony said. "Then that makes it your lead."

"The committee will recommend to the ACBL that you be barred from play in national, regional, sectional and local tournaments for a period of one year. You have the right of appeal."

Tony shrugged. "The way I figure it, most of the people who would hear the appeal are in front of me now."

"I believe that is correct," the chairman said. "At least half of the members of the National Conduct, Deportment and Ethics Committee are sitting on this Tournament Committee."

Tony got up. They weren't slugging him any harder than he expected. "All right," he said. "Goodby for a year, folks."

Outside, he angled through the room in which the finals were still being played, and allowed himself a smile at the thought that now he could look at the cards openly. Well, he had known it was a risk to work all those stunts; too many people had tried them in the past. In spite of that, he'd almost pulled off the job. It was the stunt he didn't try, the corner signals, that had trapped him. If Ace hadn't thought they were using corner signals, the Clark dame wouldn't have cut herself into the game, and that would have left Katy's squawk standing by itself, a bleat that could be ignored. So the whole thing was a bad joke, like having the horn of your car short-circuit and start blasting while you were quietly robbing a bank.

He went out to the patio and leaned over the seawall and stared at the tarnished ocean and wondered again what gave with Katy, who wasn't the type to get religion and start singing hymns. He couldn't figure the answer.

Somebody walked up behind him and a voice like a drill cutting steel said, "Well, *there* you are, Tony. I've been looking all over for you."

He turned and saw Katy. "If you forgot your knife," he said, "you'll find it in the middle of my back."

"My, my," Katy said. "What a sensitive back you must have. All I gave you was a love tap."

"I'll try to enjoy it, soon as I can swing a loan from a blood bank."

"Now that you mention it, you do look pale and anemic. Have you thought of taking a trip for your health? Waldo tells me you'll have time for a nice trip. A year, isn't it?"

Tony stared at her lumpy white face and wondered if it really would feel like slugging a mound of cottage cheese. "I don't get it," he said. "You and me, we never had any trouble. So what gives?"

Katy let out a laugh that shrilled up the scale like a fire siren. "Of course we haven't had any trouble. I think you're wonderful, Tony. You're my kind of rat. Don't you remember I said I'm planning a trip around the world? And how nice it would be to have you along, to keep me company and play bridge? We lonely old ladies love good company."

"So that was your angle."

Katy patted a strand of her silvery-purple hair back into place, and paused to admire the way the silver snake of her turquoise ring caught the starlight. "You must admit I had your best interests at heart," she said. "I really did go to a bit of trouble to get you time off for the trip. As I said before, I'll pay all expenses and let you have some pocket money, fifty dollars a week. How else can you make a living during the next year, and have a good bridge partner besides?"

"Don't you figure you're taking a little risk, putting the arm on a guy like me?"

Her eyes looked very bright and eager. "Indeed I do," she said. "Have you ever killed anyone, Tony?"

"Not so far."

"I find the idea simply fascinating," she said, with an odd husky note in her voice. "I don't really think you're the type, but if you're shoved around a bit too much, who knows?"

"Yeah. And you're just the dame to do some shoving, huh?"

"Let's not look only on the bright side of things, Tony. Let's look on the dark side, too. Let's consider the fact that I might turn into a silly old woman who can't let you out of her sight and who showers you with presents and leaves you all her money."

"I wouldn't want to bid a grand slam on those cards."

"You might luck out the bid. Anyway, what other cards do you hold?"

They stared at each other for a moment, the glitter in the keen blue eyes matching the glow in the dark ones behind the sunglasses, a pair of gamblers working out the odds. "All right," Tony said in a flat voice. "When do we leave?" It was going to be quite a game.

21

LATER THAT EVENING two more people walked to the seawall, also working out the odds for and against things that might happen. Vicky Summers looked at Ben Aarons and wondered what the chances were that she might ever have another date with him. Perhaps the chances were about as good as those of being dealt four aces, the odds against which were three hundred and seventy-eight to one. The thought should have depressed her but tonight nothing could make her feel that way. In the future, no doubt, she would go back to those horrible swings between hopefulness and despair that she had always known, but tonight she was relaxed and happy.

The hours had been glorious ever since Ben asked her to go swimming and she found courage to accept. She squandered twenty dollars for a bathing suit in the sportswear shop of the Xanadu, reluctantly giving up a nice yellow one that the sales-girl insisted was bright orange and not right for her, and accepting a pale gray suit that the salesgirl claimed was yellow and just perfect for her skin. Anyway, whatever the color was, Ben hadn't winced when he saw her in it. They had a fine time in the pool and ate dinner together and, when they went up to get their entries for the side game, an unusual thing happened. The director asked Ben if they would mind substituting in the finals of the Open Pairs. It seemed that Ace McKinley, who had been leading the event with his partner, was ill and unable to play. Of course they would not be eligible for an overall rating but they would get any points they won in their section. Vicky had never played in the finals of a national event and ordinarily would have been numb with fear. But, since nothing was really at stake, she enjoyed it and played better than usual, and Ben said they might have come in as high as second in section.

While Vicky considered the odds against four aces and another date with him, Ben was considering the odds on winning the McKenney if he gave up everything else and concentrated on it. He had increased his lead during the Spring Nationals, picking up eighty points for a grand total of five hundred and two. Maybe —surprise, surprise—he even got several tonight with Vicky. The odds were perhaps two to one in his favor that he could win the McKenney by devoting all his time to it.

He said, "Hey, you know what, the owner of that hotel where I work in the Catskills phoned last night, all excited about me winning the Mixed with Carola. He figures it won't do business any harm to have a bridge director who won a national title, and he's giving me a raise. And he says he'll fix up my schedule so I can have all the time off I need for big-time bridge."

"That's just wonderful!"

"Yeah, and Prentice-Hall phoned too, and said I could have another advance any time. So listen, the two of us can play in some more tournaments."

Vicky peered at him and wished her eyes would stop blinking so rapidly, because the blinking made it hard to see. "I didn't quite catch that," she said.

"The two of us can play in some more tournaments."

"I thought you said that, but it doesn't make sense."

"Why doesn't it?"

"Oh Ben, I played way over my head tonight! You've got to play with top people in order to win the McKenney. Besides I'll be in Philadelphia and—"

"Uh, speaking of Philadelphia, they're holding a Sectional the week after next. I'd like to come down and play a few events with you. How about it?"

She didn't believe this at all. There was no reason why a man should cross a street to see her, let alone travel from the Catskills to Philadelphia. "I think I'm going to be busy," she said weakly.

"Yes ma'am. Busy playing bridge with me."

"But you can't! It's a waste of your time. You've got to win things, not come in way down the line with me."

"It's only a Sectional," he said patiently. "There aren't many points to be won in it anyway. And there isn't any big tournament I could go to that week. So what am I losing? Fact is, it'll do me good to play bridge with you. I enjoy it, see? It's relaxing. Bridge shouldn't be work all the time, should it?"

"Well, no, but—"

"Then it's all settled, right?"

Up in her head something was shuffling her thoughts like mad and preventing her from arranging them in proper order. Was it possible that Ben did enjoy playing bridge with her? And that it relaxed him? If it would be good for him, then of course it would be wonderful for her. "All right," she said. "It's settled." Then the something in her head that was shuffling her thoughts suddenly dealt one out to her, and she put it into spoken words before realizing what a vain and brazen idea it was. "Ben," she said, "I'm beginning to think that you like me."

"Got any objections?"

"Well, no," she said, trying to be calm and practical about such an impossible notion. "Except that I don't want to get in your way and keep you from winning the McKenney. You are going to win it, aren't you?"

"Sure, sure," he said, taking her into his arms gently, so that their sharp joints and thinly covered bones wouldn't get bruised. But he had already worked out the odds about the McKenney. He was not going to win it. He couldn't offer much to the memory of Sammy Rothberg, and to the girl in his arms, but he could offer that.

♠ ♥ ♦ ♣ 22

IT WAS MONDAY MORNING and, from most points of view, the Spring Nationals were ending. It was true that the Vanderbilt would resume in the afternoon, but only eight teams remained in it including the Dukes and Ashcrafts, who in the course of winning it were going to commit enough atrocities on their opponents to make Attila the Hun seem like Good King Wenceslaus. People were checking out of the Xanadu in crowds: the Life Masters, the Advanced Senior Masters, the Senior Masters, the National Masters, the Masters, the Junior Masters, and two maiden ladies who had arrived with no points at all and were leaving with none.

Carola Clark sat on a couch beside a mound of blue-and-white airplane luggage and watched the cashiers' windows. Finally she saw a man in a pearl-gray Stetson walk up to a window. Ordinarily he wore his Stetson at a jaunty angle but today it sat on him like a candle snuffer. His eyes were usually a bright blue, like the sky over Laredo, but this morning they had red streaks. He paid his bill and turned and saw her, and hesitated.

Then he straightened his shoulders and marched over to her and said, "Howdy, Carola. You getting ready to leave?"

"Yes," she said. "Where did you go last night?"

"Last night? Now let's see . . . oh yes. Well, I had a little drinking I wanted to catch up on. Uh, by the way, thanks for helping me out of that mess."

"You could at least have answered your phone. You were in your room, weren't you?"

"I didn't have much to say to anybody, I reckon. Well, I got to catch a plane. Can't give you a lift anywhere, can I?"

Carola got up. "Yes, you can."

He hesitated again, and then wrenched his face into a smile. "Good. Fine. Where to?"

"I don't know," she said coolly. "Where are we going?"

"Well, I'm going to New York and . . . and . . . whoa there! What's that mean, Carola? You're not hinting at anything, are you?"

She gave him her look of faint interest. "No, I'm not hinting at anything. I'm just saying I'd like to go with you, wherever it is, if you have no objections."

He lowered his head and peered at her like a tired old bull studying a picador. "I'd just as soon you didn't make any jokes."

She laughed, a sound like a fingernail tapped on thin crystal. "It's not a joke. We used to play some fair bridge together. I'd like to try it again."

"You mean all the tournaments?"

"All the tournaments."

"Now listen," he said, "we did that once before, remember? Back when you were a kid just off the stage? We went around everywhere and I never even made a pass at you for a year, not that anybody believed I didn't. It was kind of rough going for me. Remember that crack that went the rounds? Ace is making a Life Master out of Carola, but when is he going to make an honest woman out of her?"

She sighed and said, "Maybe it wouldn't take you a year this time."

"Oh, shoot," he said, rather helplessly. "I reckon you're serious. But is it going to work out?"

"I don't know. Is it?"

"Well, I admit you're playing nice bridge and had some big wins since we split up, but bridge is a partnership game, see, and just because I had a little bad luck with my game lately don't mean you got me roped and tied. From time to time you got to listen to me."

23

25

"Do you have any special listening in mind, Ace?"

"You remember that fight we had over you leading that single-ton diamond king? You wouldn't admit it, but it was a real bad lead."

For a moment she was tempted to argue, but then she saw the flicker of worry in his bloodshot eyes. He didn't quite believe his statement. But the thing was, he *needed* to believe it. "I'll admit it now," she said softly. "It was a bad lead."

"Well, shoot!" he cried. "You'll learn this game yet, Carola. Son," he called gaily to a bellboy, "get our stuff out to a taxi, will you?" He tucked an arm through Carola's and led her to the door-way, and the famous McKinley laugh rumbled through the lobby like the sound of a cattle stampede.

The morning wore on and the players continued to stream out of the Xanadu, heading for Boston and Seattle and Fort Worth and Toronto and Los Angeles and elsewhere. P. J. Hoffmeister tramped across the lobby with his suitcase, staring at a far hori-zon, heading for a land where the miracle might happen and the people would listen. Katy Edmunds made her way to the exit with battleship firmness, while a slim young man in dark glasses kept station on her like a destroyer. Vicky Summers and Ben Aarons went out hand in hand, and at the doorway Vicky gave Ben a little tug so that for once he did not bump into it. Runa Montez, tall and regal, crossed the lobby with Jake clinging to her arm as if afraid he might lose her, which of course he would eventually, although not just yet and perhaps not even at the Summer Nationals, where they had agreed to meet.

Behind one of the grilled windows in the lobby, a cashier studied a bill and frowned and went to the assistant manager, J. B. Rothman, to check the amount. He looked at the name of the guest, and thought again of what the auditor would say, and muttered, "Yes, six dollars a day." So Mary Rose Rutledge paid her six-dollar-a-day charge and walked lightly and happily to the exit, not looking back at the jungled walls or the inch-thick rug on which vivid raised designs floated like lily pads, not looking back at anything, because she believed in looking ahead, and up ahead were more tournaments and more red points and possibly a wonderful wonderful partner.

Juan Gomez, the bellboy, found a pack of cards that someone had left in a corner of the ballroom. Nobody was watching him, and he quickly dealt four hands and studied them, his lips moving as he pronounced the names of the cards.